'So,' the Sergeant said, dipping a look quickly back over his shoulder to make sure his every word was being closely followed. 'So, miss, you don't attempt to deny that this particular handkerchief is your particular property?'

'I do not, Sergeant. Why should – '

'Then, miss, do you deny what this handkerchief is stained with?'

With a flick of the wrist that would have done credit to a professional conjuror Sergeant Drewd turned the fragment of cambric so that the larger part of it, until now hidden inside his fist, was visible.

On it Miss Unwin saw a dark brownish stain which she knew at once was blood.

The Governess

H. R. F. KEATING

writing as

EVELYN HERVEY

SPHERE BOOKS LIMITED
London and Sydney

First published in Great Britain by
George Weidenfeld & Nicolson Limited 1984
Copyright © 1984 by Evelyn Hervey
Published by Sphere Books Ltd 1986
30–32 Gray's Inn Road, London WC1X 8JL

TRADE
MARK

Printed and bound in Great Britain by
Collins, Glasgow

Chapter One

The first crime committed at No 3 Northumberland Gardens, London West, in the July of the year 1870 was the theft of a sugar-mouse. A headless sugar-mouse.

When little Pelham Thackerton saw that the sweet had disappeared from the table on the landing outside the schoolroom where he had put it hardly twenty minutes before he burst into tears.

Miss Unwin, his new young governess, at once gave up puzzling about how the mouse could have vanished from a place where at that time of the evening no one should have occasion to be.

'Come,' she said. 'No need to cry, you silly boy. You earned that mouse with your recitation for your Mama down in the drawing-room, so I'll go and fetch you another.'

Little Pelham's tears came to a gasping halt.

'But won't Grandpapa be cross if you go down now?' he asked.

'You go and see if Mary has brought up the water for your bath,' Miss Unwin replied. 'Little boys shouldn't speculate about their elders and betters, you know that. Now, off you go.'

She gave Pelham a push in the direction of his bedroom, where Mary, the second housemaid, would have begun to fill his tin bathtub, and set briskly off down the broad main stairs of the house.

But she was not feeling as confident as she looked. Pelham's grandfather, Mr William Thackerton, sole proprietor of the flourishing firm of Thackerton's Patent Steam-moulded Hats, might well be angered at her returning to the drawing-room again after her attendance with Pelham at his nightly appearance there. Mr Thackerton had firm views about those beneath his own station in society keeping to their place, and he had an explosive temper.

So far she had avoided his wrath. But an intrusion now when

the family were waiting for dinner to be announced might bring about just such an outburst and could end even with her summary dismissal. Only just on the lowest rungs of the ladder of society, the thought of anything that could send her tumbling back into the mire again was cause for palpitating inner anxiety.

Yet little Pelham had been unjustly deprived of his treat. How that could have happened she still could not understand. But she was not going to let any lack of courage on her own part prevent her putting it right.

Yet, in front of the tall and solid mahogany door of the drawing-room, she hesitated once again.

All she had to do was to turn its large brass knob and go in, to seek out Pelham's mother wherever she was seated and ask her if she could take a second sugar-mouse from the little wheeled chiffonier where they were kept, then to murmur some apology and to leave. It ought to be simple enough. But what if Mr Thackerton, standing no doubt as usual in front of the wide marble fireplace, thumbs stuck characteristically into the pockets of his waistcoat, large-featured face flushed with good living, were to grind out at the sight of her some such question as 'What the devil are you doing here, miss?' Whatever answer she gave might well lead to one of those explosions of anger and perhaps to the end of a career hardly yet begun.

But why should little Pelham suffer?

Miss Unwin put her hand on to the big brass doorknob and turned it.

The room she entered had never seemed so crowded with obstacles. There were chairs everywhere, large and small, tall-backed in dark wood and heavily buttoned upholstery, low in Utrecht velvet framed by painted papier-mâché. There were sofas. There were screens. And beside almost every chair and sofa there was a table, some with fringed chenille cloths covering them, some without, one with a large Paisley shawl draped over it, another there simply to provide a stand for a great glass-domed display of wax fruits, yet another so filled with silver-framed photographs that to go anywhere near it was to invite calamity.

But past all these obstacles she must thread her way to reach

Pelham's mother reclining on the ottoman at the far side of the big room, an illustrated newspaper held languidly in her long white hands, her pearl-grey dress spread like a pallid lake on the rich crimson upholstery.

Yet at least there was only her and Mr Thackerton in the room. Apparently this was one of the evenings when there were no visitors and when Mr Arthur Thackerton, Pelham's father, was not dining at home, something in fact that he seldom seemed to do.

So it was watched in ominous silence by the master of the house from his position in front of the marble fireplace that Miss Unwin skirted all the tables and chairs that lay between her and Pelham's mother and at last was able to make her request.

'Another mouse? But surely, Miss Unwin, he should not have two in one evening?'

'Oh, no. Of course he should not. But the one that you gave him disappeared from the table on the landing outside the schoolroom while he was eating his supper.'

Mrs Arthur Thackerton frowned.

'But why was the mouse outside on the landing?' she asked.

Miss Unwin, always conscious of the silent, red-faced figure leaning against the mantelpiece in front of its array of plaster statuettes, silver ornaments and china vases, hastened to explain.

'You will remember that I found that if Master Pelham was allowed to eat the whole mouse he had earned as a reward for his evening recitation he did not finish his bread-and-milk. So we agreed that he should take one piece of it only.'

'Ha.'

A grunt of something – was it anger or was it amusement? – came from the direction of the mantelpiece.

'And the boy munches off the mouse's head in one good bite each night,' Mr Thackerton said.

His eyes shone with vigorous pride.

'He'll do,' he added. 'The boy'll do when he comes to take his place as head of the firm. He won't let anyone put anything past him. Not my muncher.'

'Yes,' Pelham's mother put in, with more than a trace of petul-

3

ance. 'But why was that mouse left outside the schoolroom, Miss Unwin?'

'That is quite simple,' Miss Unwin replied. 'I found that looking at his treat to come still stopped Pelham from eating up his supper. So he and I agreed it should be left outside until he had finished.'

From the mantelpiece there came a fierce snort.

'And now this evening's mouse has been taken away?'

Mr Thackerton's voice had begun to show an edge of anger. Miss Unwin stepped in quickly as she could to soften it. She well knew that any hint of his possessions being abused could produce the dreaded thunderbolt that might in the end strike at her as easily as at some more deserving target.

'I have only just found the mouse has gone,' she said. 'Of course I shall make inquiries. But poor Pelham is much distressed, and I wanted to put it right as quickly as might be.'

'Yes, yes,' Mr Thackerton said. 'Give the boy another mouse, quick as you like.'

As swiftly as she could without allowing her skirts to brush against some delicately poised object Miss Unwin went to the chiffonier, extracted from it a new sugar-mouse and with a murmured 'good night' made her escape.

But she was more than a little puzzled about how she was to fulfil the pledge she had given to find out how the first mouse had disappeared. She felt it very probable, too, that Mr Thackerton would not fail to ask her at some later date who had had the temerity to make away with something paid for ultimately out of his own pocket.

For who could have taken that sparkling white, headless little sweet? No one had any reason to come up the main staircase of the house as far as the landing that led only to the schoolroom, Pelham's bedroom and her own. The servants should, of course, use the back stairs if any one of them had occasion to go to their rooms in the attics on the floor above.

True, there was nothing to have prevented Pelham's father coming up to the schoolroom landing before he had left the house. But that was something he had not done once in all the three months of her own time in the house. Nor was it any more likely that the only other member of the household, Mrs William Thackerton, would appear there. She hardly ever left her bedroom on the floor below or the invalid's sitting-room next door to it with its constant ammonia odour of hartshorn and tang of eau-de-cologne.

So, Miss Unwin pondered slowly mounting the wide staircase with the little glittering sugar-mouse in her hand, so that leaves only one person with any right to be outside the schoolroom at this hour of the day. Mary, with her cans of hot water for Pelham's bath.

But Miss Unwin had a very special reason for knowing that Mary would not have played such a trick on Pelham and on herself.

Because Mary was Vilkins.

Mary being Vilkins had come as a terrible shock to Miss Unwin on her very first day in the house. She had scarcely made little Pelham's acquaintance and was standing, mercifully on her own, looking in at the bedroom that was to be hers lost in a dream of her future there. She had barely been aware that someone had come up the servants' stairs and through the green baize door cutting them off from the rest of the house.

Then from behind her there had come a sound something between a gasp and a shriek and a voice had said 'Unwin.'

She had turned.

There at the doorway was a young woman of much her own age wearing a housemaid's lavender cotton dress and with a housemaid's dusting-cap jammed on her head. And the face beneath the cap was one she had known as well as any face she had ever seen, a broad plain full-coloured countenance with jutting out from it like a rock in a swelling sea a great big red dab of a nose.

'Vilkins,' she had said. 'You? Here?'

'But you. You, Unwin. What about you here? An' you the governess, the new governess what I come to ask was there anything you wanted. An' you ain't her. Or you is. Oh, lawks, I don't know one from t'other.'

Well might Vilkins be in turmoil, Miss Unwin had thought then, her mind going back to her very earliest days when she had been a parish orphan farmed out to the care of an old woman who took in small children on a small allowance from the board of parish guardians and kept them on a short allowance of bread and a large allowance of slops. It was there that she and Vilkins had met, when she had been plain Unwin and nothing more and Vilkins had been equally plain Vilkins, each named by the parish beadle in a regular order. The orphan falling on the parish before Unwin had been a boy and had been given a name beginning with T, the orphan coming immediately after her had been Vilkins (the beadle, though a stickler for the alphabet, was not much of a scholar).

Confronted at almost the first instant of her arrival at highly respectable No 3 Northumberland Gardens in the post of governess with this reminder of her appallingly humble origins, Miss Unwin had for a moment wanted to repudiate the spectre that had risen up, red nosed, before her. But that had been for a moment only. She and Vilkins had been much too good friends in those first evil days of theirs for her not to welcome this altogether unexpected reunion.

Little had she thought then, however, that the day would come before very long when the presence in the house of one person she could trust through and through was to be perhaps all that saved her from disaster. But that was to be when a crime a great deal more serious than the theft of a sugar-mouse had taken place beneath the roof of No 3 Northumberland Gardens.

Chapter Two

Other crimes, no more serious than that first small theft, were to be committed in the house before Miss Unwin was faced with the crumbling of all her cherished hopes of advancement. The first sugar-mouse to disappear so mysteriously was not the last.

The second occasion a mouse disappeared was two evenings later when Miss Unwin knew there were visitors for dinner and she had to tell Pelham that there could be no replacement brought up from the drawing-room.

'You must learn to bear the disappointment, you know. We all have to accept those at times. Even when they are quite unjust.'

She believed what she had told the boy. The world, she well knew, by no means always rewarded merit or compensated for ill luck. Even the rich had to learn that. But she was to look back on these words of hers to Pelham with bitter irony before many days had passed. Injustice awaited her, sharper by far than the loss of a decapitated sugar-mouse.

But Pelham's mouth had shaped itself into a wide O, ready to bawl.

'No, Pelham. No tears. Show me how brave and sensible you can be, and tomorrow I will try to find out just what happened to your mouse tonight and see that it does not happen again.'

'Yes, miss,' Pelham said, swallowing hard. 'I will be good, and tomorrow you'll catch that beastly thief and then I'll tell Grand-papa and he'll be as angry as angry.'

'Well, we'll see about that when it happens. That will be the time to think about who we tell and who we don't.'

So, allowing Pelham one extra game of his favourite Snakes and Ladders, Miss Unwin saw him safely through bath and pray-ers, drew the heavy curtains of his bedroom to shut out the still strong evening light, lit the tiny nightlight on his mantelpiece and left him on the point of sleep. Then she spent a little time thinking how she might catch the sugar-mouse thief if next evening the same trick was tried.

She decided that all that would be necessary would be to leave the schoolroom door ajar, as it were by mistake, and to station herself somewhere inside the room where she could keep the table by the banisters outside cautiously under her eye.

But when it came to it the plan did not prove altogether easy to put into action. Wherever she placed herself in the schoolroom she was hardly able to see the sugar-mouse and she guessed that if she moved its table to a better position the thief would take warning. Nor was Pelham any help. After every other mouthful of his bread-and-milk there came a penetrating whisper.

'Miss, are they there yet?'

'No, Pelham. Now, you finish up your supper like a good boy.'

So, going to peer through the quarter-open door for a fifth or sixth time, Miss Unwin was not much surprised to find that once again Pelham's treat had been whisked away.

She ran over to the stairs and peered down them hoping to catch at least a glimpse of the retreating thief. But she saw no one and heard only a muffled scurry of feet on the rich stair carpet below.

Once more, after Pelham had been put to bed soothed with promises that next evening she would produce a better plan, she gave herself over to trying to account for the mystery of the disappearing mice.

Of one thing she had made certain. The thief, whoever it was, must come from inside the house. No 3 Northumberland Gardens was a jealously guarded place. Mr Thackerton's often repeated orders had seen to that. Every window on the ground floor was protected by thick iron bars, as was the window of the servants' hall in the basement looking out on to the area below the front steps. The servants' door down there was, too, never left unbolted by day or by night. Any servant returning from an outing or an errand had to mount the steps and ring there at the servants' bell beneath that labelled 'Visitors'. Then he or she had to go down the area steps and wait patiently for admission. The wide front door, too, was kept as carefully locked. Only Mr Thackerton himself and his son were permitted to have latch keys. Otherwise any member of the family had to ring and wait for one of the household's two footmen to come and let them in.

So, as she sat in the schoolroom eating her own modest supper which Mary, or Vilkins, had brought up to her, Miss Unwin reviewed in her mind what she knew of the servants in the house. That the sugar-mouse thief was one of the family was unthinkable.

But her review did not much help her. In the time she had been in the house she had not got to know any of the servants, except Vilkins, at all well. They distrusted her and did what they could to keep their distance. It was no more than she had expected, for all that this was her first post as a governess. But she had been warned by the lady in the country, to whose house she had gone long ago as a kitchen-maid and in whose service she had step by step mounted up, that a governess's lot was not always an easy one. The servants in a house, although they were in duty bound to acknowledge a governess as a lady, knew always that she was a paid employee like themselves, often not much better paid, and they had many ways of showing how aware they were of this.

So even Hannah, the first housemaid, with whom Miss Unwin came into most contact, was still much of an unknown quantity. While Nancy, the scullery maid, was someone she hardly saw except across the dining-room at Morning Prayers, since she had few occasions to visit the kitchen with its great white-scrubbed table and its ever-glowing three-fire range nor the pantry beside it with its deep shelves piled with china and its heavy sink steamy with washing-up water, nor the larder next to that where as often as not there would be hanging a pair of hares – Mr Thackerton's favourite rich dish – softly dripping blood for the full eight days needed to give them their gamiest taste.

Mrs Breakspear, the cook, who had charge of the hares and all the mighty piles of good things in the larder, was yet less well known to her. She had spoken to her a few times, a stout, cheerful person, but hardly more. Yet the thought of her creeping up the stairs and snatching a sugar-mouse from its resting place was ridiculous. Equally ridiculous, somehow, was the notion of the sole other maidservant doing the same thing, although Simmons,

9

old Mrs Thackerton's lady's-maid, was the very opposite of stout Mrs Breakspear, a thin, papery-faced individual, long in the family, who moved about the house always in particular silence.

Miss Unwin knew her rather better than any of the other maids except Vilkins since she came upon her most afternoons when, while Pelham was having his nap, it was her duty to go to Mrs Thackerton's sitting-room to read to her, a task which it had taken her some weeks to feel comfortable about. Simmons would greet her then, giving her a smile, a sudden glimpse of long incurved yellowy teeth in her papery face. Yet they were smiles that seemed always to leave her feeling less cheerful than she had been before.

The men servants Miss Unwin felt she knew even less than the maids. There was old Mellings, the butler, distant and stately. There was Peters, Mr Thackerton's valet, reserved and private. There was Henry, the first footman, distinguished only by being – to Miss Unwin's eyes – no more than a six-foot tall clothes-horse for his imposing green plush uniform. There was Joseph, the second footman, rather less of a clothes-horse and rather worse at his duties. Last of all there was John, the page, almost as tall as Joseph, looking a little lubberly in his tight, button-decorated suit, and almost as much of a newcomer to the house as herself, a sign of yet another upward step for the thriving Thackertons. If she must suspect someone, Miss Unwin thought, John was the most likely one of them all to cast in the mould of sugar-mouse thief. She had seen him looking with envy at the dishes of sweets being carried into the dining-room to round off the eight-course dinners Mr Thackerton offered to his guests.

But suspicion, she told herself, was not enough. She must have proof.

'Miss Unwin, have you thought?' Pelham inquired of her as, next evening, they went up the broad, thickly carpeted stairs together, Pelham with his latest reward, its head taken off in one clean bite, dangling by its soft white string tail in his chubby little hand.

Miss Unwin had no difficulty in knowing what it was she was meant to have thought of.

'Yes, Pelham,' she said. 'But wait until we get to the school-room. We don't want any long ears to hear what our plan is, do we?'

Pelham tiptoed the rest of the way up the stairs.

In the schoolroom Miss Unwin took a reel of strong black thread from her work-basket, a farewell present from her protect-tress in the country given to mark her jump from being lady's-maid to the daughter of the house there, now married, to the status of governess and lady herself. From Pelham's little desk she took a couple of sheets of paper.

Then, watched by her charge in silent awe, she tied the thread to the end of the sugar-mouse's tail, put the sparkling sweet in the customary place on the table by the banisters at the head of the stairs, hid the thread under the sheets of paper and led it, concealed by the landing rug into the schoolroom through the gap at the door hinges. To the end of the thread inside the room, so that neither of them should miss the faintest twitch on it, she tied a large bow of crumpled paper.

In a minute Mary brought up Pelham's bowl of bread-and-milk.

'Now, eat it up every drop,' Miss Unwin said. 'Or I'm sure nothing will happen.'

Pelham began to eat. But between each mouthful he gave the paper bow a long hard stare. Each time, however, it stayed as frozenly still as it had been when Miss Unwin had first put it down on the floor. At last the bread-and-milk was eaten to the last piece.

'Miss,' Pelham said, pointing with his spoon at the door.

Miss Unwin did not rebuke him for this lapse in manners. Instead, quietly as she could, she went over to the door and flung it suddenly open wide.

The sheets of paper lay on the table by the banisters exactly as she had placed them there. But the sparkling white sugar-mouse had disappeared.

Miss Unwin hurried across, Pelham scuttling after her. She lifted the piece of paper nearest the place where the mouse had been. The end of its tail had been neatly snipped off.

Little Pelham's face went horrendously red with rage. Miss Unwin felt almost as furious. But her fury was at once followed by a sharp inner sinking. If the thief succeeded in repeating his thefts again and again, her position in the house might well become intolerable. So far Mr Thackerton had not remembered to inquire into that first disappearance. But now Pelham might well say something to him, and then his anger could well be directed not so much against the actual perpetrator of the deed as against the person who had failed to protect his property.

But, almost as disquieting, there were the servants, too, to think about. Whichever one of them it was who had first stolen Pelham's treat, in perhaps a moment of greed, was acting now from a very different motive. They were acting out of a desire to score over her. They might for a while keep silent about their repeated victories, but they would not stay silent in the servants' hall for ever. Sooner or later they would begin to boast. And then her stock in the house, not very high at the best, would sink yet lower. Her orders and requests would be ignored, and that in turn would make her task as Pelham's governess less and less easy to carry out.

The thought of dismissal entered her mind. And the ugly, charity-cold Home for Unemployed Governesses that would follow.

She had seen herself when she began her new duties as on the foot of a long, rising slope. She would become a more and more accomplished governess, learning from books and from experience. She would gradually accumulate some savings. One day she would open a school. Perhaps that school would grow in reputation. In her most secret dreams she had seen herself ending her days as a person honoured in society.

And now all that was in peril. Because of a stolen sugar-mouse.

She forced herself not to let tears come into her eyes.

'Well, Pelham,' she said with what briskness she could muster, 'the thief has beaten us once more. But we're not going to be beaten in the end, are we?'

'No, we're not. We're jolly well not. And, when we've caught the person, Grandpapa will make it so hot for them they'll roast and roast and roast.'

'As to that, my lad,' Miss Unwin said, mistress of herself once more, 'we'll see when the time comes. But it's bed for you now, bath and prayers and bed, and tomorrow we'll see if I haven't thought of a better trap than today's.'

But she could not bring herself to rebuke Pelham when those prayers ended 'And please God let Miss Unwin and me catch the thief and make Grandpapa roast him.'

So the next day when it came to that regular part of Pelham's education called the Object Lesson – Pelham had enjoyed 'How A Pin Is Made' the week before so much that he had spoken about nothing else all the rest of the day – she told him that their new subject was to be 'How We Make Toffee'.

'Can I eat it when we've made it, Miss Unwin?'

'Well, perhaps if you're good you may have some. But most of it I shall need for another purpose altogether.'

Pelham looked disappointed.

'For the purpose of trapping,' Miss Unwin said.

Pelham's eyes lit up. But before he could produce any more threats of roasting Miss Unwin rang for Vilkins – carefully addressed as Mary in Pelham's presence – and got her to bring up from the kitchen a saucepan and sugar and to light a fire in the narrow schoolroom grate. Together then they manufactured a quantity of toffee nicely judged to be as sticky and glutinous as black road tar. Miss Unwin would have liked to complete her trap there and then, but to spend more time on it would have interfered too much with Pelham's instruction, and she was determined that by the time he was nine, in something under two years more, he would be as ready to go to Eton and shine there as any boy in the land.

So she reconciled herself to the loss of another headless sugar-mouse. And so, after a little persuasion, did Pelham.

But when after his supper they went out on to the landing and found his unprotected treat had once more been made away with she could not resist leaning over the banisters and whispering fiercely 'Just you wait.'

'Just you jolly well wait,' Pelham echoed, more loudly.

The next day's Object Lesson was 'How to Make A Cast with Plaster of Paris' and by the end of that day Miss Unwin and Pelham were in possession of a fine representation of a headless sugar-mouse that had been carefully filled with gluey toffee and as carefully dusted with icing sugar brought up with Pelham's bread-and-milk by Vilkins, whom together they had sworn to secrecy.

Not many days later Miss Unwin was to look back on that giggling, cheerful ceremony and contrast it bitterly with pledges she had to ask of Vilkins in a matter a thousand times more serious than the theft of any number of sugar-mice.

But now the new trap was ready to be sprung. The plaster-mouse was carefully put in the exact place that the sugar-mice had hitherto occupied and Miss Unwin and Pelham retreated to the schoolroom and all but closed its door.

There they waited, Pelham's bread-and-milk this time gobbled up in two minutes.

Then, at the precise moment Miss Unwin had expected, shortly after Vilkins had gone clumping down the back stairs to collect her second pair of hot-water cans for Pelham's bath, there came from the front stairs just a few yards away a single, ear-splitting roar of outrage. A roar oddly stifled and muted.

Pelham slipped down from his chair and darted for the door. But Miss Unwin was quicker. She swept the door wide but at the same time protected Pelham with her skirts from any unexpectedly disconcerting sight he might see there.

But she had no need to worry on that score. The culprit, standing half-way down the first flight of the stairs with only his face showing through the banisters, was the second footman, Joseph, someone who had never been even remotely a favourite among the servants with Pelham. From the little she knew of the fellow, he was not much of a favourite with herself. She suspected him of more slyness than she had actually seen in him and she had heard him once, somewhat to her amazement, tell young John that one day he would be butler in the house.

She looked at him now with distaste. His long, bold-featured face was dark with rage as his teeth, large and yellow as a horse's, stayed clamped on the sticky toffee inside the now broken plaster-mouse whose soft string tail was dangling from his lips.

'Well, Joseph,' she said, 'you're caught red-handed, are you not? How could you have played such a nasty trick on Master Pelham night after night?'

Through the banisters Joseph glared back at her, working his big teeth to free himself. At last, tearing off one of his white gloves, he managed to get a finger into his mouth and eject most of the sticky mess.

'You could always have fetched the boy a new one, couldn't you?' he snarled unexpectedly. 'You got him one soon enough the first time. I was watching you. But you didn't dare face 'em in the drawing-room again, did you?'

Miss Unwin felt a small jab of shame. It was true that she had not wanted to ask more than once for new mice for Pelham. But, she told herself, her share of the blame for depriving the boy of his treat was tiny compared to Joseph's.

She turned to Pelham now.

'Run along to your room then,' she said to him. 'I must have a word with Joseph, but you go and begin getting ready for your bath. Mary will help you when she comes back.'

Pelham crossed the landing to his bedroom, went in and shut the door without a word. Miss Unwin felt that her fears that confrontation with the sugar-mouse thief would not be as much of a pleasure as the boy had thought had turned out to be justified. But this was something she would have to try and put right at some other time. Now there was Joseph's sullen face looking at her defiantly from the other side of the banisters.

'I had hoped that this was something that could be settled here and now,' she said to him. 'But if you take that attitude I shall have to tell Mrs Arthur what you have done.'

Joseph looked at her for a little in silence.

'Don't do that, miss,' he said at last. 'I might be dismissed.'

There did not seem to be a great deal of repentance in his tone. But Miss Unwin seized on it. She could not easily bring herself to say anything which would cause the dismissal of even as sly a servant as Joseph. Anyone dismissed without a letter of reference faced a bleak future.

'Very well,' she said. 'We will say no more about it.'

Joseph's long teeth, still with brown toffee smears on them, showed in a brief smile.

'Thank you very much, miss, I'm sure,' he said.

He came up the remaining stairs to the landing, slouched over to the green baize door to the servants' stairs and vanished.

Miss Unwin went to watch over Pelham's bath, feeling uneasily that the encounter had not been exactly satisfactory. Pelham had got into a fearful muddle trying to take off his undervest and it took her a full two minutes to sort it out and rather longer to put the discovery of Joseph's mischief into a light in the boy's mind that he could deal with. She felt, when at last she sat down in the schoolroom with her own supper, more than a little exhausted.

So it was all the more infuriating, next evening, when going with Pelham to collect his new headless mouse from the table by the banister she found that once again the sweet treat had disappeared.

Chapter Three

Miss Unwin felt outraged and at the same time more than a little afraid. She had no doubt that Joseph had stolen this mouse just as he had stolen all the others. All his talk about losing his place had been so much dust to throw in her eyes, and it was the fact that he was calmly prepared to ignore her that filled her abruptly with doubts. How could she go on in this house if she was being treated with such contempt? Yet go on she must. She would not easily get another such chance in life again.

Little Pelham, however, plainly felt rage unclouded by any doubts at all. His cheeks were getting moment by moment redder and redder preparatory to some furious outburst.

'Now Pelham,' Miss Unwin said hastily, 'I am going down this moment to your Mama, and if you are a good boy and make no fuss I dare say she will let me have another mouse for you.'

'Yes please, Miss Unwin. And, Miss Unwin, you will tell her to send Joseph away, won't you?'

'What I tell your mother, Pelham, is something for me to decide. Now, you hurry along and begin getting ready for your bath, and, remember, when you come to your undervest, cross your arms over, take it by the bottom edge and pull it off you like a rabbit skin.'

'Yes, Miss Unwin.'

Pelham went briskly across to his room and his waiting bath. Miss Unwin made her way down to the drawing-room with much less determination.

It was not braving the assembled family and the dinner guests she knew were there this evening that made her steps slow. If something had to be done, it had to be done. But she found herself now reluctant, despite Joseph's blatant snub to her, to condemn him to dismissal, something she thought more than likely if Mrs Arthur was told of this repeated offence. She could not quite contemplate the idea of anyone in much her own hazardous circumstances trudging the streets, basket of belongings on shoulder, looking for a bed in some servants' lurk while begging and scraping for a new chance somewhere without a 'character', that necessary letter from a previous employer.

But if she kept silent about Joseph, would not that be neglecting her duty towards the family who had entrusted their child to her? To know that one of the servants of the house was an habitual thief, to have proof of it, and to say nothing: that would be to commit a crime herself.

So once again she turned the heavy brass knob of the drawing-room door and entered.

There were tonight some half dozen guests sitting among the many chairs of the big room, elegantly dressed, talking and laughing. Mr Thackerton was standing in his customary place in front of the ornament-crowded mantelpiece. Mr Arthur was present too, leaning over one of the lady guests, his long face intent in its frame of fashionable Piccadilly Weeper sidewhiskers. His wife was where she too usually chose to be, on the ottoman at the far side of the room, reclining languidly and playing with the heavy amber necklace round her throat as she listened to what one of the gentlemen guests was telling her.

Miss Unwin crossed the room, unobtrusively as she could, and, waiting her chance, intervened and asked if she could have a word in private.

'I'm sure, Miss Unwin, you can have nothing to say to me that cannot be said here. Or, rather, cannot it in any case wait until tomorrow?'

'No. I am sorry, but I do not think that it can.'

'But dinner will be announced at any moment. I'm sure I hear Mellings at the door.'

'I do not think so. It is only twenty to seven by the clock on the mantelpiece. There is a full quarter of an hour, and I shall not need more than two or three minutes of your time.'

Miss Unwin's heart beneath her calmly respectful exterior was beating like a tattoo. Was she being too insistent? Would the gentleman standing now a little aloof put her down as a subordinate showing something like impudence? But Pelham must have his treat restored to him, and Mrs Arthur must learn why that was necessary.

'Oh, very well.'

With a sigh and a pout Mrs Arthur rose from the ottoman, murmured something to her cavalier and led the way out to the hall.

'Well? What is it then?'

Miss Unwin pulled the drawing-room door closed.

'You will remember,' she said hurriedly, 'that not long ago I had to ask you for another sugar-mouse for Pelham when the one you had given him had mysteriously disappeared?'

'Yes, yes. Has the same thing happened again? Do you want another one now? I don't see why you could not have quietly fetched that without taking me away from my guests to tell me about it.'

Miss Unwin hurried on.

'The same thing has happened a good many times since that first incident,' she said. 'But I have discovered who was the person responsible. It was Joseph.'

'Well, if you have found that out, well and good. But I still do not see why I should be bothered over it.'

'I had hoped that catching Joseph in the act would be enough to bring the business to a halt. But this evening he has taken yet another of the mice.'

Miss Unwin waited for her announcement to receive its due. It was Mrs Arthur's duty to deal with Joseph now.

But Mrs Arthur remained silent.

'Shall I tell Mellings that Joseph is to come and see you in the morning?' Miss Unwin asked at last.

'Yes. No. No, Miss Unwin, I really cannot have all this nonsense put upon me. Joseph has done this, Joseph has done that. I don't know what to believe. And there are our guests, let me remind you. You are keeping me away from them.'

'I can assure you that Joseph has stolen Master Pelham's sweets,' Miss Unwin said, with more firmness than she had thought herself capable of. 'I caught him doing so last night, and he did not deny that he had done so each night before.'

'No, really, I cannot understand all that rigmarole. I am sure Joseph is not half as much to blame as you seem to think. Now, come and fetch poor little Pelham a fresh sugar-mouse. I cannot understand why you have kept him waiting so long. The poor lamb.'

Miss Unwin recognised that she could do no more. Meekly she followed Mrs Arthur back into the drawing-room, took a new mouse from the chiffonier and carefully carried it upstairs. But inwardly she resolved that the matter was not going to end like this. If she let it, her position in the house would become yet more intolerable.

But she had no immediate opportunity of putting matters right. Before she could act at all she had, indeed, to experience the humiliation of having Joseph almost openly triumph over her.

The encounter took place just after Morning Prayers next day. The whole household habitually gathered for this short ceremony at a quarter to nine each morning, with only Mrs Thackerton senior, the privileged invalid, absent. By that time the servants had got through all their first duties. The three fires of the kitchen range had been lit, and in winter fires in all the downstairs rooms as well. Hot water had been taken up to all the family bedrooms. The front steps had been holystoned to dazzling whiteness and the brass doorknob and the bells polished to a glitter. The table had been laid in the breakfast-room, and the servants' own hasty meal eaten. Promptly at the quarter hour then they all filed into the dining-room and took up their positions in a line against the far wall – where in winter a sharp draught was apt to come in at the windows.

Mellings, broad and solemn-faced, stooping slightly with age and long service, headed the line. Next to him, plump and comfortable, stood Mrs Breakspear, red-faced already from bending over the hot range. Next, forming a curious contrast by her withdrawn paper-pale face, came Simmons, as yet unwanted by Mrs Thackerton upstairs in bed. Then came Peters, fresh from having seen his master dressed, reserved as ever. Beside him stood Henry, resplendent in his green plush and white waistcoat, plainly conscious of every inch of his six feet. And next to Henry, and noticeably shorter in height in his matching livery, was Joseph, who when Miss Unwin had entered the room with Pelham clutching her hand had given her a long, cool stare, his boldly featured, waxy face a mask of blandness.

20

Miss Unwin had felt able to ignore that look. But she guessed it was only a foretaste of what was to come. Nor would there be insolent looks from Joseph alone before much longer. There would be such glances from every single one of the servants, except poor Vilkins, as well as deliberate failure to accept the orders she was bound from time to time to give.

Next to Joseph in the servants' rank stood Hannah, the first housemaid, already little inclined to do what she was asked. Vilkins, standing next to her, a drip on the end of her big red dab of a nose, would not be support enough if all the house was set against her. Even Nancy, the scullery maid, would no doubt find occasion for some display of contempt, and lubberly John, last in the line in his tight-fitting, button-sparkling uniform, could well play some trick or other on her.

Mr Thackerton, having left as was his custom a minute's pause after the family had entered and taken their places, came striding in.

He marched, heavy-footed, to the top of the long table where on the thick green cloth that covered it at this hour there had been placed the large family Bible, opened at the page he was to read from. His arrival at the head of the table was the signal for all to kneel while he recited the Lord's Prayer, to which they all in their different ways murmured accompaniment.

Miss Unwin, with as usual her eyes only half-closed so that she could keep a watch on little Pelham, was able to detect across the width of the cloth-covered table that Joseph's voice this morning was noticeably louder and clearer, almost as loud indeed as the Master's at the table's head.

A reading from the Bible followed. Next Mr Thackerton was accustomed to intone a short prayer commending them all to their duties for the day. He finished, as usual, by closing the Good Book with a resounding bang as much as to say 'That's that'. At once the servants got to their feet and filed out to start again on the duties to which they had been so firmly directed. The family waited for them to have gone and then Pelham's mother and grandfather wished him good morning. His father seldom remembered.

It was while they were all moving across to the breakfast-room and its laid table that Miss Unwin was greeted directly by Joseph.

'Good morning, miss,' he said, putting himself in her path as she followed the others and even for a moment sticking his thumbs into the pockets of his white uniform in a cocksure parody of Mr Thackerton's customary stance.

'Good morning, Joseph,' Miss Unwin replied, loudly and clearly.

She looked straight back at him, her expression as devoid of feeling as she could make it. He smiled, the long teeth curving between the pale lips of his large-featured face.

Miss Unwin resolved then that, before the day was out, she would have done something to see that this triumph was short-lived.

She took the first step to achieving that end when she went in the afternoon to read to Mrs Thackerton senior. Generally, few words were exchanged on these occasions. Mrs Thackerton often would do no more than extend a thin hand towards the book they were working their way through. Then, fighting off the torpid heat of the blinds-darkened room, it would be Miss Unwin's duty to read steadily on until asked to stop. Yet sometimes Mrs Thackerton liked a little undemanding talk. She would ask how Pelham's lessons were progressing, comment in mildly shocked tones on the weather, or boast feebly that she had gone for a whole week without having had to summon the doctor.

So Miss Unwin acted quickly now to forestall the long, bone-thin fingers pointing towards the book.

'Did you hear about poor little Pelham and his sugar-mice?' she asked, making the question as casual as she could.

'No. No, I hear nothing of what goes on in the house.'

Miss Unwin gave her a quick glance in the gloom, and was struck not for the first time by the thought of how young 'old Mrs Thackerton' really was. Though her face was lined there was hardly a grey strand in her pale golden hair. She must be no older than her husband, vigorous in his mid-fifties. Yet, seldom moving away from the special, Paris-imported invalid sofa where she now lay, she had all the appearance of someone almost old enough to be his mother, even of someone indeed not long for this world.

22

Would she have enough force to deal with the affair of the stolen sugar-mice, now that it had been brought to her notice?

Concisely as she could, Miss Unwin retailed the whole history. Certainly her hearer seemed to take it all in. But how would she respond?

The response, when it came, was unexpected.

'You say that you made Pelham go without his treat for so many nights?'

'Why, yes. He must learn to accept the setbacks of life, after all.'

It seemed to be Mrs Thackerton's turn to be surprised.

'Yes. Yes, I know that he ought to. But . . . But . . . Well, he has not been prepared to accept setbacks very much up to now. His previous governess had to be sent away, you know, because he was so wilful and she could not control him. Is he not disobedient with you?'

'Well, I see to it that he is not. He is a good-hearted little fellow once he understands how things must be.'

Mrs Thackerton, careworn on her French sofa, sighed deeply.

'If only I could have been as firm as that with Arthur,' she said, as much to herself as to Miss Unwin.

She turned her head then.

'We had no governess for him, you know,' she said. 'Mr Thackerton was not so prosperous in the days before he was able to use the invention for making steam-moulded hats.'

Miss Unwin murmured something in acknowledgement of the confidence she was being favoured with. She would rather have pushed forward with her scheme to persuade Mrs Thackerton to deal with Joseph. But she saw that this was not the moment.

'Yes,' Mrs Thackerton murmured on, her eyes fixed now on the slumbering fire that was making the room so oppressive. 'Yes, Arthur was always a troublesome boy. He was a trouble at home, and he was a trouble at Eton when he went away to school. He was fast there. He was fast at Oxford, and I sadly fear he is fast yet.'

Miss Unwin sat still as she could on her low chair near the

window and turned her mind away from the whole conversation. She had heard more than she should.

A silence fell. The coals settled in the grate. Outside in the sun a pigeon cooed and cooed and cooed.

At last Miss Unwin thought she might venture to speak again. Perhaps firmly changing the subject back to what she had wanted to discuss in the first place would obliterate in Mrs Thackerton's mind that indiscretion of hers.

'I had occasion to tell Mrs Arthur about Joseph last night,' she said, 'and I am very much afraid that she does not intend to take up the matter with him. Do you think that you could see him?'

'See him? You mean speak to him? Dismiss Joseph myself?'

Mrs Thackerton raised her thin hands in dismay.

'No, no, my dear girl,' she said. 'You are asking too much. You know that the affairs of the house are out of my keeping. Oh, I have my set of keys still. I am Mr Thackerton's wife after all. But Mrs Arthur has the keys that are used. She orders everything now. I cannot do it. I cannot.'

'Yes, I understand,' Miss Unwin answered, a little desperately. 'But it truly seems that Mrs Arthur is unwilling even to speak to Joseph. So, if you could . . .'

But Mrs Thackerton shook her head.

'You are right, my dear. Joseph's misdemeanours should not go unchecked, and I admire you for your courage in attempting to see that they do not. But there are things that I can no longer do. Many, many things. And to speak to Joseph is one of them. It would be beyond me, beyond me altogether.'

'Yes, I see,' Miss Unwin replied.

She felt suddenly very much alone. Was there no one in this house she could rely upon? Was there, at best, only dear, cheerful, willing but incapable Vilkins on her side? And could she succeed in doing what must be her duty if all were so set against her?

Yes, she could. She must.

'Yes,' she repeated. 'I can see that such a task is beyond you, Mrs Thackerton, and since Mrs Arthur will not take it up there is only one thing I can do. I shall have to go to Mr Thackerton himself.'

It was a brave boast. But had she realised that in carrying it out she would come to place herself in a situation that held for her far more dangers than all the hostility of the house could bring to bear, would she have spoken with so much determination?

Chapter Four

Late that evening Miss Unwin was listening from near the top of the stairs for Henry, down below, to take in to Mr Thackerton in the library his nightly whisky and seltzer. She had decided that this last quiet hour of the day would be the time when, if ever, the Master of the house would be disposed to give his grandson's governess a hearing.

If she still did not know a great deal about the servants under the roof of No 3 Northumberland Gardens, she had long before taken care to find out as much as she could about the man whose word in the house was law. His lightest shaft of anger could, she knew, send her sliding down from her hardly won position as swiftly as if she had landed on a long snake on the board game that was little Pelham's favourite.

Of all she had learned about Mr Thackerton one thing stood out: he was terribly quick to look down on anyone lower than himself in the social scale. Miss Unwin thought she knew why. Mr Thackerton's beginnings had not been all that high. They were by no means as utterly low as her own, but they had been low enough. His father had been a hatter, owner of a business that provided no more than modest comforts, but shortly after Mr Thackerton himself had inherited the concern the remarkable invention that produced Thackerton's Patent Steam-moulded Hats had been introduced. From then on progress had been extraordinary and now Thackerton hats put all their rivals to shame. Advertisements for them were to be seen everywhere, plastered on every poster-covered wall, blazoned on the sides of horse-buses, boldly inserted in half a dozen varieties of fancy type in every magazine and newspaper.

The Thackerton family had soon moved from the mild prosperity of Lambeth across the stinking waters of the Thames (which had nevertheless somehow washed away all traces of humble origins) to the dignity and massive respectability of Bayswater.

All this piecemeal gathered information had made Miss Unwin certain that if Mr Thackerton was to be approached at all on the matter of Joseph and the stolen sugar-mice it would have to be done at the most propitious moment.

So now she listened for Henry to enter the library carrying in his white-gloved hands the silver salver on which there would be resting a tumbler, the whisky decanter and the seltzer siphon. She would wait, she had decided, until he came out and then for three minutes more. At that point, if she had guessed correctly, Mr Thackerton would be moderately at ease but not so much so that an interruption would be furiously resented.

She had had to give herself a long vigil. There were some occasions, she knew, when Mr Thackerton received a visitor in the library and his nightcap was postponed. This visitor was a confidential clerk from the firm's London office, one Ephraim Brattle, a young man of singularly dour appearance, black-haired, with a set round face that reminded her of nothing so much as the front of a steam locomotive so strongly determined was its expression. It was his task to go from London to the works in Lancashire with whatever orders were necessary, leaving by the first train from Euston Station having slept the night in a spare servants' bedroom. His interviews in the library might be short or might be long, so Miss Unwin had had to station herself at her chosen post well in advance.

It seemed, however, that this was not one of Ephraim Brattle's nights. At quarter to eleven, exact to the minute, she heard Henry knock on the library door below and enter.

He was inside for barely two minutes. Miss Unwin saw in her mind's eye the whisky and the seltzer poured into the tumbler, the tumbler set down beside Mr Thackerton and Henry quietly leaving with the salver. From the moment she heard him close the heavy door of the library behind him she began to count the seconds. Up to sixty. Then up to sixty again and then once more.

At last, her calculated three minutes up, she drew back her shoulders and set off down the stairs. At the tall library door she paused for an instant. On the far side she heard Mr Thackerton's little dry cough.

Was she asking for trouble? Would she irritate to fury the person who held over her something approaching powers of life or death, or at least of an aspiring life and an existence of deadly poverty? Was she risking all this simply for a point of petty principle?

Then, no, she told herself. This was not petty. For one thing Joseph had clearly done wrong, considerable wrong though on a trifling material scale. He ought not to escape without paying some penalty. But, as important, if he were allowed to go scot-free, her own position in the house would rapidly become impossible.

She knocked at the gleamingly polished door. Two raps, not sharp, but not timid at all.

She heard Mr Thackerton call out 'Come in.' Was there already a note of anger in his voice? Well, if there was she must do her best to dispel it.

She entered.

'Miss Unwin!'

The whole room, which she had been inside only once before, was formidably impressive. Round its walls in tall glass-fronted bookcases volume upon calf-bound volume was ranged. Miss Unwin had never seen any one of them taken outside the library, but nevertheless, even bought by the yard as they may well have been, the impact of so many books, of so much stored learning, was awesome. Then, a more blatant piece of splendour, down the middle of the big room there ran a magnificent table, wide and well-polished, its legs ornately carved. On it there was a shining array of every article a man of substance might be thought to need in his library. There were three enormous silver inkwells. There were two large wooden racks holding thick wads of heavy cream-laid notepaper and envelopes. Two smaller racks, though not much smaller, held pens, a full dozen in each, and little leather-bound penwipers. There were four blotting-pads, all un-blemished by any ink-stain, their corners rich in gold-tooled leather, and scattered here and there as well were half a dozen little attendant semi-circular blotters with dark rosewood handles. There was a large and ornate brass letter-scales. There were two fine Italian-work paper-knives, one at each of the table's ends.

But the crown of the whole was the object that stood at the centre. Mrs Arthur, when she had shown the new governess over the house – drawing-room, morning-room, library, billiard-room, dining-room, breakfast-room – had been at particular pains to draw attention to it. It was a Testimonial. A noble piece of jeweller's work in silver and modelled plaster, it stood some two or three feet high. Its theme was Industry and Endeavour, illustrated in various figures mounting up to the silver representation of the machine – it was called the Thackerton Tube – that had been the making of the steam-moulded hat. At the base of the whole a large silver plate proclaimed that it had been presented to Mr William Thackerton on the occasion of his twentieth year as Sole Proprietor of the firm, subscribed for by its managers, the clerks in its office and the hands at its works.

Mr Thackerton had not stirred at Miss Unwin's entrance from his deep easy chair within comfortable reach of a corner of the wide table where there rested his glass of whisky, its bubbles lazily rising.

'I am sorry to trouble you at this hour, sir,' Miss Unwin said, hearing with inner pleasure that her voice was steady and quiet. 'But there is a certain matter which I think it my duty to bring to your attention.'

'Indeed?'

Mr Thackerton spoke without removing the glowing cigar from between his lips. Its scent came, heavy and aromatic, to Miss Unwin's nostrils.

'It is a matter concerning one of the servants, sir,' Miss Unwin said, steadily pursuing her object.

'One of the servants? Surely if it is a matter concerning a servant Mrs Arthur will deal with it.'

Miss Unwin hesitated now for an instant. Here, before she had at all paved the way for what she was going to have to say, she was confronted by her dilemma at its sharpest. To tell Mr Thackerton bluntly that his daughter-in-law had declined to do what she ought to have done would very likely antagonise him at once. But not to speak would clearly involve her in half-truths that were almost bound to be shown-up. Then what little credibility she had would be blown away in an instant.

She hesitated. And plunged. For the truth, however dangerous.

'I am sorry to say, Mr Thackerton, that I have already brought the matter to Mrs Arthur's notice but that she has not pursued it.'

She saw the dark colour come flooding up in Mr Thackerton's already reddened cheeks. But another emotion than anger was plainly in his mind, an emotion she had pinned her hopes on. Curiosity.

Curiosity won.

'Pray, what is this matter that you seem to consider so serious, Miss Unwin?'

There was a good deal of contempt in the 'you' but Miss Unwin had been determined before she had even entered the room not to let anything of that kind affect her.

'I am sure you will agree,' she said, 'that theft, even of trifling objects, is a serious matter, especially when it is repeated more than once.'

Had she appealed sufficiently to her employer's pride in his property? In every single item of it?

She had.

'One of the servants is stealing?' Mr Thackerton replied, bringing his legs rapidly up to crash down on the rich Turkey carpet under him. 'Who is this? Man or woman, neither shall remain a day longer under this roof.'

'Yes, I am sorry to say that one of the servants has been stealing. It is Joseph.'

Once more Miss Unwin recounted the history of the missing sugar-mice, and again, thanks to the concise manner of her telling, it appeared to make its full impact.

Mr Thackerton, when her recital was over, pushed himself to his feet and went striding up and down the length of the long central table.

'Well, ma'am,' he said at last, 'I have not heard anything to Joseph's detriment before this.'

'There may have been nothing to hear,' Miss Unwin answered, a little surprised at the calmly judicial tone Mr Thackerton had fallen into. 'But, I can assure you that he has been responsible for taking Master Pelham's treats night after night.'

'Will Pelham verify that?'

'He would, of course. But, let me say, I do not think he ought to be questioned about the matter. Already, I am afraid, he is not a little disturbed over it.'

'I dare say. I dare say. So, we shall have to take your word for it then.'

Miss Unwin pushed back a sharp retort about her word being as good as anybody's. She stood looking at Mr Thackerton in nun-like silence.

He sighed heavily and pushed his thumbs into the pockets of his waistcoat. But for once the characteristic gesture seemed to lack its customary air of abounding confidence.

'Very well,' he said at last. 'I shall see the fellow tomorrow, and take whatever steps I think necessary. Believe me. And now, good night, Miss Unwin.'

'Good night, sir.'

Miss Unwin, lying a little later in her narrow and uncomfortable lumpy bed, admitted to herself that the interview with her employer had not somehow gone quite as she had hoped. Mr Thackerton's first fire seemed to have become dampened in the course of listening to her recital of the facts concerning Joseph's thefts. Could she have presented that recital in a better way? Have taken less time to set out what had happened? But to have done that would have meant omitting links in her chain of proof. It might have made the whole business look like the invention of an hysterical young woman. Would Mr Thackerton even come to regard it as such now, when he saw it in the cold light of morning? Then all the risks she had taken would become worthless.

Uneasily she let sleep overtake her.

Next day, however, her fears seemed groundless. As soon as Morning Prayers were over – Joseph had again intoned the words of the Lord's Prayer in a way that sounded much more triumphant than humble – Mr Thackerton announced in a single barked sentence that he wished to see Joseph in the library immediately.

Miss Unwin took care not to look at the fellow as he made his way out of the dining-room in advance of the family. But, to her surprise, scarcely had Henry begun to serve the breakfast when Joseph appeared in the breakfast-room to assist him, apparently in no way downcast.

Had he not been dismissed then? It certainly seemed as if he had not. It looked even as if he had not been threatened with dismissal. He had nothing of the air of someone who five minutes before had been faced with the loss of his livelihood.

But if he had escaped Mr Thackerton's wrath in some unaccountable manner, what did that portend for her own future in the house? If Joseph felt he had got away with those tricks of his, would he not eventually tell the tale in the servants' hall? And then her own foot would be on the slippery slope.

She must discover what Mr Thackerton had said to Joseph. But to find that out from him himself was, of course, an impossibility. She could not question her employer.

So she must tackle Joseph. It was not a pleasant prospect. She would have liked not ever to have had to hold converse with him again, beyond perhaps to give him what orders might be necessary when Henry had his half day off and he was the sole footman in the house.

Henry, and his half day off. An idea sprang into her mind. This was the very day that Henry was off duty in the evening. So it would be Joseph who took to Mr Thackerton in the library his whisky nightcap, and when Joseph left that room he would be alone and in a place where she could speak to him without any chance of interruption. She would tackle him then. A few sharp questions: that might be all that was needed. Then at least he would know quite clearly that it had been herself who had been the cause of his being spoken to by the Master. Perhaps then he would think twice before tittle-tattling to his fellow servants.

She feared at first, that evening, that she might miss her opportunity. It had proved to be one of the occasions when Ephraim Brattle was to be in the house prior to going to Lancashire with orders for the factory. The young, determined-looking confidential clerk had arrived shortly after the family had finished eating dinner – no guests tonight, but Mr Arthur had sat for once at his own table – and Miss Unwin, waiting with the schoolroom door wide open as she read a French story-book to improve her knowledge of that language, had known Ephraim Brattle had entered the library when she had heard the sound of his voice floating up the stairs from below. She had gone across then and opened the baize-covered door to the servants' stairs just a crack. She felt confident that when the dour young clerk made his way up to the attic bedroom he used on these occasions she would hear him.

Nor did his interview with Mr Thackerton last so long that the hour of the whisky and seltzer had to be postponed. Just before the clock of St Stephen's Church struck ten Miss Unwin detected the sound of the clerk's steps tramping heavily up towards the attics.

She sat on in the schoolroom in the growing darkness of the summer evening, her book abandoned. When St Stephen's clock chimed the half hour she waited for what she judged to be ten minutes more and then went and stationed herself on the stairs where she could be sure of hearing Joseph on his way to the library with the tray of whisky and be ready to intercept him when he came out.

She experienced a moment of alarm when she thought she had failed to hear the library door opened for Joseph to go in. But hardly had she begun to wonder whether she had misjudged the time and was venturing to creep further down the stairs to a point where she could see the library door when it was opened and Joseph came out.

She hurried down the remaining stairs to intercept him.

'Joseph,' she called. 'I want a word with you.'

Joseph wheeled round towards her. His long, bold-featured face seemed drained to an extraordinary whiteness.

A sheet, she thought. Why, he's white as a sheet. I cannot have startled him so much as that.

'Joseph,' she said. 'What is it?'

Joseph's mouth opened once or twice on his long yellow teeth but no words emerged.

'Joseph?'

'The Master. Miss. Miss. The Master, he's dead. Murdered, miss. Stabbed. Murdered.'

Chapter Five

Miss Unwin was entirely unable to believe what she had heard. In her earliest days down in the harsh world of the workhouse she had been acquainted well enough with brutal violence, and sudden death. Men she knew of had died in brawls. Many others, men and women, had died before their time from drink or disease. Plain starvation had carried off more. But, as she had hauled herself part of the way up the long, long ladder from those depths to the place where she now clung, a lady, she had shaken off much that had once seemed to be an engrained part of her life.

So now the shock of Joseph's stark announcement had struck at her devastatingly.

'Joseph,' she said, hearing the words as if another person was speaking them, someone else at some different time, 'Joseph, tell me: what did the Master say to you when he saw you this morning?'

'Say to me?' Joseph echoed her, his dead-white face contorting in a sudden grimace. 'Say to me? What do you mean: say to me?'

'This morning. This morning. What did Mr Thackerton say to you when he summoned you to see him before breakfast?'

Afterwards Miss Unwin was to demand of herself again and again why she had asked this extraordinary question at that moment. What was it that had come over her? Why, in face of the fearful news she had just been told, had she been able to do nothing but repeat mechanically the question she had come down the stairs to put to Joseph? How could such an absurdly silly business as the theft of the sugar-mice have stayed stuck fast in her mind, confronted as she was by the appalling calamity?

But her insistent demand did at least bring Joseph out of his apparent state of numbed shock.

'Oh, this morning, miss. This morning.' He almost smiled at her suddenly, in a flash of long incurved teeth. 'Why, this morning the Master just gave me a good wigging. That's all. Told me if he ever heard the like again I'd catch it. That's all, miss. That's all.'

They stood looking at each other then in silence. Miss Unwin still had not really taken in the terrible words Joseph had blurted out when he had turned at the library door and seen her. Joseph himself seemed caught now in a curious state of embarrassment. He stood there, twisting the silver salver which he still held in front of himself round and round in his sweaty hands leaving the imprint of his fingers smudged all over its rim, as if he was the statue of a footman at some exhibition of automata.

The silence in fact lasted only a few seconds, though to Miss Unwin, looking back on it, it seemed far longer. But, quickly enough, the shock had worn off in her mind.

'Stabbed?' she said. 'Did you tell me that Mr Thackerton has been stabbed? That he is dead?'

She still could not entirely believe Joseph the liar.

'Yes, miss,' he repeated. 'Stabbed. With one of the library paper-knives, miss. Stabbed.'

At last the words released something in Miss Unwin. She turned at once to the library door and, without hesitation, swept it open.

She had, as she moved, prepared herself against a shock, and the sight that met her eyes did not therefore discompose her. Mr Thackerton lay sprawled back in the same armchair he had been sitting in when, at almost this hour the night before, she had gone to tell him the ridiculous tale of the missing sugar-mice. But at his throat one of the Italian-work paper-knives from the wide writing-table was deeply embedded. From the wound it had made blood had gouted out in a wide stream down the pure starched white of his shirt front below. There could be no question that the Master of No 3 Northumberland Gardens was dead.

Murdered.

Miss Unwin repeated in her mind the word Joseph had used to her. She could well understand how he had come to blurt it out. There was every sign that Mr Thackerton had indeed been foully murdered.

At once she looked all round the long, book-lined room. Who had done this appalling thing? Where had he come from? Where had he gone?

Both the two tall windows were open at top and bottom with their curtains left undrawn on this sultry summer night and Miss Unwin hurried over towards them. In her mind's eye she saw some dark, indistinct crouching figure entering through one of them, striking that one deadly blow and then retreating the way he had come still in an ominous, dark crouch.

But even before she had reached the nearer window she realised that this imaginary scene could not possibly have taken place. She had failed to remember, picturing it, that the windows on the first floor of the house were all entirely inaccessible from below. There was not even a stout creeper up which a desperate burglar might have climbed. There was not so much surely – Miss Unwin halted and closed her eyes for an instant the better to recall the familiar house front – as a waterspout anywhere near either of these two library windows.

She stepped forward, knelt and thrust her head outside to make sure. A quick glance to either side confirmed her memories. The cream-painted stucco of the house fell away immediately below, and to either side its blank expanse was as obviously unclimbable. Even the dark mass of the laurels in the garden underneath was too far down to make it in any way possible for anyone escaping to have jumped into them without breaking a limb.

Did this mean then that the murderer was still in the house?

Miss Unwin blanched at the thought. But she made herself act on it. How long before had that blow with the paper-knife been struck?

She walked firmly over to the sprawled body and bent close to examine the wound. Yes, the blood from it was still wet and freshly scarlet. The murder could not have long been committed.

Perhaps whoever was responsible had hardly left the room when Joseph had arrived with the whisky and seltzer. Had she herself been only a little earlier in going down to listen for the library door she might have heard the murderer leaving.

Hurriedly she went out into the corridor again. Joseph was still standing where she had left him, looking for all the world, with the salver in his hands, as if he was about to knock discreetly at the door once more and wait to hear his Master call 'Come in.'

'Joseph,' she said with urgency. 'Rouse the house. It's very possible the murderer is still within doors. Mr Thackerton cannot have been long dead. Hurry, man. Hurry. Find Mr Arthur. Tell him what has happened, and then go and get Mellings and examine every door and window.'

Joseph stared at her, his pale face for a moment registering nothing. But then he obeyed.

'Yes, miss. Yes. Oh God, I made sure the villain got away by the windows. But I'll go, miss. I'll go.'

From that moment everything for Miss Unwin became a blur of confusion. As she waited for Mr Arthur to come her mind jumped from thought to thought in a manner she despised in herself but could not now help.

Why had Mr Thackerton been killed? What senseless murderer could it have been who had struck him down? How on earth had it been that when Joseph had told her what had happened she had thought of nothing else but the sugar-mice business? What had possessed her then? And the house, was there really at this moment a man hiding somewhere in it? Prowling? His hands red with the blood of murder, seeking some way of escape? And what was to happen next? Ought she to have summoned the police herself instead of sending Joseph to Mr Arthur? He was no longer Mr Arthur: he was Mr Thackerton now, head of the house. Should she call him that when he came?

Oh why, why, was she thinking about such trifles when death had struck on the other side of that well-polished door behind her?

Mercifully, before yet wilder thoughts overwhelmed her, Mr Arthur did appear, striding along the corridor, tall, commanding, in elegant evening dress, white shirt front sweeping towards her in the gloom like the sail of a man-o'-war.

'Miss Unwin. What is this? Joseph blubbering and mouthing. Something about my father. Is he ill? What's the matter? Do you know anything about it?'

'Yes, sir. I do. I am sorry to have to tell you that your father is dead. He has been killed.'

'Killed? What nonsense, woman.'

Mr Arthur nevertheless hesitated with his hand on the brass knob of the library door and seemed to have to gather up resolution before entering.

Miss Unwin decided that she ought to go back in with him.

Mr Arthur came to a halt a good yard away from his father's sprawled, blood-stained body. His normally ruddy cheeks – wine-ruddy, Miss Unwin had concluded shortly after her arrival in the house – turned almost mud-brown within the dark frame of his elaborate Piccadilly Weeper whiskers.

'Good God,' he said. 'Good God. Who has done this?'

He shot a wild glance at the open windows.

'No, sir,' Miss Unwin said. 'No one could have got in that way. Or have got out. The windows are too high. It is . . . it is possible, sir, I think, that whoever did this is still in the house. I have told Joseph to make a search with Mellings. Peters and Henry are out tonight, you know. It is hardly possible for anyone to have escaped as soon as this. The downstairs windows are barred or shuttered and the doors are kept locked. I had occasion only recently to think about that.'

She felt she was jabbering, but could not prevent herself.

Mr Arthur turned slowly and looked at her.

'What are you saying, you foolish woman?' he snapped. 'You are asserting that someone within the household is responsible for this terrible crime. I order you to silence.'

Miss Unwin felt the full force of this rebuke. It was true: she had been doing no more than think aloud and had by no means seen the consequences of what she had said, that no one could have entered the house to commit the deed. If she had, she hoped she would have had the sense to stay silent. The accusation she had gone more than half-way to making was not one to be voiced lightly.

'I – I will go now, sir,' she stammered. 'Pelham. I must see that he has not been disturbed.'

She turned and almost ran from the murder chamber. But even as she did so her mind was not to be prevented from telling her that, however serious the accusation was that she had inadvertently made, it was yet most likely to be true.

It was impossible for anyone to have gained access to the house in secret. She had thought about that long enough when she had been attempting to lay the blame for the stolen sugar-mice on the right head. No, she had hit on the correct and only answer. The

38

person who had killed Mr Thackerton was someone already inside the house.

Yet, softly opening the door of Pelham's room and peering into its darkness, alleviated only by the tiny nightlight burning on the mantelpiece, she could not bring her mind even to consider who among those in the house might have struck that fierce and sudden blow.

Pelham was lying flat on his back, his arms above his head. His long child's eyelashes rested gently on his soft cheeks. Perfect repose.

Miss Unwin gave thanks for it.

And as to the person, she thought, the police officers who come will have to meet with that problem.

It seemed to Miss Unwin that hardly any time had passed before the police, in the shape of one Sergeant Drewd, did indeed arrive. Mr Arthur, she gathered, had sent a note by Joseph in a hansom direct to Great Scotland Yard. So it was, in fact, a full hour before in response to a message delivered by Henry, back from his outing with Peters and looking odd without the green livery that his six-foot frame was such a fine clothes-horse for, she went down to the dining-room where she found the whole household assembled. Only Pelham, it seemed, sleeping his innocent sleep, had been excused attendance. Even Mr Thackerton's new-made widow was there, sitting huddled in the chair from the head of the table pulled from its place for her, a woollen wrapper drawn round her and Simmons, even more papery-faced at this late hour of the night, at her side, whispering. Ephraim Brattle, too, had been woken from his bed up in the attic and brought to stand at the far end of the room, half-way between the family and the servants lined up in their Morning Prayer places in front of the shuttered windows.

They did not have many minutes to wait before Sergeant Drewd came in with Mr Arthur.

Miss Unwin's first thought on seeing him was that he was too small. He had much the build of a jockey, and his air of the Turfite was added to by the brown suit he wore in the biggest and loudest checks she had ever seen. His manner, too, smacked of the jockey. His eyes constantly darted here and there as if he had a certain winner gripped between his knees and the path to the post was blocked by slower, stupider horses. Only a pair of moustaches, waxed to the sharpest points, somewhat went against the racecourse flavour with a touch of the military.

'Now, sir,' he said to Mr Arthur, who had preceded him to the head of the table and was standing there looking very much as if, were the heavy Bible in its place, he was about to conduct Morning Prayers in his father's stead. 'Now, sir, I have had my account of the bare bones of this business from your man Joseph as we drove over here, and I have made my examination of the cadaver. So I propose here and now to put a few questions up and down to whoever I choose to ask them of.'

Mr Arthur, haggard of face between his exaggerated whiskers, jerked his head back in swift anger. Such brusqueness was no way for a paid policeman to address a gentleman in his own house.

'I see you are offended, sir,' Sergeant Drewd instantly countered, raising a hand as if he was bringing to a halt a loose horse in the paddock. 'But I make no bones about offending you, standing at the head of your own table though you may be. A murder has been committed, Mr Thackerton, and I am here in this house of yours to see that its perpetrator is brought to justice.'

He darted one of his quick looks this way and that round the room, towards the rank of servants under the windows, towards the two Mrs Thackertons seated on the other side.

'Now, there are two ways I might go about this business, sir,' he went on. 'I could go about it in your way or I could go about it in mine. If I go about it in your way I should question each member of the household in turn starting with your good self and working my way down to –'

He swung round and pointed his finger, like a quivering magnet spike, at John, his page's tunic only half-buttoned, his big hands dangling rawly at his sides.

'To that young lad there.'

John, pinned by the Sergeant's extended finger like a butterfly stabbed down on to cork, positively trembled as if he was indeed a flutteringly caught victim.

'And what should I discover by this process, sir?' Sergeant Drewd asked, swinging round again to the new head of the house.

'I will tell you. Nothing. Nothing whatsoever. Each one of those here present from top to bottom' – he darted a glance again at John, who actually uttered a loud gasp as if it had pierced his very flesh – 'each one of you would tell me what he or she thought he or she ought to tell me. That, and no more.'

The Sergeant at this last 'she' had sent his darting glance straight out towards Miss Unwin.

If I were not clear in my conscience, she thought as his eye caught hers, would I quail now? Perhaps I might. Perhaps I would.

'But, sir,' Sergeant Drewd went on, whipping round once more to face Mr Arthur, 'if I proceed in my own manner, by asking my own questions here and there as the fit takes me, as my experience tells me that I should, how do you think I shall get along then?'

He actually had the temerity to pause and leave his question for Mr Arthur to answer.

After a silence that lasted all too long he did so.

'I suppose you would get along all the better, Sergeant.'

'That's it, sir. That's the ticket. You've hit the nail right on the head, as a gentleman should. We shall get along very much better if I tackle this sad affair in the way I have tackled – I won't say hundreds, but I will say dozens – in the way I have tackled dozens of sad affairs before.'

'Carry on then, Sergeant. You know best,' Mr Arthur said in an effort to re-assert his authority.

Miss Unwin could not help registering that the effort was not a successful one. But she had no time for much other reflection. Sergeant Drewd was putting into practice the process he had described.

From person to person he darted. Sometimes he seemed to gallop round the wide dining table as if he was rounding the last bend before the finishing-post. Sometimes he swung aside, leant across the broad cloth-covered expanse of the table and shot one of his questions across it as if it were a billiard-ball and he was sending it streaking into a far pocket.

All the while, Miss Unwin saw as she followed his thought processes as well as she could, he was accumulating knowledge. Most of it she realised the reasons for. But sometimes, tease her brain as she might, she could not discover the relevance of something he had asked, with every bit as much sharp significance as with his other more obvious questions.

One thing certainly became crystal clear to her. Mellings, assisted on their return by Henry and the ever-reserved Peters, had conducted a thorough search of the house and had confirmed that no door or window had been left open.

So - she could only half-admit the thought to her head - the person who had killed Mr Thackerton must be in this very room at this very moment.

An extra snap in Sergeant Drewd's voice brought her attention fully back to him. He was standing in front of John, looking, although he was an inch or two the shorter, altogether cockily dominating.

'And now, young fellow-me-lad, we come to the heart of it. That door beside the larder, the door out into the area, you drew back the bolt on that, didn't you? You drew it back after Mr Mellings here had seen to it that that door was locked and bolted fast and then you bolted it up again? I know you did it, lad. None of your lies is the least bit of good with me. Come on now, out with it.'

John, who had been on the verge of tears for the past twenty minutes, burst now into a howl of wailing that would have convinced almost anyone that the Sergeant had suddenly hit on a simple and convincing solution to the way the murderer had got into the house.

It would have convinced almost anyone: it did not convince Miss Unwin.

She left her place at the foot of the family side of the wide table and whisked round in a moment to where John was standing at the foot of the servants' rank.

'John,' she said, stepping up close to his noisily wailing figure so that her mouth was almost up against one of his burning red ears. 'Stop that noise. Stop it at once.'

John's wailing ceased as abruptly as if his vocal chords had been snatched out of his throat.

'Now, John,' Miss Unwin went on, 'just tell the Sergeant the exact truth. Did you draw back that bolt? Or did you never go anywhere near the door as you had no reason whatsoever to do? Now, John, the truth. Just the simple truth.'

But John, though plainly he was slowly seeing salvation just ahead, never got the chance to produce his answer.

'Yes,' Sergeant Drewd suddenly snapped out, 'it's time for the truth now, if it's ever time for the truth. And the truth is here, staring every one of us in the face.'

Each person in the whole large room was frozen into immobility.

The truth? Staring them in the face? The truth already?

'Yes,' the Sergeant said, giving the two waxed points of his little sharp moustache twirls that seemed as if they would send them spinning like two miniature driving shafts. 'Yes, the truth. The truth here and now. The truth in blood.'

'Blood? Oh-h-h, blood.'

It was John. His face, which had been red as a turkey cock's under the Sergeant's battering a moment before, had gone suddenly a sickly green.

'Yes,' said the Sergeant, not sparing him so much as a glance. 'Yes, the truth. In blood. Here.'

And he shot out a hand and seized hold of the sleeve of Miss Unwin's modest brown alpaca dress.

She looked down to where the Sergeant held the material of the sleeve to the light. There, true enough, unnoticed by her up to now, was a dark stain.

'The woman of blood,' Sergeant Drewd said. 'The woman of blood here before us.'

Chapter Six

Miss Unwin, for all her guiltlessness, could not suppress an inner dart of fear at the Sergeant's dramatic accusation. Blood on her dress. The blood of the murdered man. It did indeed seem to cry out for justice.

But her flutter of panic was only momentary. Then bedrock commonsense re-asserted itself.

'Yes, Sergeant,' she said, finding her voice in answering every bit as steady as she could wish. 'Yes, no doubt that is blood on my dress. You saw it, although I had not noticed it. But I told you not ten minutes ago, did I not, that in the library I looked carefully at Mr Thackerton to try to see how much time had passed since that dagger blow had been struck. It must have been then that the sleeve of my dress brushed against – against the blood. There is nothing more sinister in the stain than that.'

But if she had thought her words would silence the Sergeant she was mistaken.

'That may be so,' he shot back at her. 'Or it may not. Who's to tell? Without evidence who's to tell? And what is it that we're lacking in this affair? Evidence. Evidence, miss. Was there any other person in the library with you? There was not. I have heard as much already. For that I have got evidence. I have got the evidence of Joseph Green, footman. You were in the library entirely on your own. Were you not?'

He fired a pointing finger at Miss Unwin dramatically as if it was a bullet from a pistol.

'Yes,' she answered, steadily still, 'I was in the library on my own. I do not deny it. But, Sergeant, that was after Mr Thackerton had been stabbed. You know that.'

'Do I know it? You ask me if I know a certain fact, and I reply: I know what I have evidence for, and I know nothing more.'

'But you have evidence. You have Joseph's evidence. He went

44

into the library and saw Mr Thackerton lying there. It was only when he came out that I went in.'

'Yes,' said the Sergeant.

Fingers and thumbs went up to the points of his little waxed moustache and twirled like very demons.

'Yes, miss. The man Joseph went into the library and saw his Master there. But did he see him dead? I took particular care to question him upon just that point as we made our way here by hansom cab. And what was his answer?'

Miss Unwin felt a chill foreboding. But she spoke as calmly as she could.

'His answer can only have been that he did see his Master dead,' she replied. 'He came out of the library, and he told me that Mr Thackerton had been stabbed. He said that he had been murdered.'

'Did he now? Did he indeed? And I suppose that you have witnesses for that assertion?'

'You know very well that, apart from Joseph, no one else was there.'

'Yes, indeed. I do know that. I know it very well, and I know too that Joseph said nothing to me about "stabbed" and "murdered". Nothing at all did he say.'

With the sense of foreboding gathering within her like some rapidly darkening storm cloud Miss Unwin turned to her sugar-mouse thief of not so long ago.

'Joseph,' she said sharply. 'Tell the Sergeant exactly what you said to me outside the library door.'

'Outside the library door, miss?'

She saw a quick flash of Joseph's long teeth.

'Yes, you know very well where I mean, and when. Tell the Sergeant, tell us all, exactly what it was that you said to me.'

'Why, I'm not sure as how I can recollect exactly, miss.'

It was then that Miss Unwin felt as if the darkening storm cloud had burst in a chilling downpour.

Joseph was not going to say that he had seen Mr Thackerton dead. This was to be his revenge for her having caught him out over his ridiculous thefts. A petty revenge. But one that could be terribly serious for her.

'Come,' she said, drawing on her courage once more. 'Come, did you or did you not say to me: "The Master's dead, miss, stabb –"'

'Stop!'

Sergeant Drewd had jumped in front of her and was holding up his hand as if he was ready to catch a bolting thoroughbred by the bridle.

'Not one word more, ma'am,' he said. 'Not one word more. You were about to put a reply into the mouth of a witness. Now, I won't have that. That I will not have. Let the man say what he has got to say of his own free will. That's the way Sergeant Drewd goes about obtaining evidence, and that's the way Her Majesty's Judges in their wisdom like to hear evidence given.'

Miss Unwin took half a step backwards.

'Very well, Sergeant,' she said, 'if that is what you want.'

'It is what I want. And it is what Her Majesty's Judges want. So let that be the way they are going to get it.'

Despondency settled on Miss Unwin then, sullen and resistant to any sun as black ice. *What Her Majesty's Judges want.* Could it really be that she was in danger of appearing before one of those Judges? That she was going to find herself charged with murder? Impossible. She was innocent. She had not – she had not – plunged that Italian paper-knife into Mr Thackerton's throat. Yet was innocence enough to prevent that charge being made against her? She hoped, she prayed, that if she did find herself charged with this terrible crime her innocence would at the last shine through. But simple reasoning told her that mere innocence might not be enough to prevent the charge being made if Sergeant Drewd, that formidably sure-of-himself figure, had got it into his head that he had in one short hour of triumphant questioning discovered William Thackerton's murderer.

It seemed, too, that he was convinced. There was a look of unmistakable joy in his quick-darting eyes.

He was turning back to Joseph now.

'Well, my man, since the lady is no longer putting words into your mouth, let's hear what you've got to say. Did you see William Thackerton Esquire dead in his library before Miss Unwin entered that room, or not?'

Joseph lowered his gaze to the richly patterned carpet at his feet.

'I will say no more than what I said in the cab, Sergeant,' he answered. 'No more and no less, so help me. And that is this: I cannot recollect seeing any paper-knife nor any dagger in the body of my Master when I entered the library of this his house in order to take him his nightcap which he took regular at that time o' night.'

Miss Unwin felt the prevaricating words as if they were so many knots in a noose being tied round her neck. She realised, too, that there was nothing she could do to rebut them. Joseph was asserting that he had not seen Mr Thackerton dead. She knew perfectly well that he had. He had blurted out to her the very words 'stabbed' and 'murdered'. But she could not prove he had done so. It was at best his word against hers.

And Sergeant Drewd, for whatever reasons, seemed a great deal more inclined to believe Joseph than to believe her.

She straightened her shoulders.

'Well, Sergeant,' she said, 'there's your plain statement, unaffected by anything I might have said to influence it. You have heard it said that no one saw Mr Thackerton dead before I entered the library. You yourself pointed to the stain of blood here on my sleeve. Are you going to arrest me now for Mr Thackerton's murder?'

Sergeant Drewd stood in front of her, a confidently diminutive figure. He twirled once at his wax-pointed military moustache.

'No, miss,' he said. 'I have no intention whatsoever of arresting you.'

At his words there happened to Miss Unwin something that had not in the whole course of a life of painfully raising herself up by her own efforts ever happened to her before. A sudden grey dizziness swirled up within her.

She had only just time to think to herself *I am going to faint*, only just time to hear as from a far distance a voice oddly echoing aloud the very words she had thought in her head, before blackness overwhelmed her.

'She is going to faint. Catch her one of you. Quick. Quick.'

It had seemed to be, of all people, Mrs Thackerton, the aged-before-her-time, afflicted, new-made widow, who had seen what

47

was about to happen and had called out, in a voice a good deal stronger than she had shown herself capable of using in all those afternoons of reading aloud.

But this was a thought that had scarcely impinged before the swirling darkness had blotted everything out.

Miss Unwin did not remain unconscious for long.

It must, she decided, have been only a minute or so before she had some notion of herself being helped out of the dining-room in the sturdy grasp of Vilkins, of being half-carried up the stairs by those same rough arms.

She was in full possession of her faculties, certainly, when Vilkins, with clumsy carefulness, laid her down on her own bed and began to loosen her dress.

'It's all right, Vilkins,' she said. 'I – I feel better now. I can manage.'

'Oh, lawks, Unwi – Oh, lawks, miss, I ain't half glad to hear your voice, that I am. Are you really in the land o' the living again?'

Miss Unwin found herself smiling.

'I don't think I was ever out of that land,' she said. 'Though I did faint. For the first time in my life.'

She smiled again.

'Fainting,' she said. 'That would never have done for us when we were little, would it? We learnt to be tougher than that, didn't we?'

'We did an' all. If we didn't never learn nothing else.'

Cautiously Miss Unwin swung her legs off the bed and managed to heave herself up to sit on its edge.

'Well, I suppose if I was going to faint I had reason enough,' she said. 'It cannot happen to everyone to hear themselves accused of murder.'

'Why, no more it can't. An' what that devil of a Sergeant wanted to go a-doing that for is more nor I can say. But you didn't faint away when you heard that, you know. You had more of the old work'us spirit in you nor that.'

'Well, perhaps I did. But nevertheless I had good cause to faint then, I think.'

'P'raps you did. P'raps you did. That Sergeant turning on you like that. Why, I almost believed –'

Poor Vilkins came to an abrupt halt and looked every which way in confusion.

Miss Unwin gave her a sad smile.

'You almost believed, dear Vilkins, that your old friend had committed that terrible crime,' she said. 'For all that you know me better than anyone, the circumstances the Sergeant brought to light almost convinced you. Wasn't that the way of it?'

'Oh, Lord forgive me, Unwin. It was. It was.'

Vilkins's confession, which she was too unskilled in the ways of the world to have wrapped up in any evasive phrase, brought home in its full force to Miss Unwin the precariousness of her position.

'I really don't know why the Sergeant did not arrest me,' she said. 'He seemed to have so much evidence against me, false though the worst part of it was.'

'That Joseph,' Vilkins said. 'I knew it. He was lying, weren't he? He's one o' the sort that can't stop hisself lying, no, not never so much as he might want to speak the truth.'

'Yes.' Miss Unwin gave a long sigh. 'Yes, Vilkins, Joseph was lying, and you can guess why he wanted to spite me in telling his lies. But the Sergeant believes him. Joseph had the chance to get his word in first while they were coming here in the cab from Great Scotland Yard, and he made good use of it.'

'That villain. I could put me 'ands around his throat an' strangle him.'

Another smile, despite herself, broke through for Miss Unwin.

'I don't think you should do that, Vilkins dear. Really I don't. Not however hard-pressed your friend of old is.'

'Well, but Unwin, what can we do? What can I do?'

The momentary light that had gleamed over the landscape of Miss Unwin's mind gave way to overcast gloom again.

'I don't know what's to be done,' she answered. 'I don't know what I can do. I don't believe there is anything you can do, my dear, much though you may wish to. But, tell me, did the Sergeant say anything after I had fainted as to why he did not arrest me?'

'Well, he did, in a sort of way, though I was too busy a-holding you up and a-taking you out to pay much heed.'

'But you heard something, Vilkins? You caught a few words?'

'Oh, yes, I did. An' I'd have liked to have stuffed 'em back down inside of him till he was fair choked to death, so I would.'

'Yes. But what did he say?'

'He said –' Vilkins creased her cheerful, broad brow in a mighty frown of effort. 'He said there was three on 'em.'

'Three of what, Vilkins dear? Are there two others the Sergeant suspects?'

'Oh, no. No, Unwin, it's only you what he's got his eye on. You can be sure o' that.'

She looked delighted. Pleased to have one thing certain in the difficult course she had been asked to set out on.

'Well, if the Sergeant is so certain that I am the one he ought to have his eye on, what three things is it, so it seems, that are stopping him arresting me?'

'Oh, no, it ain't three things as is stopping him. That I do know. Two on 'em's all right by him. I'm sure o' that.'

'So it is only one thing that lies between me and a prison cell. Is that it?'

'Yes. Yes, that's right,' said Vilkins.

'But what is that thing? Can you remember at all? Please.'

'It's one o' the three, that I do know.'

'Yes? Well, what are the three then? Can you remember one single thing about any one of them?'

Vilkins stood frowning like a gridiron, plainly hoping that the very intensity of that operation would somehow bring into her mind again whatever words it was the Sergeant had spoken.

'Come, just one thing, Vilkins dear.'

'Mean! That was one of 'em. He said he was going to be mean ...'

But her voice had faded away into uncertainty.

'Mean?' Miss Unwin said. 'But not, am I not right, that he was going to be mean? Are you sure he said he was going to be mean?'

'No,' Vilkins brought out in triumph, her red nose pointing up to the ceiling in exultation. 'No, I'm sure o' that now. He didn't say as how he was going to be mean. He said something else altogether. But I'm blessed if I know what.'

'Try to get at it another way. Mean was one thing, but what went with?'

'No. No, I got it now. It weren't mean at all.'

Miss Unwin's spirits, hardly stirred by this quest even when it looked as if it might lead her to understand something of Sergeant Drewd's aims, sank back abruptly into hopelessness.

'No,' said Vilkins, failing to notice that her friend had flopped back miserably on to her pillow. 'No, it weren't mean at all. It were lots on 'em. It were means, he talked about. Means. Yes, means.'

Miss Unwin straightened up as if a galvanic shock had jerked through her.

'Means?' she said. 'Did the Sergeant say that I had had the means to commit murder?'

'Yes,' Vilkins replied, her eyes brightly shining. 'Yes, them was his very words almost. She had the means, he said, an' – an' she had the – the – the opportunity. But what is lacking is . . .'

'Is what, Vilkins?'

Vilkins's fiery dab of a nose sank floorwards.

'Can't remember, Unwin. Can't bring it to mind at all.'

But Miss Unwin was hot on the scent now. Her grasp of logic, if it had been smothered by her troubles before, was firmly back in place again.

'Means,' she said. 'The means to commit the crime. That must be the paper-knife that was so conveniently to hand there. That's one necessity. And opportunity. That there was no one else present, or so the Sergeant believes. That's the second necessity. So the third . . .? The third . . .? Yes, I have it. A reason, a motive, for my supposed act. Yes, a motive.'

'That's it. That's it, Unwin. You ain't got no motive. That's what he said. You ain't got no motive, or not anything he knows about. An' without a motive, whatever that may be when it's at 'ome, he ain't a-going to risk arresting you.'

'Well, I suppose there's something to be thankful for there.'

'Yes, but all the same, what're we going to do? That's a poser if you like.'

'Yes. Yes, it is. I can think of nothing but to hope the Sergeant never succeeds in finding me a motive for having done that horrible thing. Yet I cannot believe he will not find something sooner or later. I very much suspect he is the sort of person who must have success, cost what it may.'

'Yes, I dare say you've the right on it there. He's got the look.'

Vilkins lapsed into a gloom almost as thickly pervading as Miss Unwin's.

But she it was, strangely, who came out of it first.

After two or three minutes of grim, if companionable, silent misery she suddenly lifted up her big nose like a dog scenting dinner.

'There's only one thing for it, Unwin,' she said. 'Only one thing for it.'

Miss Unwin scarcely stirred. But Vilkins went on undismayed.

'Only one thing to be done. An' you're the one to do it. You're the one what solved the mystery o' the missing sugar-mice, an' you're the one what's got to solve the mystery o' the dead Master. You've got to do it, to save yore own skin.'

'No. No, Vilkins, you don't understand. The sugar-mice were one thing. But this ... This is serious, deadly serious.'

'Why then, all the more reason why you got to settle it. You can do it. I knows that. I knew you when we was only a pair o' tiddlers, don't forget. I knows as how you got the brains for anything. I knows that from long ago. But it's up to you to use 'em, Unwin. That's just up to you.'

Miss Unwin sat there on the edge of her narrow bed, and bit by bit into her mind there crept a feeling of resolution.

Until at last she looked up.

'Yes, Vilkins,' she said, 'you're right. And bless you for making me know it. You're right. I am the only one who can help myself now. It is up to me to find who did kill Mr Thackerton before Sergeant Drewd charges me with the crime. It's up to me, and I will do it.'

Chapter Seven

Miss Unwin, her resolution taken, found herself overwhelmed at once by immense tiredness. She was hardly able to mutter to Vilkins how much she longed suddenly for sleep. Willingly she allowed her friend of old to help her off with her blood-marked dress and into her nightgown. Before Vilkins had left the room with a last 'You get a good night, you've earned it,' sleep had overtaken her.

She woke from it, deep and seemingly dreamless, well before her usual time next morning and at once began going over in her mind the whole train of events that had led her to within an inch of being arrested for murder. For a murder she had been as far from committing as she was from flying to the moon.

Then, with horrible abruptness, she found in her mind the inescapable question that her resolution to discover herself who had killed Mr Thackerton confronted her with. Who, under this same roof, was that murderer?

Because it was certain that the murderer was one of the people in the house itself. Her own inquiries and observations at the time of the first sugar-mouse theft had convinced her that it was not possible for anyone to enter the premises unbeknown. The search which Mellings had conducted almost immediately after the murder, accompanied both by tall Henry and Mr Thackerton's quiet valet Peters when they had been admitted to the house after their joint outing, had confirmed the fact. Sergeant Drewd's here-and-there questioning of the whole household in the dining-room had underlined it twice over. No one could have got into the house to kill its Master.

So his murderer must be one amongst them now.

But, faced squarely with the thought, Miss Unwin could not bring herself, even within the privacy of her own mind, to name a name.

The Sergeant the night before, in front of the whole family and all the servants, had accused her to her face of being 'the woman of blood'. It was not something she could do to anyone else, however much her sense of logic rebuked her.

She was being weak. She knew it. Worse, she was allowing herself to be absurd. She was not using the mind God had given her. But she could not bring herself even to think of a single name.

She looked across at the battered alarm-clock on the chest of drawers that served as dressing-table in her small room. It was still much too early to get up and dress and to go to little Pelham with the dreadful news that his Grandpapa was dead. Best, she thought, to keep from him for as long as possible the manner in which that death had taken place. But important to tell him the bare fact before others, less careful than herself, broke it to him.

In the cool early morning light penetrating the thin curtains over her window she tried to lie still and think of nothing.

A forlorn hope.

The image of Mr Thackerton's blood-splashed white shirt front came battering back at once into her mind.

She must force herself to examine rationally who it could be who – No. No, there was a better way of getting at it. She would not try to decide who in the house was a murderer: she would take a leaf out of Sergeant Drewd's book and consider only whom she could clearly eliminate on the grounds of lack of either means, motive or opportunity.

Yes, she could approach the dread question in that circuitous way.

So, first, means. But everybody in the house, whoever they were, surely had the means to do that foul deed if they but had the will. The means were the Italian paper-knife so conveniently to hand at the end of the long library table. Whoever had gone into the library to speak to Mr Thackerton for whatever reason could have snatched up that appallingly sharp weapon and have plunged it fatally into his throat. Even the frailest of them all could have done that, old Mrs Thackerton, invalid as she was, or young Nancy from the scullery, young and tender as she was.

So, opportunity.

And, yes, it looked as though opportunity eliminated nobody either. From Sergeant Drewd's rain of questions as he had stalked up and down the dining-room, firing them off at random, it had been clear eventually that no one had had occasion to be in the corridor outside the library from the time Ephraim Brattle had left it, his instructions for the Lancashire works complete, till the time for Mr Thackerton's nightly whisky and seltzer.

Nor, as it chanced, had there been anybody who had been in someone else's attested presence for the whole of that time. The servants had had various duties to perform that had taken them away from their fellows at different times, some short, some longer. Mrs Thackerton had been alone in her sitting-room. Mr Arthur had been alone in the billiards-room, his wife alone in the drawing-room. So on the score of opportunity, in strict logic, no one except the two men servants outside the house could be ruled out, unlikely though it was to think of old Mrs Thackerton or young lubberly John taking advantage of the opportunity to enter the library and strike the blow.

It came down to motive then. At once Miss Unwin felt inclined to dismiss all the servants under that consideration. Perhaps Peters, in the curiously close links between Master and personal valet, might be thought of as possibly possessing some reason for hating Mr Thackerton so much that he could come to wish to kill him. But Peters had been safely locked out.

Surely, surely Mellings, old and faithful, could have no possible reason for murdering his employer. Mrs Breakspear, fat and comfortable, was a yet more ridiculous conjecture. Simmons, too, for all her habit of moving silently and secretively about the house, was an old retainer, in the employ of the family ever since they had come to Bayswater. No reason why now suddenly she should murder. Even Joseph, proven liar, had no good reason to kill his Master. He had been rebuked by him, warned by him, in the library on the morning of his death. But not by the most far-fetched reasoning could that constitute a motive for murder.

As for the maidservants, none of them ever had anything to do with Mr Thackerton, except perhaps to move out of his way should he come upon them at work in the house somewhere and to hear his prayers for them each morning. So neither Hannah nor Nancy, in her scullery, nor, least of all, Vilkins, could be taken into account. John, too, was as much out of the question. Yes, in her own early knowledge, boys of fifteen had taken lives. But why should John, little more than three months in the house, want to kill Mr Thackerton?

So that left the family.

A member of the family to have a reason for killing its head? Unthinkable. But it must be thought, sensibly and step by step.

First of all Mrs Thackerton. And, yes, looked at in cold logic, she could be said to have a motive for the murder. The old, old motive. A motive she herself in her young days in the lower depths had been acquainted with well enough, if only by rumour: the hatred of one person for another in what should be the most sacred relationship known to man. Yes, appalling though the idea might look seen from the quiet respectability which was her way of life now, a husband was the most likely murderer of his wife and a wife, woman though she was, the most likely killer of her husband.

But Mrs Thackerton, who so seldom left her two rooms, a murderess? It was in the highest degree unlikely.

On to the next in strict order. To Mr Arthur.

At once there forced itself into Miss Unwin's mind, though she half-wanted to exclude it altogether, a very sound motive for Mr Arthur to have murdered his father. It came in the form of a Latin tag she had picked up in the course of her hungry reading. She had learnt what it meant, even though Latin itself was a masculine preserve she had not yet ventured to penetrate. *Cui bono?* To whom the good of it? And the answer was plain. The good of Mr William Thackerton's possessions and wealth was to his son and heir, Mr Arthur Thackerton. To Mr Arthur, of whom she had heard his own mother say 'fast at Eton, fast at Oxford and fast still'.

Yet, Miss Unwin recognised, Mr Thackerton had always been ready to dispense largesse, where it showed. He would not have been at all niggardly with his son, as he was for instance to the governess in his employ.

Nevertheless, proceed in an orderly fashion. After Mr Arthur, his wife. Hard to find any reason why she should have attacked her father-in-law, even supposing her to possess the necessary strength of will, and the person who had evaded reprimanding Joseph over the sugar-mice was as weak-willed as could be.

That left only, hovering between servants and family, Ephraim Brattle, confidential clerk. Could there have been some extraordinary quarrel concerning the firm's activities that had led to murder? Business could be cruel enough, from all she had heard. But never in the newspapers or elsewhere had she come across any account of a business dispute leading to the striking of a desperate knife blow. No, leave Ephraim Brattle, tramping past the schoolroom landing on his way to bed, out of account.

Then was the only real possibility Mr Arthur? But if he was indeed his father's murderer what could she herself do about it? Sergeant Drewd was plainly convinced that she was the guilty party. How on earth could she demonstrate to him that it was the new head of the house? If that was the case even.

The hands of the old clock on the chest of drawers that had seemed to be moving so slowly when she had first wakened, were now already almost at the time she should leave her bed.

Pelham. Poor little Pelham. He had to be rudely hauled out of his everyday happiness with the grim news.

Miss Unwin flung back the bedcover and hurried across to the wash-stand and its tall ewer of cold water.

It was the beginning for her of a day of expected anxiety that was to be marked, too, by unexpected events. But the thing she had dreaded most on waking, the need to break the news to little Pelham, passed off with quite unexpected ease.

'Has he gone to heaven?' Pelham inquired simply when she had told him.

For a moment Miss Unwin hesitated before replying. Had William Thackerton been a man deserving of heaven? Or even, making allowance for divine mercy, a reasonably good man? Well, no, he had not been. He had been overbearing to his family, indulgent to his son, yet more indulgent towards his grandson, seldom ever speaking to his invalid wife, contemptuous towards his daughter-in-law. To his servants he had been abrupt, if not harsh, with that sole, odd exception of his having let go unpunished Joseph, the sugar-mouse thief. He had been generous only when his generosity could be openly seen as a sign of how far he had risen in the world.

No, if there was justice in the end, William Thackerton was hardly now in heaven. But his little grandson was here, in this vale of tears.

'Yes, Pelham,' she answered at last. 'We must all believe Grandpapa is in heaven now.'

'Then that's all right.'

Yet, though Miss Unwin had expected a difficult day, some of its complications she found yet more daunting than she had been prepared for. She had known that the whole household would have to go into mourning clothes. But what that involved altogether surprised her expectations. The appropriate garments for everyone in the house were ordered by telegraph from Messrs Peter Robinson in Oxford Street, to be delivered within twenty-four hours at the latest. For the wife of the deceased and his daughter-in-law there had to be dresses in unrelieved black made of that dullest of materials, stuff. For herself and all the maids there had to be new dresses in half-mourning made out of the same napless, unshiny stuff, lavender-coloured for the servants, a dark-grey for herself. Even little Pelham's sailor-suit had to be put away in favour of proper black.

The blinds at every window had, of course, been lowered and would stay so until after the funeral. This was no less than Miss Unwin had expected. But she had never before been inside a house where the custom had had to be kept, and she found the physical gloom everywhere added heavily to the lowness of spirits she felt, especially when her duties allowed her a moment or two to consider her own position.

At about the time she would, in the ordinary way, have been reading to Mrs Thackerton in her stuffy, overheated sitting-room she had yet more cause to think about how she stood. It was when the inquest was held.

To her considerable surprise she had been informed by Mr Arthur at luncheon that this was to take place that very afternoon.

'I am naturally much concerned that the terrible event of last night should be referred to as little as possible outside,' he had said stiffly. 'Happily my father was well acquainted with the Coroner and he has been most helpful. The hour has been fixed for three o'clock. It will be held here in the house.'

Miss Unwin had felt more than a little disconcerted. But she had said nothing.

She was yet more surprised when she realised that the jury of respectable tradesmen in the neighbourhood – she recognised the local corn-chandler from whom the family bought supplies for the horses kept in the nearby mews – were to hear only three witnesses, Mr Arthur who would state formally that the dead man was his father, Sergeant Drewd to say what inquiries the police were making and herself to detail the circumstances of her discovery of the body.

Told of this by Mr Arthur only when she had presented herself outside the dining-room where the proceedings were to take place, her first thought was that she ought to say, firmly as she could, that she had not been the person to have discovered the dead man. That had been Joseph.

But a moment's caution made her stop. If she made that claim, Joseph could do nothing other than repeat his assertion of the night before, and his claim would be backed as it had been before by Sergeant Drewd. She decided to see what happened when the Coroner put his questions to her. If she could answer them truthfully without mentioning Joseph she would do so. After all, she could certainly describe the wound in Mr Thackerton's throat and the position of his body in his chair as well as anybody.

'Very well,' Mr Arthur said. 'Shall we go in? I believe they are ready to begin.'

He stood aside for her to enter, the gentleman according proper courtesy to the lady.

Or, Miss Unwin thought with a sudden flutter of panic, the murderer pretending to accord courtesy to the person, only doubtfully a lady, who was most likely to be accused eventually of the murder. Perhaps even accused in a very short time by that jury of solemn-faced tradesmen gathered in front of the blinds-shaded windows, looking not unlike the servants waiting for Morning Prayers.

She did her best not to regard the short figure of Sergeant

Drewd, his vivid brown suit looking screamingly out of place in the gloom, standing in a far corner, his head moving to and fro incessantly as he darted his glances around.

No sooner had the two of them entered than the Coroner opened the proceedings. Three or four short sentences sufficed and then Mr Arthur was asked to take his place at the foot of the table to give his evidence.

One question and one answer was apparently enough.

'Mr Thackerton, you have seen the body on which this inquest is being held: will you tell us whose it is?'

'It is that of my father, Mr William Thackerton, of this address.'

'Thank you.'

The Coroner gave a dry little cough.

'Miss Harriet Unwin,' he said.

Miss Unwin went to the place at the foot of the table where Mr Arthur had stood.

In a quiet, precise voice the Coroner began putting questions to her. Her name. Her position in the house.

Before she knew it she was answering yes or no to questions about her discovery in the library. Once she attempted to expand on a reply. The Coroner cut her short.

It has all been arranged, she thought. The Coroner has been told exactly what to expect. He is asking me questions that will bring out those circumstances thought fit to be brought to light and nothing else.

Should I try to say something more?

'Thank you, Miss Unwin. I do not think we need to trouble you further.'

'But –'

'Thank you, Miss Unwin. You may step down.'

She moved back from the table. She had thought she would have to stay in the room until the jury had pronounced a verdict. She had prepared herself even to hear the foreman of that collection of glum-looking tradesmen solemnly bring in not 'Murder by A Person or Persons Unknown' but a verdict naming herself. But, as soon as she had stepped away from the table, Mr Arthur indicated to her with a single sparse gesture that she should leave the room. She went to the door, opened it and went out.

Then, bewildered by the unexpectedness of everything, she stood trying to gather her thoughts in the hall in the deeper gloom by the stairs next to the loudly ticking long-case clock. In a very short time, hardly ten minutes later, the door of the dining-room was opened once more and the jurymen came filing out, only just daring to give subdued, curious glances round about them.

They were followed by Mr Arthur and the Coroner. She just heard the Coroner murmur 'Person or Persons Unknown, we could have hoped for nothing less scandalous, I'm afraid'. Then Mr Arthur suggested a glass of madeira and they went off in the direction of the drawing-room.

The last to leave the scene was Sergeant Drewd. He gave her, for all that she was almost hidden in the darkness beside the stairs, one of his sharp glances and she felt she could almost hear the words *Motive? What motive, I should like to know* being uttered in his head. But a moment later a similar darting glance shot towards Henry, standing holding the front door open for the departing jury, and Henry was provenly out of accounts.

She shook her head vigorously. She must not let herself fall prey to fancies. For one thing, she was not simply the woman Sergeant Drewd had all but arrested. She was, first of all, little Pelham's governess. She had duties towards him. And towards herself. If she was not as good a governess for Pelham as it was possible to be, she would not deserve one day to be rewarded with a more demanding post and to move on from that to yet higher and yet more demanding things.

She turned and hurried up the broad, carpeted staircase to the schoolroom where Pelham had been left in the temporary care of Mary, alias Vilkins. And until Pelham's head was lying on his pillow that evening, his long lashes safely resting on his delicate cheeks, she let nothing else but his needs occupy her.

But, once Pelham was soundly asleep, she decided that it would be expected of her to offer what help she could in the business of putting the house and family into a proper state of mourning. Perhaps there would still be black-bordered envelopes to address for the many thick, black-edged mourning cards that had been ordered that morning and had arrived, elaborately printed, during the afternoon. Or there might be tasks for her needle in addition to the work of the busy-fingered seamstresses at Messrs Peter Robinson's.

As she reached the hall on her way to find Mrs Arthur, there, standing close against the wall just beside the loud-ticking long-case clock, was a man, a stranger. He was dressed in much-worn black and carried, clasped to his stomach, a tall silk hat that looked as if it was battered down to one side.

The undertaker.

That was her first thought. The funeral was to be next day, and what could be more likely than that the undertaker would need to visit the house, even at this comparatively late hour?

But something in the way the man had first, at the sound of her feet on the stairs, shrunk hastily back even closer to the wall and had then stepped forward and directed up towards her a look of brazen confidence made her abruptly less sure of his occupation.

'Good evening,' she said. 'Have the servants left you standing here? I am afraid they are not as they should be after the sad event that has taken place. What can I do for you?'

The man smiled at her then. A sudden smile, suddenly cut off.

'And who might I be addressing, madam?' he asked, giving a little bob of a bow as he spoke, like a wooden toy.

'I am Miss Un –'

Miss Unwin checked herself. The man had evaded replying to her own direct question, and he could have had little straight-forward reason for doing so.

'No, sir,' she countered. 'Who are you?'

The man gave quick looks to left and right, as if perhaps he was hoping that some intervention would save him the necessity of answering. But none came.

He licked his pale lips.

'Hopkinson,' he said, with another quick-come, quick-go smile. 'Hopkinson, of the *Mercury*.'

'A newspaper reporter? And were you let into the house by one of the servants? Yes or no, sir?'

Reporters had gathered outside from as early as the middle of the morning. But Mr Arthur had at once given orders that none was on any account to be admitted and that no one was to speak with them.

Hopkinson of the *Mercury* dipped out another of his little bobs of a bow.

'No need for the peremptory,' he said. 'No need at all. If not welcome, ready at once to retire from the scene. Always ready to do the correct.'

'Then, sir, I suggest you leave directly.'

'Yes, yes.'

Hopkinson moved his silk hat towards his head – it was very much down at one side – thought better of it, turned, made for the front door at a sharp pace, fumbled lengthily with its lock, got it open at last, sidled out and walked, with ever increasing speed, down the path to the gate.

Miss Unwin watched him from the threshold until he had reached the pavement and then closed the heavy door behind him.

Good riddance, she thought. And thought no more.

But this was not the last unexpected event of that long and wearisome day.

No sooner had she entered the drawing-room to ask Mrs Arthur what help she could give her than she found herself confronted with a new turn of events. It was a situation that, having first somewhat embarrassed her, soon occupied her mind in no uncertain way.

Mrs Arthur, already wearing her deep black mourning, her fingers playing now not with the heavy amber necklace she generally wore but with a newly arrived one in glittering jet, seemed not to have heard the polite inquiry she had made.

She repeated it.

'Mrs Thackerton, is there anything you wish me to do?'

Then Mrs Arthur – Mrs Thackerton now – raised her head with a look of unmistakable fury on her usually languid features.

'Do?' she said. 'Do? Why should any of us do anything when the head of the house cannot stay within doors but must go to that person? Why should I care about my duties? Does he? Does he?'

Miss Unwin felt, first, simply shocked by this revelation of marital discord, hitherto scrupulously avoided. She had an impulse to cross the furniture-crowded room and put an arm round Mrs

63

Arthur's shoulders. But at once she realised that the gesture would not be welcomed. Mrs Arthur, no sooner had those impulsive and angry words been spoken, would wish that they could be treated as if they had never been uttered.

'Perhaps,' Miss Unwin said hastily, 'Mrs Thackerton senior will find me useful.'

She turned and left, quickly and discreetly.

But, standing with her back to the closed drawing-room door, she let the thoughts which that single outburst had given rise to run pell-mell in her head.

When the head of the house cannot stay within doors but must go to that person. So Mr Arthur's frequent absences from the family dinner table were explained. By *that person.* That person, surely, must be a mistress. So, Mr Arthur had a mistress, and one to whom he was so violently attached that he could sink all considerations of propriety and go to her on the evening after his father's death.

Did not this, suddenly, provide him with a real motive for having himself taken his father's life? Until this moment she had thought that *Cui bono?* could be the only reason for his having committed the appalling deed, and it had hardly seemed a sufficient one. Mr Arthur had appeared to have had from his father all the money he could possibly want. His clothes alone spoke of that.

But would a father pay happily for his son to keep a mistress? More to the point, would Mr William Thackerton have paid for that? No, most certainly he would not have done. Conscious as he was at every hour of his position in society, of where he had come from and where he plainly hoped to get to, respectability had always been at the forefront of everything he said.

Why, even little Pelham had not escaped that law. In her earliest days with the family she had been sharply reprimanded for allowing Pelham to join in play in Kensington Gardens with a youngster of his own age who, it had turned out, was not of the same social standing as the Thackertons. The two had been seen together by one of the visitors to the house and Mrs Arthur had been instructed to visit Mr Thackerton's wrath on her head. After that she had had, afternoon after afternoon, to steer Pelham away from this playmate until the other boy's nursemaid had taken the hint.

No, the claims of respectability would never have allowed William Thackerton to have paid his son's expenses in keeping a mistress, however discreetly. Yet such expenses would certainly be heavy.

So Arthur Thackerton would frequently be in need of ready money. Perhaps he had taken out post-obits on his father's life, or was being pressed by the moneylenders. It was possible, then, really possible that Mr Arthur had been the person in the library who had quarrelled with the head of the house a few minutes before Joseph had gone into the room with the Master's whisky and seltzer.

But how to convey that to Sergeant Drewd? How could she somehow get such clear proof of it all that the Sergeant could not ignore it? She would certainly have to do no less to alter that implacable little man's fixed conviction of her own guilt.

Then, even as she asked herself the question, an answer came ready-made into her head.

Chapter Eight

It would be necessary, Miss Unwin had thought, to find out who Mr Arthur Thackerton's mistress was and where she was to be found. That was a task which would require first following him one evening when he left Northumberland Gardens to see where it was that he went. That was something that she could perhaps do. It would mean only leaving a little earlier than the new master of the house, securing a hansom and persuading its cabbie to follow the hansom Mr Arthur was in the habit of taking on his evening expeditions.

But it was what would have to come next that had seemed to present her with major difficulties. It would not be enough to observe, if it could be done, just which house in whatever district of London it was that Mr Arthur went to. It would be necessary to find out a great deal about who lived in that house, her name, her reputation, her circumstances.

This was something that Miss Unwin could hardly see herself accomplishing. To begin with, it would almost certainly necessitate her being away from Northumberland Gardens for a considerable period, and her duties towards little Pelham made that difficult, at the least. Then, too, it would mean putting questions to people in the neighbourhood of whatever house had been discovered, and Miss Unwin, the lady, would find it hard indeed to extract easy confidences from tradesmen and others whose affairs took them to the immediate neighbourhood of such a house, a crossing-sweeper perhaps or a policeman or the servants of the place.

But – the inspiration had come to her in an instant – there was someone, someone she could trust through and through, who would carry out such a task admirably. Vilkins. Vilkins with her ready friendliness, with her sturdy frame that could spend a long evening tramping here and there to make inquiries. Vilkins would be ideal. She was a woman of the people. She could pick up the

66

gossip of a neighbourhood as easily as she picked up the dirt and dust of the house at Northumberland Gardens with her pan and brush.

Yes, Vilkins was the one. She would be her substitute prying eyes, her eagerly listening ears.

But, as she went soberly up the stairs, to ask Mrs Thackerton whether she could be of any assistance to her in the business of going into mourning, Miss Unwin made herself look on the bleaker side once more. It was possible, surely, that Vilkins, however clever she was at following Mr Arthur and poking and prying in the neighbourhood, would find nothing. Mrs Arthur might be mistaken. Her husband might have no mistress. He might do no more in the evenings than visit his club.

It was a notion she felt bound to scare herself with so as to ward off any bad luck that might come after the piece of extraordinary fortune she had seemed to have when Mrs Arthur had burst out with her secret. But it was a mental precaution she need not have taken. Ill-luck was to descend on her all too soon again, and enough to weigh the scale hard down.

The bombshell burst soon after breakfast next morning, the day of the funeral. It came in the form of Vilkins's companion housemaid, Hannah, bustling into the schoolroom where Miss Unwin had just begun Pelham's lessons, as much to take his mind off the funeral procession due to leave the house some two hours later as to impart instruction.

'You're wanted in the morning-room, miss,' the girl said with an insolent flirt of her hips. 'Mrs Arthur, Mrs Thackerton as is, says immediate.'

Miss Unwin stood up without haste from the table where she had a reading primer – *Jack and Jill live in a house with a red door* – open between herself and Pelham.

'Very well, Hannah. Will you sit here with Master Pelham? I dare say I shall be back directly.'

'I don't know as I can stay here. I got my work to attend to.'

'Well, that will have to wait for a little. Master Pelham is not to be left on his own today of all days.'

Hannah gave her a mutinous look, but hauled back the chair and plumped herself down, legs stuck out.

'Be a good boy, Pelham, and try to go on reading the story to yourself.'

'Yes, Miss Unwin.'

Miss Unwin went down the stairs to the morning-room wondering only a little what it was that she had been summoned for. With the whole house in disarray it could be any one of a hundred things that Mrs Arthur considered her as being the right person to deal with.

But, entering the morning-room, dim behind its lowered blinds, she did not expect to find the new mistress of the house sitting holding a newspaper. Nor was Mrs Arthur reading it, but instead she was holding it in front of herself folded with some precision into an odd shape.

'You wanted to see me?' Miss Unwin asked.

'I wanted you to see this,' Mrs Arthur replied, banging the paper down with sudden ferocity on the small table beside her chair and sending its green chenille cloth dancing in the draught it made.

'This?' Miss Unwin asked, completely puzzled.

'This newspaper, Miss Unwin. This disgraceful newspaper.'

'I am afraid that I do not understand.'

'No more do I. I do not understand how you can have acted in such a shameful way. Read it. Read it.'

Mrs Arthur thrust the paper out. Miss Unwin took it and saw that it had been folded into its curious shape so that one particular article was to the fore.

She began to read, straining a little in the gloom of the room.

Mysterious Death of Respected Hat Manufacturer. A Murder Without A Motive?

By Our Special Correspondent, Horatio Hopkinson.

Hopkinson. The name alerted her.

She opened the paper more widely and saw that it was indeed the *Mercury*. An unaccountable uneasiness invaded her.

She turned back to the article to which the paper had been folded. Rapidly her eyes ran down the column, which began with a straightforward account of Mr Thackerton's death based, it would seem from the frequent mention of Sergeant Drewd of the Criminal Investigation Department, on the Sergeant's own

68

account of the case. But soon there came paragraphs more specu-
lative.

*It appears to be irrefutably proved that the murder was committed
between the hours of 10 p.m. and 10.30 p.m. During this period only one
person is known to have entered the fatal chamber. That person is the
governess resident at No 3 Northumberland Gardens, a Miss Harriet
Unwin. Miss Unwin was introduced into the household some three or
four months ago to attend to the education of Master Pelham Thackerton,
the deceased's only grandson. Mr and Mrs Arthur Thackerton, the
deceased's son and daughter-in-law also reside in the house, and it is
understood that Mr Thackerton senior took the greatest interest in the
welfare of the boy, sole eventual heir to the family fortune.*

So far, surely, nothing to have aroused in Mrs Arthur quite the
angry distress she had shown.

Oh, but now. The next paragraph.

In an exclusive interview with Miss Unwin I learnt –

Miss Unwin lowered the paper.

'Mrs Thackerton, believe me, that man had no interview with
me, exclusive or otherwise. I cannot understand how he can claim
to have done so.'

'Miss Unwin, that is not my information.'

'Not your information? I do not understand.'

'It is very simple. You were seen talking to this individual.'

'But I –'

Miss Unwin came to a halt. She had, of course, talked to the
reporter. However briefly. In whatever terms.

'I am glad to see that you do not persist in denials.'

'Madam, I do not. It is true that I did talk to that man. I came
upon him in the hall, and . . .'

A sudden thought struck her. She had seen no one else in the
hall at the time Hopkinson of the *Mercury* had been lurking there.
So how had Mrs Arthur learnt that the two of them had exchanged
those few words?

'But who has said that I talked with that person?' she demanded.
'Let them face me. Let them tell you in my presence just how
many or how few words I addressed to him.'

'It was Jos – I cannot really see, Miss Unwin, that it is in
any way material who it was who did his duty and informed

me that my husband's strict orders concerning newspaper reporters had been disregarded. The fact remains that they were so disregarded.'

Miss Unwin felt her mind swing between fury and dread. Joseph. It had been Joseph who had seen her with Hopkinson and had found an opportunity to tell another tale against her. Would his malice never be satisfied? And Mrs Arthur. What steps did she mean to take over that obstinate conviction of hers that her husband's order had been flagrantly disobeyed?

'If you will just let me explain.'

'No explanation or excuse will meet the case. I have made up my mind.'

There was an edge of hysteria in Mrs Arthur's voice. The excitement of a weak will screwed up to take decisive action.

'But you do not understand the circumstances. Believe me, I –'

'No.'

Mrs Arthur's interruption was almost a scream.

'No, Miss Unwin, we cannot any longer tolerate under our roof, looking after the wellbeing of our child, a person who is spoken of in the newspapers in this manner. I do not know whether what the paper alleges about you is true. I presume there must be some doubt since Sergeant Drewd has not seen fit to proceed further. But it is intolerable to find ourselves publicly described as sheltering a person who may have committed that abominable crime.'

'Madam, you are not sheltering that person.'

'Miss Unwin, I must be the judge of what is or is not suitable. You will go to your room, pack your belongings and leave this house before the funeral procession sets out.'

Miss Unwin felt an iron shutter of despair descend. To have climbed inch by inch the long ladder from those depths of her earliest days. To have achieved so much progress with so much effort. And now to see it tumbled down in an instant to nothing. It was unbearable.

And she would not bear it.

At the lowest point of her misery she found in herself a small spark of determination burning still. With a little glowing residue

70

of acquired knowledge. Had she not discovered within a week of coming to the house over the matter of sugar-mice and Pelham's spoiled appetite that Mrs Arthur did not really possess a strong will? Very well, put her to the test. See who was truly the stronger, for all the difference in their stations.

She drew herself up, straight as a pikestaff.

'Mrs Thackerton, I cannot accept your decision. It is true that Sergeant Drewd appears to entertain suspicions of myself, and I suppose that this newspaper' – she slapped it against her thigh in contempt – 'repeats the vile suspicions he seemed to hold against me. But I am not guilty of that monstrous crime any more than I am guilty of having spoken to this Mr Hopkinson, and I require you to show your belief in that. You must keep me under your roof, or face whatever consequences will come of turning me away and implying utterly unjustly that I have committed the gravest of all offences.'

Mrs Arthur was silent, stunned it seemed by the outburst. But at last she turned towards the little table at her side and adjusted the position of the pink and purple glass vase that stood on it.

'Very well, Miss Unwin,' she said then. 'Since you put the matter in that light perhaps for the time being we should say no more about it.'

Miss Unwin gave her a stiff little bow, slapped the offending copy of the *Mercury* down beside the pink and purple vase and marched out of the room.

But it was all she could do, once beyond its door, to drag herself back up to the schoolroom and let Hannah resume her household tasks.

She had managed to put Mrs Arthur in the wrong and make her own continued stay in the house a point of principle. But would that state of things last very long? If Mrs Arthur told her husband what had happened, he would very likely take a much sterner line. If he called her bluff, she could not, of course, go to law against him. A lawyer's fees would eat up her scanty savings in a day.

Then there was that article in the *Mercury*. She wished abruptly she had not made the gesture of returning the paper to Mrs Arthur with such ferocity. She had not read everything its special correspondent, Horatio Hopkinson of the sudden false smiles and battered silk hat, had written about her. From what Mrs Arthur had said it seemed that he had gone on to make even more specific allegations about her.

The whole world would now be thinking that she had murdered her employer, a man who took 'the greatest interest in the welfare' of his only grandson.

She paused for a moment before entering the schoolroom and devoting herself once more to little Pelham.

Now, more than ever, she must get hold of proof, or at the very least of the strongest indication, that Mr Arthur was the person who had wielded that Italian paper-knife. If she delayed too long she could well find herself bundled unceremoniously out of the house, without any form of character reference, heading for that long downwards slope.

But there was nothing that she could do immediately. She must go to Pelham. In a very short time the first gentlemen coming to the house to follow the funeral procession would be arriving, to be shown into the library where Mellings would dispense sherry wine and cake and the undertaker would dispense his supply of black hatbands, black scarves and pairs of black gloves.

Then there would come the departure of the coffin, black and massive round its inner case, studded with shining rows of japanned brass nails. That would be a hard moment for a small boy, knowing that under all the show there would be lying the body of his grandfather so lately alive and barking out each evening his approving grunt of a laugh when a sugar-mouse's head was snapped off.

No, only when at the end of this day Pelham was safely asleep could she attend to her own troubles. Perhaps that would be time enough.

She found Pelham excited rather than distressed, at least outwardly.

'Miss Unwin, Miss Unwin, the funeral carriage has arrived. Hannah and I peeped through the blind and saw it. And can I creep down when Grandpapa goes and watch through the banisters?'

'Certainly not. And, Hannah, you can go back to your work

now. No, Pelham, your mother and your grandmother will be staying in their rooms, as is proper, and you must stay up here.'

'But, miss, must I?'

'Yes, you must. No two ways about it.'

'Well, but ... But couldn't we peek round the blinds again? The horses have all got tall black feathers on their heads.'

Miss Unwin thought for a moment. Perhaps, after all, it would be better for the boy if he did see the coffin leave. At least it would prevent him harbouring in his head unpleasantly fantastic thoughts.

'All right. You may do that. But you mustn't lift the blind more than an inch or two, mind.'

'No, Miss Unwin. I won't. Really I won't. Thank you, Miss Unwin.'

So when the procession was due to leave they each went to a window and peered downwards at the enormous hearse, its black relieved only by gold-painted skulls at each corner and gold-painted cherubs along its sides, at the four black horses in its traces nodding and tossing the ostrich plumes on their heads, at the coachman, massive in his all-black coat and hat.

'Oh, look, Miss Unwin, one of the horses is –'

'Sssh, Pelham. I can see that quite well, but a little gentleman does not mention such things.'

'No, Miss Unwin.'

Then along the path to the gate between the heavy clumps of laurel there came the big, black elm-wood coffin, carried on the shoulders of half a dozen black-clad mutes.

Miss Unwin thought she recognised them from a funeral she had encountered nearby one day when she was taking Pelham for his walk. The two of them had stood respectfully to the side then as that other coffin had been carried to the hearse and Miss Unwin had been assailed as the mutes had passed with such a reek of gin that for an instant she had been transported back to her earliest, most terrible days and the full-bellied parish beadle who on his visits to the workhouse had always exuded such an odour of juniper.

No doubt, she thought, a similar waft of sweetness is eddying along the path down there now.

But a lady, however newly arrived at that state, does not mention such things. Even to herself.

The new Mr Thackerton emerged a moment later and went down the path in the wake of the coffin and climbed stiffly into the family carriage drawn up behind the hearse. He was followed by the other mourners who had come to the house. There were not, Miss Unwin noted, all that many of them although they included a number of under-managers from the office with among them the dark, dour figure of Ephraim Brattle.

Eventually the cortège moved off in the direction of the notably respectable Kensal Green burial ground, the lumbering hearse, the mourning carriages and finally the carriages of neighbours sent empty to follow the procession as a mark of respect.

Then, just as the last carriage turned the far corner at its slow walking-pace, a four-wheeler cab came up from the other direction and tagged itself on to the end of the line. Through its window, which was opened to its fullest on this day of inappropriate sultriness, Miss Unwin caught a distorted glimpse of a vivid brown suit.

She shuddered at the sight. In a swift spasm of true fear.

But this was no time for considering her own future. Pelham had to be kept fully occupied until his head lay on his pillow in sleep. There had been certain small signs, a quick frown, a withdrawn look momentarily about the eyes, that had told her that for all his merry talk of black-plumed horses' disrespectful behaviour some decidedly unmerry thoughts had come into his head.

So in a twinkling it was out with Miss Richmal Magnall's *Questions* and learning by rote their answers. What is the largest desert in the world? The Sahara. Which is the greatest ocean in the world? The Pacific.

At last however the supper hour arrived – no visit to the drawing-room on this sad day and no reward of a sparkling sugar-mouse – and then it was bath-time and finally it was time for prayers, for a story read till sleep had almost closed the eyes of the listener. And then finally Pelham's long day was over.

Miss Unwin lit his nightlight and then went to the schoolroom and rang its bell for Vilkins.

As soon as Vilkins had come in and shut the door safely behind her Miss Unwin put her first question.

'This ought to have been your half-day off, shouldn't it?'

'Well, yes, in a manner o' speaking. Only Cook said as I'd better stay in on account o' the funeral an' everything.'

'Yes. But there's nothing to prevent you going out this evening if you want to?'

'No. She said that'd be all right. An' I might take a bit of an airing.'

'Could you do something for me instead? Though now it comes to it, I hardly like to ask you.'

'Well, if you don't ask I can hardly say as I will, can I? An' you can take it from me, whatever you does ask I'll do it. I ain't been friends with you since before almost I could talk for nothing.'

'No. No, I suppose you haven't. And, believe me, whatever has happened to me since we were little girls together, I am your friend still. Unless I felt I was, I would not dare ask what I am going to.'

'Ask away then. Ask away.'

So Miss Unwin told her friend of old about the extraordinary speech Mrs Arthur had burst out with the evening before and the inference she herself had drawn from it. Then she went on to say why she felt it was now doubly urgent for her to find proof of some sort of the supposition she had arrived at and how she thought that Vilkins could help her to that.

'Follow 'im in a hansom,' Vilkins said at the end of it all. 'Why, I'll do that an' make a pleasure of it. I ain't never rode in no hansom afore. I won't half make that cabbie go, I can tell you.'

'But, Vilkins dear, you must be careful. What if it turns out that I am quite wrong about Mr Arthur and he finds you spying on him wherever it is that he goes to? You could be dismissed.'

'Yes, an' pigs could fly. I won't let 'im see hair nor hide o' me. Don't you worry. I'll just go an' get me glad rags on, an' then I'll be off. A hansom cab, an' me in it. Oh, lawks.'

Vilkins was as good as her word, even attempting to leave the schoolroom before Miss Unwin could give her money for the expedition. In less than ten minutes her figure could be seen clattering up the steps from the front area, banging out of the gate and marching off in the direction of the nearest cab rank.

Would she succeed in following Mr Arthur when he came out, Miss Unwin asked herself. Would he even go out this evening?

The second of her questions was answered some twenty minutes later when Henry left the house and went off in the same direction as Vilkins had taken. Five minutes later he returned in the hansom he had been sent to fetch and Miss Unwin heard him through the open schoolroom window, which now that the funeral was over no longer had to be obscured with a blind, telling the driver that his master would be out directly.

Then, while the cab stood below in the dusty, left-over heat of the hot day, its ribby horse occasionally shaking its head against the flies and making its harness faintly jingle, at the far end of the street another hansom appeared. As soon as it had rounded the corner it came to a sudden rocking halt.

Miss Unwin, leaning out of the window as far as she dared without attracting attention, felt she could almost see Vilkins, in her big garishly flower-bedecked straw bonnet, thrusting her cheerful round face up to the little opening in the cab's roof to bawl out instructions to the driver on his perch above and behind her.

Then Mr Arthur came out, his silk hat freshly gleaming from the attentions of Henry's brush, a cigar between his lips. A whiff of its rich, piquant scent came all the way up to Miss Unwin as his cab clattered away down the street.

The second hansom at the far corner jolted into sudden life. Miss Unwin watched it until it disappeared at the other end of the road. Then she put Pelham's discarded Snakes and Ladders board back into the cupboard and settled down to a long wait.

But well after St Stephen's Church clock had struck ten - all the maidservants were strictly bound to be back indoors after a half-day by ten-thirty - there was still no sign of Vilkins returning.

Chapter Nine

Abruptly Miss Unwin left the schoolroom, went into her bedroom, lit her candle and by its gradually increasing light looked at the battered alarm-clock on the chest of drawers. Twenty-four minutes past ten.

She blew out the candle, turned and hurried out of the room and down the stairs. Bonnetless, she unfastened the lock on the wide front door, slipped it open a few inches and stepped out into the warm night. She went along the path to the gate and peered up and down the road.

Nothing.

Silence. The undisturbed quiet of a respectable district of London at a late hour of the night. The laurel bushes in the garden behind her were not stirred by so much as a puff of air. No dog, far or near, so much as barking. Not even the rattle of the hansom taking home some late-returning reveller in a distant street.

How long had it been, she asked herself, since she had looked at her clock. Two minutes? Probably not more. And the clock was right. She made sure of that herself when she wound it. It needed putting forward only by one minute each night, old though it was.

What should she do about Vilkins? Should she go back indoors, ask one of the men servants, any one of them but Joseph, to go to the police station and report that a girl was missing? Surely it was ridiculously early for such a dramatic measure. But then if Mr Arthur had – appalling to think of it – somehow realised that Vilkins had been following him, and if he was truly his father's murderer, would he have hesitated to ...?

She could not make up her mind to carry forward the thought.

Then, almost unbelievably, in the hushed silence of the heavy night she thought she caught the sound of a tiny tick-tocking, rapid and regular.

Footsteps. It must be footsteps beating out on the pavement as someone hurried along. Would it be Vilkins? Surely it must be.

Was the sound getting nearer?

She listened, straining.

Yes. Yes, it was. And the rapidity of the steps meant surely that they belonged to someone who was running.

But they were still a good way off, and it could not be long now – hardly two minutes, if that – before the church clock would strike the half hour and Vilkins, if this was Vilkins, would be late, would have to produce explanations, might give away their whole plan in her flustered state.

Certainly she would have no time to stand outside and tell of any news she had. If she failed to ring at the servants' bell before half past she would be in trouble.

Miss Unwin went back into the garden and pushed her way into the massed laurels beside the path until she was sure she was well out of sight.

The footsteps were loud now in the darkness, and surely they must be Vilkins's. There was a hearty clumsiness about them that, even at a distance, was somehow unmistakable.

But would she be in time?

Then at last Vilkins came into sight, running up to the gate, pushing it open and leaning on it panting loudly as a dog. Then with lurching, exhausted strides she made her way along the path, up the front steps and leant a finger on the bell beneath the visitors' one.

In time. The church clock was silent still.

Down in the area below, as Vilkins stumbled to the steps leading to it, Miss Unwin heard the heavy bolt on the basement door being drawn back.

'What time of night is this, my girl?'

The cook, for all her plump and comfortable aspect, plainly had a sharp side to her tongue on an occasion like this.

'It's not half past, Mrs Breakspear. Really it ain't.'

'And lucky for you it isn't, my girl. Otherwise you'd be in hot water good and proper.'

'Yes, Mrs Breakspear. Sorry, Mrs Breakspear.'

'Well, get along to bed with you. Straight away, mind. A fine time of night for a girl like you to be out. Off to bed. Straight away.'

Miss Unwin breathed a sigh of relief on Vilkins's behalf. She waited among the blotchy, dust-laden leaves of the laurels until she heard Mrs Breakspear bolt the basement door again and then she slipped back inside again herself, locked the front door and made her way calmly up the stairs, the lowly governess going quietly about some business of her own.

But how was she to learn now what Vilkins had found out? If Vilkins had found out anything. Had she perhaps done no more than wait hour after hour outside Mr Arthur's club somewhere in the West End while inside he ... He did whatever it was that gentlemen did in gentlemen's clubs, dined, talked, played cards, played billiards. Had Vilkins's expedition come so near to disaster for her to no purpose?

Miss Unwin longed to know. But she saw no way that she could find out.

Vilkins had been ordered up to bed straight away, and she would not dare disobey. Doubtless Mrs Breakspear would not be above going to see that her order had been carried out. Nor could there be any question of creeping up the servants' stairs to go to Vilkins when all was quiet. For one thing that part of the house was somewhere she had never penetrated to, which it would have been wrong for her to be seen in. For another, second housemaid and scullery maid shared the same small room, Vilkins had told her once, and Nancy would be in bed there already.

Miss Unwin sighed. She would have to exercise patience. That was all.

She would have to go to bed as usual now, go to sleep and in the morning when it was Vilkins's duty to sweep the schoolroom during the family breakfast hour she would have to make some excuse and go up and see her then.

But it was a long time to wait for the news which she hoped would mean so much to her.

Not surprisingly, for all her good intentions, she did not get to sleep when she had got into her narrow bed. The mattress, never at the best of times free from lumps in its much-used horsehair, seemed now intolerably uncomfortable. And the heat, which the night before she had hardly noticed, seemed so oppressive now that she felt she might be in that Sahara Desert that was the answer to one of Miss Richmal Magnall's famous questions.

Then, then when it seemed she had been lying there tossing and turning for hours, there came at her door a sharp, persistent scratching sound. She knew at once what it would be.

In a moment she had jumped out of bed, gone across in the dark to the door and opened it wide.

'Vilkins. It's you.'

'Lawks, Unwin, I thought Nancy was not never going to go to sleep. Where you been, Mary, she kept saying. You been with a young man? What's his name, Mary? What's he like? Where'd you meet him?'

Miss Unwin had hauled her into the room and closed the door behind her during all this whispered outpouring. Now she could not stop herself taking her old friend by both shoulders and positively shaking her.

'Vilkins, what did you find out? Did you find out anything? Why were you so late? Tell me. Tell me.'

In answer Vilkins gave a great gurgle of a laugh, appallingly loud in the darkness.

'Why, I found out the 'ole lot. Everything what we 'oped, lock, stock an' bloomin' barrel.'

'What, Vilkins? What?'

'He goes to a house in Maida Vale. That's what he does, an' he meets a lady there. Lady, did I say? Woman I ought to 'ave said. No better nor what she ought to be. Miss Bond she calls herself. Miss Rhoda Bond. An' I bet she was christened something a sight different, if she was christened at all. Shrimp-girl, she was once, if what I heard was true. Just a little shrimp-girl a-running in the sea with her legs as brown as a native of India's.'

'But, Vilkins, let me get it all clear. This person, this Miss Rhoda Bond, is she really a kept woman? Does Mr Arthur keep her?'

'Him now, and one or two more before, if what I heard at the pub on the corner's anything to go by. An' it is. Her house is just like a jewel-box inside, so they says. An' her little trap what she goes driving down in the Park in of an arternoon, you should just see it. I did. Went round to the mews with a chap I got talking to, a cats-meat man, an' saw it with me own eyes.'

'Vilkins dear, you didn't ... You didn't have to ...'

'Lawks, no. I knows how to talk to a chap without a-having to do that. No, I was just friendly like with him, an' he was just friendly like with me. He keeps his cats-meat cart in the same mews, an' he showed me ... A beauty of a little carriage it is, with the seat all in the skin o' some sort o' foreign animal, fawn like in colour an' with spots.'

'A leopard. In leopard skin, Vilkins dear.'

'Yeh. That's what he said, the cats-meat feller, come to think. Leopard skin. An' the harness all white leather. White like milk, an –'

'Yes, yes. But what else did you discover, you clever girl? Or was that all? Just that this Miss Bond owns a trap with a leopard-skin seat and milk-white harness?'

'Oh, bless you, no. I heard a sight more nor that. What I didn't hear about that Rhoda Bond wouldn't be worth hearing.'

'But, what, Vilkins, what?'

'Owes, Unwin. She owes, that one, high an' low. She owes at the stables for her two white ponies. She owes at the grocer an' the butcher an' the fishmonger. She owes the colourman for half the decorations in that pretty little house of hers an' the haberdasher for half the ribbons on her head. An' if she goes on the way she has just a week or two longer, she's going to have the bailiffs in, that's what.'

Miss Unwin heard Vilkins's gathered gossip as if she was listening to a Judge pronouncing her guiltless of the gravest of crimes. As perhaps, at a remove, she was.

'It is as I thought,' she said at last. 'It is really as I thought. Mr Arthur does need money, a great deal of money by the sound of it, and he needs it to give to a woman of that sort. She must have been pressing him for it, threatening to tell Mr Thackerton perhaps. If only I could be sure of that. If only I could go to Sergeant Drewd and tell him that for a fact. Then, surely, he would begin to direct his investigations where he should, instead of anywhere but at the head of the house.'

'So he would, Unwin. So he would. Only . . .'

Vilkins's cheerful voice faded away on a note of plain discouragement.

'Yes, Vilkins, you are right, alas,' Miss Unwin said. 'Only, I have not got anything more to go with to the Sergeant than some gossip you have picked up in a public house. He would laugh it to scorn, my dear. It's no use blinking that.'

'Yeh. That old Sergeant wouldn't believe me, not if he was paid to.'

Vilkins could not have sounded more despondent.

'My dear, it's not your fault. You did splendidly. No one but you could have found out all that you did, and so quickly.'

'I did find it quick, too,' Vilkins chimed in, still lugubrious. 'I found it so quick I thought I could take a bus back instead of a hansom. But that old bus, why, the horses must have been due at the knacker's yard ten year ago. An' the way that driver would stop to pick up a fare, even if he so much as saw somebody walking down the next side-street . . . That's why I was so late, an' all. An' it was for nothing in the end, I s'pose. Nothing at all.'

'No, Vilkins dear, it was not for nothing. Don't you believe that. What you found out is almost certainly the truth. Or the truth only a little exaggerated. Why should it be anything else?'

'Oh, yes, it's the truth all right. I know that. But the thing is, it ain't no good to you, Unwin. It ain't one bit o' good.'

'Oh, yes, it is. It certainly is. If it's the truth it can be substantiated. It can be substantiated from Miss Rhoda Bond's own lips, and I mean to make her own to it, Vilkins. I must. I see now that I must. I must go as soon as possible and talk, woman to woman, with that creature. There's no help for it. No hope for me unless I do.'

But it was to be some time before Miss Unwin, little Pelham Thackerton's paid governess, could do anything to put her new resolution to the test. And before she had had any opportunity to do so yet worse troubles than those that had already gathered like heavy thunder-clouds above her were to break over her lonely head.

Chapter Ten

It was not Mrs Arthur, ready to hit out with anger, who showed Miss Unwin next day that morning's copy of *The Times*. Miss Unwin heard about what was in it from Vilkins.

"'Ere, miss, has any o' them said anything to you about the paper?"

'What paper, Vilk – What paper, Mary? I don't understand.'

They were out on the landing beside the schoolroom. Miss Unwin with her bonnet on, neatly gloved, had just sent Pelham into his room to fetch the new black cap that went with his mourning suit before they went for their walk. Vilkins was on her way to Miss Unwin's room, a broad red hand grasping dustpan and brush.

She stood twisting a foot round her ankles and dropped her voice as she glanced in the direction of Pelham's room.

'I don't know as I rightly know what it's all about meself,' she said. 'Only that there's this paper and it's something about you, so they say.'

'Who says, Mary? What paper is this? Is it a newspaper?'

'Oh, yes. It's a newspaper all right, though why there should be a letter about you wrapped up in it is more nor I can say.'

Miss Unwin sighed.

'If it's a letter about me in a newspaper,' she explained, finding it hard to keep patient even with her old friend and daring helper of the evening before, 'it will be something that someone has written to the editor and he has printed it. But which paper is it? Are you sure that there's a letter about me?'

'Oh, yes. I see it all now. Mr Mellings always has a read of it while he's ironing it before it goes to the Master. Well, before it goes to Mr Arthur now, 'cos now he is the Master, ain't –'

'Yes, yes, of course he is. And you've told me quite enough already. Mr Thackerton always used to take *The Times*. That would be the paper Mellings ironed for him, and now Mr

83

Arthur has it. But how am I to see it and find out what's there about me?'

Vilkins gave a great grin. She leant towards Miss Unwin and whispered, spittily. But then she had whispered spittily even when they had been little girls together.

'That's easy, Unwin. I'll pinch it out o' the library directly an' put it at the top o' the area steps for you. Under me apron. It's always left in the library till evening. It'll be all right.'

Miss Unwin wondered whether such illicit borrowing would indeed be all right. Vilkins's scheme seemed riddled with holes to her. But her faithful accomplice had darted away down the servants' stairs and it was too late to devise any better plan.

Besides, a letter in *The Times* about herself: it was worth taking a risk to see it.

What could the person who had written it have said? It seemed as if the murder must have become one of those cases that everyone discussed, that newspaper correspondents delighted to air their views about. And she had known nothing of all the hubbub, beyond having had that one short look at Horatio Hopkinson's lying account in the *Mercury*.

Had the letter writer in *The Times* attempted to contradict that baseless notion that Horatio Hopkinson had, surely, put forward? Or did his letter do the opposite? Had he produced extra reasons why the police should arrest her?

She must find out.

She realised that Pelham had failed to appear with his cap, and swept into his room in a gust of impatience. He was sitting on the bed playing with his box of glass marbles.

'Pelham, I told you to get your cap. What are you doing? I shall have to take those marbles away.'

The boy burst into tears. In the whole time she had been looking after him she had never spoken as sharply.

She pulled herself together.

'Now, come along, Pelham. There's nothing to cry about. You get your cap and I'll put the marbles back in the toy cupboard.'

But the toy cupboard was in the schoolroom and Pelham's muttered 'No' indicated clearly that he no longer trusted her not to whisk away his precious playthings instead of putting them in their proper place. So, however keenly she wanted to get off on their walk with the purloined copy of *The Times* under her arm, she felt she must allow him to put the marbles away himself, delay her as that might.

She waited, reining herself in, while Pelham trotted through to the schoolroom, opened the toy cupboard – its door gave a small grunt of a squeak – put the box of marbles in its place, began to come back, realised he had forgotten to shut the toy cupboard door, went in again to do so – that grunt again – and at last returned.

'Now then, my lad, get that cap. Quick sticks. Or we shall be too late to get to the Gardens.'

Too late, too, perhaps, she thought, to reach the area steps before Mellings or someone else notices Vilkins's apron lying there, picks it up and discovers *The Times*. And then there would be a great inquiry as to how it got there.

'Good boy. Off we go now. Run, run, run.'

'But, please Miss Unwin, can't I take my hoop with me?'

'No, no. Not today, Pelham. We're all in mourning, remember. The hoop will have to wait for a few days more yet.'

'Yes, Miss Unwin.'

Thank goodness, she had established the habit of obedience right from the outset.

So they went tripping down the stairs, both of them, in a decidedly unrestrained way and waited, dancing with impatience while Henry opened the front door for them. Then out into the sunshine, already hot, and a swift glance down to the area steps.

And, yes, Vilkins's white morning apron folded up, not at all neatly, at the corner of the top step but one.

'Stop a minute, Pelham. What's that on the area steps there?'

'Oh, Miss Unwin, it's only a horrid old rag, and you said we'd be late for the Gardens.'

'No. I think I'll just pick it up. It might belong to somebody.'

'But, Miss Unwin . . .'

Pelham was hopping from foot to foot in agitation. But that could be ignored.

Hastily Miss Unwin ran across to the steps, stooped, picked up the apron and from underneath it *The Times*.

'It seems to be one of the servants' aprons. They must have left it there for some reason. I think I'd better just put it back where it was. They're bound to remember and come back for it.'

'That's Grandpapa's *Times*, Miss Unwin.'

For a moment Miss Unwin's mind went blank. She saw herself having to restore the paper under little Pelham's stern eye to its proper place in the library. Then commonsense reasserted itself.

'Why, what a clever boy you are to recognise that. Did you read the big letters on the front?'

'Well, I more sort of just knew.'

'Never mind, it was still clever. Now, off we go or we really won't get to the Gardens.'

Miss Unwin shooed Pelham down the path in front of her before any question arose of taking *The Times* back into the house. She would have liked to have opened it where she stood. The desire to do so was sharp almost as a pain in her side. But she knew that to stand there in full view of anyone who might look out of the window of the house would be too much tempting fate.

But once round the first corner on the way to Kensington Gardens. That would be a different matter.

'Oh, Miss Unwin, what are we stopping for? We won't never ever get to the Gardens if you read that paper.'

'You mustn't say "never ever", Pelham. Just "ever". We won't ever get to the Gardens if – Well, never mind.'

'But, Miss Unwin, you're still looking at the paper.'

Pelham stamped his foot in frustration.

He's quite right, Miss Unwin thought. After all, I was the one who put the idea into his head that we might be too late to get to the Gardens.

She folded *The Times* back, tucked it under her arm and set off again in the direction of Kensington Gardens as briskly as the hot sun would allow.

But at last they reached their rather dusty destination and Pelham could be left to run about on the grass. Miss Unwin seated herself hastily on a bench and once more opened *The Times*, nearly tearing its pages in her anxiety to get to the Letters to the Editor.

The Northumberland Gardens Tragedy

There it was.

She read, oblivious of the heat of the sun, of the other governesses and nursemaids and their charges, of everything.

Sir, It seems to be the general opinion that this murder was committed by some inmate or inmates of the house. In examining the evidence against all possible culprits it will be necessary to discard the argument that has been pretty extensively pressed – that a crime of such brutality can have been committed only by a member of the male sex. We know that women have murdered men, especially that women scorned have murdered their lovers, since the world began and will do so again before the world ends, and it remains to be seen whether a crime of that atrocity has been committed in Northumberland Gardens. Great stress has been laid upon the fact that Mr Thackerton was known as a person of the utmost respectability, but it is also known that his wife has been an invalid for many years and we have too many instances of men in that situation seeking solace elsewhere to be able to discount such a possibility altogether.

No traces of the murder have been found on the premises with the single exception of the blood that was observed on the sleeve of the governess's dress. Such a trace undoubtedly proves that she was in the library at some period, whether after the murder as she is said to have asserted or before it, as is equally likely, there is no evidence. What is clear, however, is that she is a person with entrée to that room, and it must be asked how often was she accustomed to avail herself of this privilege at those hours when, by the custom of the household, Mr Thackerton was alone there and had given orders that he was not to be disturbed.

It is very possible that some or all of these questions have been answered satisfactorily, but it does not appear from the actions of the official investigators that they have been; they are in everybody's mouth and in everybody's mind, and it is in the interest of the governess, if she be innocent, that they shall be publicly met and dealt with.

The letter was signed simply *Commonsense*.

Miss Unwin felt an appalled, outraged sense of invasion. It was as if a stranger, no, more, a whole band of strangers, had burst into her bedroom while she was in a state of undress. The inmost circumstances of her life were being bandied about 'in everybody's mouth'. She was being discussed in every detail as if she was the latest drama in the theatre or the price of shares in the Stock

Market. And, worse, things had been invented about her, wicked, impossible, evil things. Just for pleasure. For the pleasure of speculating.

About her. About herself.

In the strong sunshine she suddenly felt cold, as if she was sitting out on her bench on the bleakest day of winter.

These thoughts, which idle people were idly indulging in, must also be in the mind of someone as little idle as Sergeant Drewd.

Perhaps the Sergeant had read the letter. No, it was certain that he had. Perhaps he was even at this moment discussing with some superior officer at Great Scotland Yard whether the public outcry the letter represented gave them cause enough to make an arrest. Perhaps some such consultation had been responsible for the Sergeant's curious absence from Northumberland Gardens ever since she had seen him, in his fearfully out-of-place brown suit, following the funeral procession in that four-wheeler.

She had found his absence, when she had had time to think about it, almost as disconcerting as his earlier presence. Could he be away investigating her own origins? Tracing back her life? And, if he were to find out the secret of her birth, would he see that as the famous motive he had said he needed in order to complete the case against her? Would he believe that Mr Thackerton had come to discover her lowly birth and, eager to protect his precious grandson from such contamination, was on the point of dismissing her, and that she had struck that dagger blow to keep her situation? Would that seem cause enough in his eyes for her to have committed murder? And if it did, would it in the hands of a savage prosecuting counsel be enough to damn her in court?

She told herself she was being foolish. And knew that this was only half-true.

Sergeant Drewd was a man who depended on success, and would snatch at anything to obtain it. This she was fully aware of, as aware as if he had boasted of it to her directly. His whole manner betrayed it.

Would Mr Commonsense's letter in *The Times* added to what might have been found out about her past be enough to make the Sergeant arrest her?

And what could she do now to prevent him? Could she fly?

That was something she could certainly manage to do. The Sergeant, for all his suspicions, had done almost nothing to put a watch on her. No doubt he had calculated earlier that someone who was both a lady and a governess was not the stuff a fugitive was made of. As a lady she would be quickly enough traced, as a governess she would hardly have the resources to go far.

But she was, in truth, neither wholly lady nor wholly governess. True, she had scant resources, but she knew well how to live on the barest of means. She could make her way to St Giles's or some other rookery where the police were afraid to venture except in raiding parties and find some way there to earn enough to keep body and soul together. Yes, and without sinking to the utmost degradation either. And as for the easily recognisable appearance of the lady, however much she had struggled to attain that, she could cast it off in an instant if the need were pressing enough.

Yet she knew that she was not going to run. She was not going to be chased from the field of battle by anybody, and especially not by Mr Commonsense of *The Times*. No, she must fight back.

The only pity of it was that she had had to delay as long as she had in her plan of going out to Maida Vale and there confronting Miss Rhoda Bond. Certainly, now she must make whatever excuses for absence she could and leave the house this very afternoon.

If Sergeant Drewd would let her.

She got up briskly from her bench, tucked the copy of *The Times*, hateful, hateful sheet, under her arm and went over to where Pelham was running backwards and forwards on the grass absorbed in pretending to be a railway train.

'Shall we go down to see the boats at the Round Pond before we go home?' she asked him.

She gave the boy his due share of time at the pond and brought him back to Northumberland Gardens just in time to wash before luncheon. No point in asking for permission to be away for an hour or two until later. Vilkins had said that Miss Bond went out driving in the Park each afternoon.

Nothing else to do to advance her case for the present than to make a quick dart into the library – everything there in its place as it had been before the murder, the heavy armchair in front of the fireplace, the long table with its burden of writing necessities and that tall silverwork Testimonial – and to restore the copy of *The Times* to where it belonged.

Time, too, after luncheon and when Pelham had been settled down for his nap for her customary hour of reading to old Mrs Thackerton. Miss Unwin found her, in the heavy atmosphere of her sitting-room, where on this most sultry of days the fire had not for once been lit, even less inclined for conversation than usual. She wondered, indeed, whether she was not more seriously ill than her ordinary state of invalidism. Was she, perhaps, likely to join her dead husband before too long? Certainly she looked dreadfully pale and seemed, too, deeply preoccupied.

But this was not unwelcome. Had conversation been required, Miss Unwin doubted whether she would have been very coherent. The nearer she got to the time when she might leave to tackle Arthur Thackerton's mistress and try to wring from her the truth about their relationship the more the danger of her situation crowded into her mind.

Would Sergeant Drewd, if he came back to the house now with proof of her own secret, penetrate to this room itself to make his arrest? Or would a servant merely be sent to request her presence somewhere else?

She brought herself back to Keble's *Christian Year*, whose pious pages Mrs Thackerton had, since her bereavement, declared to be her sole reading matter.

> '*Far better they should sleep awhile*
> *Within the church's shade,*
> *Nor wake, until new heaven, new earth,*
> *Meet for their eternal birth . . .*'

But perhaps the Sergeant would not make an actual arrest. Perhaps she would be requested only to accompany him to the police station to be questioned there.

> '*Then, pass, ye mourners, cheerly on*
> *Through prayer unto the tomb,*
> *Still, as ye watch life's falling leaf,*
> *Gathering for ever loss and grief,*
> *Hope of new spring and endless home.*'

'That will do, child. You may go now.'

So, now to ask Mrs Arthur for permission to be absent for the second half of the afternoon. But would it be granted? What if it wasn't? Would Mrs Arthur be unwilling to take the slight risk of leaving Mary to go with Pelham for his second walk of the day? Or had perhaps Sergeant Drewd requested her to see that their distrusted governess never left the house on her own?

At the door of the room, on the point of leaving, she stopped.

'Mrs Thackerton?'

She had spoken quietly so as not to alarm, and there came no reply.

She half-turned back to the door again. The promise of some fresh air out in the corridor after the oppressive, medicaments-scented closeness of the sitting-room was a temptation in itself. But the thought of Mrs Arthur's likely reception of her request drove her back inside again.

'Mrs Thackerton?'

She had spoken quite loudly, more loudly indeed than she had intended.

'What – What – What was that?'

'It's only me, Mrs Thackerton. I wanted to ask you something.'

Mrs Thackerton shook her head in pallid rejection.

'Not now, my dear. I'm very weak today. I – I have undergone a great strain, a great strain.'

Again Miss Unwin almost lost heart. And again she thought of the consequences of a refusal from Mrs Arthur.

'It's only a small matter,' she said hastily. 'I wanted to go out shortly, and . . .'

For a moment inspiration failed her. But it was for a moment only.

'I want to visit an old friend,' she said. 'A friend of my childhood days who has fallen into poor circumstances and is ill. I thought that Mary could take little Pelham for his walk this afternoon. She has done so before, and she is a reliable girl.'

Mrs Thackerton raised her head a little from the plump dark silk cushion of the invalid sofa behind her.

'My dear, you ought not to be asking me this. Especially not now when I am twice over no longer mistress of the house.'

There was a note of bitterness in her voice. Miss Unwin decided, in an instant, on a daring stroke.

'Mrs Thackerton,' she said, 'I know that I ought to go to Pelham's mother to ask this. But – but, may I be frank, I much suspect she would forbid my going. It would inconvenience her only a little, but it would . . .'

'No. You have said enough.'

Had she failed?

A sudden cough shook Mrs Thackerton's tired frame. Miss Unwin hastened to offer her the glass of sugar-sweetened water that stood on the little pie-crust table beside her sofa. She took a careful sip.

Then she spoke again.

'My dear, there are some things that ought to be understood between people without the necessity of speech. Go to your sick friend when you wish, and if the need arises I shall say that I gave you permission.'

'Oh, thank you. Thank you.'

Miss Unwin, leaving the sickly, overheated room, felt a jab of shame at having taken advantage of the kindness she had realised that Mrs Thackerton felt towards her, for whatever reason. But her back was to the wall.

Yes, she thought to herself as rather more than an hour later, she approached a small and very attractive house in Maida Vale, I must fight with any weapon that comes to hand now. Even to the point of trying to prove that Mrs Thackerton's son – Mrs Thackerton who has never been other than kind to me – is the person who killed her husband. I must do it. Or Sergeant Drewd will try to prove that that person was myself. And, however guiltless I am, it is not impossible that, before a Judge and jury, he could succeed.

Miss Rhoda Bond's house had a brightly polished brass bell beside a little door surrounded by bounteous, free-growing yellow roses. Miss Unwin took the bell-pull between two gloved fingers and tugged firmly.

Chapter Eleven

Miss Unwin was left a long time waiting in the still oppressive sun outside Rhoda Bond's neat little house for her pull at the bell to be answered. But she had no doubt that it should be answered. A twitch at a curtain as she had walked up the garden path had told her that.

The scent of all the yellow roses bowing and tumbling round the door, which had at first seemed delightfully sweet, soon became overpoweringly sickly to her. Her mind filled with more and more disquieting half-visions of the woman she had come to see. A kept woman. A person outside the bounds of society. Pitch, to touch which was to be defiled. And especially so for anyone who was only precariously in the world of the genteel and the respectable.

She wanted to put up the cotton umbrella she had brought with her to act as a parasol and shade herself from the hot sun's rays. But to do that would be to admit to the watcher inside that she was being kept waiting longer than she found pleasant, and this was something she was not going to admit.

Before long she even began to want to turn and walk back along the path to the gate, to close it irrevocably behind her and to hurry, hurry, hurry away till she found a street where there were clopping horse-buses plying – perhaps carrying enamelled advertisements for Thackerton's Hats – and she could get herself back home.

To No 3 Northumberland Gardens.

No, she was not going to draw back. What awaited her there was something she had to fight to free herself from, to fight however besmirched the battlefield.

Then at last, just before she was going to concede at least a second pull at the brightly polished bell, the door was opened. A pretty little maidservant stood there, a girl scarcely out of her teens dressed in a pink print frock that made even the dresses of the maids at Northumberland Gardens before they had been put into half-mourning look drab as sackcloth, with an apron that though it was not lace was as deeply frilled as if it had been.

'Yes?' the girl said. 'Madam?' she added.

'I wish to see Miss Bond.'

'Miss Bond's resting. She's been out driving and she always rests then till dinner time.'

'Very well. But will you please nevertheless go to her and say that a lady has called on urgent business concerning –'

Miss Unwin drew in a quick breath.

'On urgent business concerning Mr Arthur Thackerton.'

At the mention of the name, to Miss Unwin's considerable relief, a fleeting look appeared on the apple-rosy cheeks of the pretty, and pert, girl blocking her entrance to the house. It was only the briefest of passing expressions. But Miss Unwin had learnt by sharp necessity to read everything in people's faces long before she had learnt the pleasure of reading print.

Mr Arthur Thackerton was certainly known in this pretty little house. That she had learnt for certain now. He was known here in a special way, an intimate way, even a disgraceful way. The flick of extra pertness on that pert and pretty face had told Miss Unwin that.

'I'll see,' said the girl.

She stood back from the door.

Miss Unwin stepped quickly forward, without any lack of dignity but with determination.

Inside, she found a charming, small hallway, papered with other roses, pink ones. There was, too, the neatest of hall-stands with a mirror in a gracefully carved frame and with, each hanging on its own hook, brushes with delicate china backs painted in a pattern of forget-me-nots, a hat brush, a clothes brush, a mud brush.

The little maid went trippingly up the stairs. Miss Unwin set herself to wait again, grateful now for the coolness inside the house.

She waited for nearly ten minutes.

Once she looked longingly at the closed front door. But she had not overcome the obstacles she had surmounted to lose heart now, even though what lay immediately ahead was almost certain to be a task more formidable than anything she had encountered yet.

Then at last the little maid came mincing down the stairs again.

'You're to wait in the drawing-room. This way.'

A door was opened for her, a door decorated with china finger-plates and doorknob, here with roses and forget-me-nots intertwined.

The drawing-room of the little house was by no means as imposing as that at No 3 Northumberland Gardens, and it was by no means as pleasant as the drawing-room at the house in the country, the first such Miss Unwin had ever seen, a room she had learned to love and regard as the centre of her world. But it was a pretty room, an elegant room. Its walls were lined with padded satin in a soft pink. The curtains, looped deeply over the two tall windows, were of a paler satin and the lace behind them was of the richest workmanship, reducing the sunshine outside to a cool opalescence. All the chairs and the single little sofa were covered in heavily embroidered material and the side furniture was of ebony, intricately patterned with brass. There were pictures close-packed on every wall, paintings of elegant ladies on swings, in boats, with little dogs.

A room that has cost someone a great deal of money, Miss Unwin said to herself.

Then the door behind her opened and the person who had caused all that money to be spent stood before her as she wheeled round.

She was tiny. Her lack of height struck Miss Unwin with almost as much surprise as if the newcomer had been blown into the room in an explosion of conjuror's smoke. But in the next instant she saw something else about Rhoda Bond. Tiny she might be, but she was every quarter-inch a woman. Her figure was, despite the smallness of her body, if anything too full, too womanly. She was dressed, too, in a manner that did everything that could be done with tight-laced stays, artful pleats and stiffening at the hips to emphasise and present that full womanly figure.

She would be a difficult person indeed to deal with. Her very assurance of dress, her very lack of any self-consciousness about the smallness of her stature, told Miss Unwin that at once.

'My maid says you come from Mr Arthur Thackerton.'

The voice was not unladylike. But it was as contrived, Miss Unwin thought, as her figure. This gave her a small burst of hope. If contrivance was there it could be broken. However iron-reinforced underneath, that which had been manufactured could, given enough will, be broken.

As within the next few minutes it might well have to be.

'Then I am afraid that your maid misunderstood me,' Miss Unwin answered her. 'I did not say that I came from Mr Thackerton. I said that I came on business concerning him.'

The soft womanliness of the face atop that tiny, full, womanly body hardened for an instant into a smile. It was a smile that in part acknowledged that in response to an invitation to tell a half-truth a truth had been told, and it was in part a smile that flung down a challenge.

'I believe,' said Rhoda Bond, 'that you told the girl your business was urgent.'

'Yes. Yes, I said that. My business is urgent. It is perhaps even a matter of life and death.'

Again Rhoda Bond's soft, round face in its frame of dark curls smiled a swift, hard smile.

'Not a matter of life and death for me, I trust.'

'No. For myself.'

'Then I hope you'll not find yourself disappointed.'

Miss Unwin allowed her gaze to drop for a moment to the pretty round rug at her feet. Then she lifted it once more to face her opponent.

For she had no doubt now, if ever she had had any doubts, that it was by an opponent that she was confronted.

'I have omitted to tell you my name,' she said. 'It is Unwin, Miss Harriet Unwin, and I am –'

'The governess,' Rhoda Bond broke in. 'I thought as much. The governess there's been all the talk about in the *Mercury*.'

'Yes. There has been talk, as you call it. There, and elsewhere. It is because of that talk, because it is nothing less than the most atrocious falsehoods, that I have dared to come and call on you.'

'You have dared?' Rhoda Bond sounded thoughtful. 'Yes, I was beginning to wonder about that. Calling here's a daring enough thing to have done. A very daring thing for a governess, a governess in the employ of Mr Arthur Thackerton.'

'For Mr Thackerton's employee to call on ...'

Miss Unwin let the end of her retort hang in the air. But if she had hoped that she had said enough to Mr Arthur Thackerton's mistress she was to be disappointed.

Rhoda Bond simply let the sentence hang.

At last Miss Unwin was constrained to admit defeat and finish it.

'Yes, daring enough to call on another woman who depends for her daily existence on Mr Thackerton.'

'Oh, don't think I deny what I am,' Rhoda Bond answered. 'But, you know, there's a difference between the two of us. Quite a difference. Mr Thackerton would dismiss you at a moment's notice if he found any cause to do so. But I don't think he's any intention of dismissing me.'

'No? Perhaps you have had recent reason for believing that?'

'I –'

Rhoda Bond, a tiny extra flush of colour on her softly rounded cheeks, had plainly been on the point of claiming that she did have a recent reason for believing Arthur Thackerton's interest in her had not waned. Of that Miss Unwin was as certain as she was that four fours made sixteen.

But she knew, too, that Rhoda Bond had stopped herself making the admission, and that, once seen as a danger, such an avowal would be doubly and trebly hard to wring out of her.

Indeed, she was standing there now quite silent and waiting. If the negotiations were to be kept open then the next move would not come from her.

If 'negotiations' was at all the word for one whose position was so altogether weak.

Miss Unwin took a breath.

'Miss Bond, you know what is being said about me, that I was the person who gave the alarm over Mr William Thackerton's death and that this means that, in a closed household, I am the most likely person to have struck the fatal blow? That and worse.

97

It is not true. None of it is true. But what is true is that some-one, some person within those four walls, did strike that blow. I know that. None better. I was the one responsible in the first place for making it plain that the house is as impregnable to any burglar or even to an unannounced visitor as it is possible to be.'

'Miss Governess, if I wanted to hear any of that I could read it in the paper.'

'And it seems that you have done so,' Miss Unwin retorted. 'But you have read to poor purpose. Will you let me tell you what are the consequences of what I have just explained? The conse-quences for you?'

Rhoda Bond did not reply. Yet her silence now was an open admission that she did indeed want to know what the conse-quences were. For her.

Again Miss Unwin gathered her resources.

'Admit for one moment that that which I have sworn to you is the simple truth,' she said. 'That I was not the person who com-mitted that act. What follows? That it was some other person in the household. And now consider it all, quite coolly and disinter-estedly, as if ' – she could not stop the tiniest bitter trace of a laugh colouring her voice – 'as if you were a newspaper reader who knew nothing of the people concerned, or someone who had written a letter to the editor and believed he had as much right as anybody to speculate on the matter.'

'Come on, you said there'd be consequences for me. I don't see them so far. None at all.'

'Not even that the most likely individual within that house to have needed to commit the crime would be Mr Arthur Thacker-ton?'

Rhoda Bond stepped back half a pace. The high colour which had stayed on her full rounded cheeks left them as abruptly as if her very heart had ceased for a moment to beat.

'What – what do you mean?' she said at last.

'My meaning is quite clear,' Miss Unwin replied. 'I do not propose to discuss with you every person under the roof at Northumberland Gardens, but it must be plain with only the very least thought that the one who stood to gain most from old Mr

Thackerton's death is his son and heir. He needed money. He needed it badly, did he not?'

'Yes. No. No. Why should he need money? What do you mean?'

Miss Unwin had kept hold of her umbrella when she had been shown into the room and now she lifted its point a little from the floor and swept it round in a gentle arc.

'This is what I mean, Miss Bond. That here is a room that must have cost a very great deal to furnish so prettily, and it is in a house that must cost more than a little each month in rent. Where does the money come from?'

'Where it comes from is no concern of yours.'

'I wish it were not. Believe me. I do not like having to come here and say the things I have to you. But I have been accused in so many words of killing Mr William Thackerton. Knowing that someone else had very much better reasons for doing that than I ever could have makes what I asked altogether my concern.'

'Well, that's as may be.' Rhoda Bond stamped her expensively shod little foot. 'That's as may be, but it's certainly no concern of mine.'

'No? Let me speak quite plainly. To have a murderer as your lover, to have it come out in court one day that he murdered his own father so as to pay your bills. I think that should very much concern you, Miss Bond.'

'But – but he isn't. He didn't. My God, what am I to do?'

'You are to tell me the whole truth. At least then you will know where you stand and can do something to make matters as easy as possible for yourself.'

'You think so? But surely –'

'Come, if that is what did happen, and there is a good deal to say that it was, then you will get nowhere by pretending that everything in the world is made of roses.'

'But I didn't want him to –'

Rhoda Bond stopped herself. She stood looking then at Miss Unwin under lowered brows, her mind plainly calculating and calculating.

It seemed a long time to Miss Unwin before she spoke again. But when she did so it was with a toss of her elegant head.

99

'Oh, no, miss. You don't catch me that way. You and your "if this happened" and your "admit for a moment". Well, I don't admit, not for one moment. It was you, you the governess, who was first to see that body. If you're to be believed. More like it was you that saw the body dead minutes and minutes before you set up a cry of murder. Oh, I know the likes of you, and don't you think I'm to be caught in any of your little traps, my miss.'

'I am setting no trap,' Miss Unwin answered.

But within she was wishing with desperation that Rhoda Bond had tumbled out the facts she needed to hear while she had still been so thoroughly frightened. Now, it was clear, any fright she had been feeling had passed away. It was going to be yet more difficult to get out of her anything at all concerning Arthur Thackerton.

'Well,' Rhoda Bond went on, 'what you done smelt devilish like a trap to me. But I won't be took. So you'd better be on your way, before I gets angry.'

'I have told you. Everything I've said has been for your good, as well as for mine. I wish to clear my name. And as for you, I suggest that if Mr Thackerton did indeed kill his father you –'

'Ah, but there you're wrong, my fine miss. Arthur Thackerton didn't never kill his father. You was the one what done that, and don't think I don't know it.'

Miss Unwin felt suddenly that all was lost. If this elegant venomous tiny creature really believed that she was the murderer at Northumberland Gardens, or even if she was determined to pretend to believe it, then she was never going to say anything about what Arthur Thackerton had told her. She was not going to admit that he had been deeply in debt because of her or, much less, that she had been pressing him for money to pay off her creditors.

But Miss Unwin did not altogether let misery overwhelm her. Some small part of her mind still worked in its old logical way. A small part that told her that something she had just heard had been somehow wrong. A small question that demanded its answer.

Then she found it. It was the way Rhoda Bond had been

talking. Under pressure the veneer of the ladylike had blistered and peeled. The shrimp-girl, long ago thrust deeply away inside, had been brought to the surface.

And the revelation showed a possible way forward still.

'Please,' Miss Unwin said abruptly, 'please think of it from my point of view. Let me tell you something. I'm not the lady of scant means working as a governess that you've probably taken me for. I'm like you. I was never a poor girl in a village by the sea making a living from my shrimp-net, but –'

'I was not. Where'd you hear that? What damned lies.'

'There's no shame in having been what you once were. I'm not ashamed that I was a foundling who came into the world with nothing at all. With less than you even. It's where you've reached to now that counts. That's what should make you proud, when you look at this room and think you've learnt to live in a way as genteel as anybody in the land.'

Rhoda Bond, born under some much less fine a name, did look as Miss Unwin had told her to at the elegant room they were standing in, facing one another. And an expression very different from the hard anger of a moment before came on to her face. Though just what it was compounded of, of pride or doubt or fear, it was hard to say.

But Miss Unwin was not going to let slip the advantage she had gained this time.

'Yes, we're two of a kind, you and I,' she said. 'Two of a kind. We're the sort who know what life's like at the bottom of the heap, and we know how hard it is to fight the way up. And something else. Neither you nor I, if I'm right in what I think, has any intention of sliding back down there again, not if it's to be helped in any way. So won't you tell me the truth? When I know it for sure, I'll be able to see what can be done, for both of us.'

'The truth? What truth?'

'Arthur Thackerton, does he have debts because of this house? Were you pressing him for money? And has he said in the last few days that he can pay and will?'

'There was a telegraph message,' Rhoda Bond said. 'It came on the morning after the murder, if you must know. It said he'd pay up after all.'

101

She flung the words out as if she did not quite know whether she should be doing so or not. But there was one thing more Miss Unwin had to be sure of.

'And you had been pressing him?' she asked.

The elegant head framed in its tumbling dark curls tossed upwards in pride.

'I'd told him if he didn't pay by next day I'd go to his old father for the money.'

Chapter Twelve

Approaching Northumberland Gardens about an hour later Miss Unwin felt she had only one more hurdle to get over. Sergeant Drewd. Would she be able to tell him what she knew before he had found out her own secret down in the country and become so doubly fixed on the notion of her guilt that he would not even listen to her?

The actual telling of her news to him was something about which she was reasonably confident. She suspected that he had all along been blankly unwilling to consider the new head of the house as a murderer, for all the bravado of his *I can go about it your way or I can go about it my way* at his first encounter with Mr Arthur. But she guessed that, if she could contrive to make him believe that the idea of investigating Mr Arthur's Maida Vale love nest was his own, then the business would be done in an instant.

Yet would he be there to be cajoled in that way? Or was he still down in the country digging out the circumstances of her own early life like some busy robin unearthing worms from a neat lawn?

However, when Henry opened the door to her ring at the visitors' bell the Sergeant was standing there in the hall almost as if he had been waiting especially to receive her.

Had he? Was this after all going to be the moment of her arrest?

'Ah, it is Miss Unwin. The very person.'

Then not a word more.

Miss Unwin realised at once what the object of his silence was. She was now expected to ask, with a display of humility, why it was that she was 'the very person'. Sergeant Drewd liked nothing better than to be danced attendance on.

Yet the very crudity of his manoeuvre reassured her. Surely the answer to the question she was to put, *Yes, Sergeant, and why, if you please, am I the very person?* could not be *Because, madam, I wish to arrest you on a charge of murder.*

So it was with an inward smile that she asked the Sergeant the exact question he had begged for.

'Because, madam,' he replied, with a little jounce of his jockey's frame, 'I feel it my duty to communicate to you a piece of important intelligence, and Sergeant Drewd is not the man to shirk his duty.'

'I am sure that you are not, Sergeant. But, please, what is it that you have such a duty to tell me?'

The Sergeant gave a quick twirl to the pointed ends of his moustache.

'It is the result of certain investigations I have been making ever since the funeral obsequies of the late Mr William Thackerton.'

'Indeed? I had noticed your absence from the house.'

'Absence from the house, yes. Absence from the scene of the crime? Well, now, that's another matter altogether. Yes, indeed, I don't think it can be said that Sergeant Drewd was absent from the scene of the crime.'

Miss Unwin repressed her impatience. The Sergeant was certainly creating plenty of difficulties in the way of her learning his 'important intelligence'. But he had, too, aroused in her a real curiosity. Away from the house but not absent from the scene of the crime, what could he mean? Where had he been? Not, surely, after all down in the country digging out her own little miserable secret?

'But Sergeant,' she said, with a touch of sharpness, 'I should have thought it was your duty to communicate any new intelligence to Mr Arthur Thackerton.'

'And so I will, miss. So I will. Yet there's one individual, I believe, who has a prior right to hear it. Yes, one individual. And that individual is yourself. I make no bones about stating that it has been yourself that I have held under the very gravest suspicion from the outset of my investigation. And not without evidence, miss. Not without evidence.'

'Yes, you saw blood on my dress. Blood that I had not noticed. Blood that had got there when I went to see if I could tell how long Mr Thackerton had been dead.'

'Yes, indeed. There's not very much that escapes my eye, I can tell you. Neither in this house, nor in such other places as I see fit to conduct my inquiries. In places such as the London premises of the Thackerton Patent Steam-moulded Hats Company.'

These last words at least were unexpected.

Inquiries in Mr Thackerton's office? What concerning the murder could possibly have occurred there? And to judge by the confident twinkle in the Sergeant's eye his inquiries had not been without success.

'In Mr Thackerton's London premises?'

Miss Unwin wished at once she had not echoed the Sergeant's words in such a simpleton way. Her question immediately put an extra bounce of pleasure into his whole carriage, as if he had a fine piece of horseflesh under him and was heading the field at odds of a hundred to one. But she had been deeply confused by what he had said: it went so contrary to what she had come back to the house determined to tell the Sergeant as soon as she could.

'Yes, indeed, miss. In Mr Thackerton's office, and in connection with a certain Mr Ephraim Brattle, confidential clerk to the deceased. As well as having something rather more to do with him.'

Ephraim Brattle.

Miss Unwin's mind leapt and darted. Ephraim Brattle who had been within the house on the night of the murder. Ephraim Brattle who had been the last person, by his own admission, to have seen William Thackerton alive. The dark-visaged, locomotive-determined person they were all of them used to seeing in the house as often as one night a week before his journeys to the Lancashire manufactory. Mr Thackerton's confidential clerk. But with something more to do with him than that. What could it possibly be?

Well, doubtless the Sergeant would tell her in his own good time.

But this must mean – the realisation came flooding in on her – that Mr Arthur Thackerton was no longer the sole person who had any real motive for the murder. Whatever it was the Sergeant had found out about Ephraim Brattle it was plainly something that was a reason for his having killed William Thackerton. That much at least had been clear from all the nods and winks.

And if Mr Arthur was no longer the only person with good

reason for having committed the crime, why then the whole tower of suppositions and inferences she had built up about him at such trouble and risk to herself and to Vilkins was all at once a heap of useless rubble. Yes, she had proved Mr Arthur had a far better reason for wanting his father dead than anything the Sergeant or anyone else could know about, but that did not mean she had proved he had actually killed his father.

She had some shreds of logic still left.

But not enough to warn her to put a look of half-admiring inquiry on to her features.

'So what is it that you have discovered about Mr Brattle, that has suddenly put me out of your reckoning, Sergeant?' she asked.

A closed look came down over the Sergeant's features like a descending curtain.

'Out of my reckoning, miss? Ah now, I don't think we can go quite as far as that. We in the detective fraternity don't put people out of our reckoning so very easily. There's no one in an affair like this that we don't suspect. From start to finish. From the very start till the moment the black cap goes on Mr Justice's head at the Old Bailey and sentence is pronounced.'

'Indeed, Sergeant?'

It crossed Miss Unwin's mind that she had just been given an excellent opportunity for suggesting to the Sergeant that he ought to be suspecting Mr Arthur Thackerton. But wasn't the time for that past? What could she tell him now that would make it more likely that Mr Arthur had been the murderer under this roof than that Ephraim Brattle had? Nothing. Nothing.

But what did the Sergeant know about Ephraim Brattle that made him the more likely suspect?

She managed now to put on the air of wheedling weakness that she should have contrived earlier.

'But you have come to suspect Mr Brattle more than anyone else, Sergeant, haven't you?' she said. 'Won't you tell me just what your inquiries at the office brought to light?'

'You may ask, miss. You may ask. But whether you'll get to know is quite another question.'

Sergeant Drewd was not to be so easily placated once any suggestion had been made about his judgement.

With a quick straightening of his little ramrod back he marched over now to the hall-stand where his brown bowler hat was hanging, took it down with a flourish, set it on his head at a cocky angle and indicated to the quietly waiting Henry that he was ready to leave.

But before Henry had quite got the door open for him he was unable to resist adding just a few words more.

'Still, if you'll take my advice, miss, you'll look in the *Mercury* newspaper tomorrow morning. I dare say you'll find something of interest there. Dear me, yes, something mighty interesting.'

So Miss Unwin was left with another long period of pricking uncertainty, made endurable only because she was kept busy until Pelham had been seen through the last hours of his day. His velvet suit with the broad lace collar had to be put on for his nightly visit to the drawing-room and the poem he had learnt earlier had to be gone over to make sure he could say it. Then down in the drawing-room a sugar-mouse's head had to be snapped off and no more – Miss Unwin found herself listening for that grunt of a laugh from the direction of the fireplace and the small fit of coughing that often accompanied it – and then, upstairs, the mouse had to be deposited in its customary place on the landing table, safe from thieving fingers now, and then, with supper finished, it had to meet its end. Next, just one game of Snakes and Ladders. Bath. Then prayers. Finally the night-light had to be lit and a soft good night said.

But at last in the schoolroom Vilkins came up with her mutton chop and pot of tea and she could turn her mind fully to consider how her situation had changed. Vilkins, of course, wanted to know how her expedition to Maida Vale had gone and had to be told about it at length and then, despite the joy at its success that had lit up her round face as if it was a turnip with a candle inside it, she had to be told of this newest, most perplexing development.

'But, Unwin, what could that Sergeant have found out about that old Brattle, go about the 'ouse and never a word to no one an' so determined you wonder where he's a-going to fetch up?'

'Vilkins, dear, I can't tell what Sergeant Drewd has in his mind, and I'm sure I never will, puzzle my brains how I may. If it had been something that could easily be guessed he would not have left me in ignorance. You may be sure of that.'

'Well, if you say so.'

'I do. I think I know that man by now. I've had to wonder so much about him.'

'I dare say you 'ave. But he's off your mind now. That's one thing.'

'Is he, my dear? I wish I could be sure of that. Did I tell you that he said to me that he always suspects everybody up till the moment the Judge passes sentence? It may have been said only to frighten, but I don't doubt he would be quick enough to go back to his old ideas about me if whatever he's found out about Ephraim Brattle proves to be a disappointment to him.'

'Would he? The devil. But, Unwin, whatever can he have found out at the office? That's what I'd like to know.'

'And I, Vilkins. And I.'

But Miss Unwin had to wait till the new day and the bright new issue of the *Mercury* to have that question answered. Even when she saw the paper lying on the breakfast table curiosity could not be satisfied.

It had been the custom in the house before violent death had come to it for Mr William Thackerton to be handed *The Times* by Mellings each morning and for Mr Arthur to be given the more raffish *Mercury*. But the day after the murder Mellings had had no hesitation in placing the freshly ironed *Times*, all smelling of printer's ink, in front of Mr Arthur. It was almost the first acknowledgement that he was now head of the house. Then Mellings had been for a moment at a loss. What should he do with the *Mercury*? Perhaps it ought to have been cancelled. But it had not been. So eventually he had placed it, not exactly in front of Mrs Arthur, but within her reach.

She had picked it up with some eagerness.

So thereafter Mellings had given it to her more directly each morning and she had glanced at its pages in the intervals between pouring coffee or tea. It had been while reading more of it after breakfast that she had come across Horatio Hopkinson's 'exclusive interview' with Miss Unwin and had broken into her frenzy of weak rage.

Nothing for it now, then, but to sit eating buttered toast and drinking tea next to Pelham and to watch Mrs Arthur toying with the *Mercury*, picking it up, reading a few lines, then putting it down again to pour more tea or coffee.

Then Pelham spilt his glass of milk.

Miss Unwin somewhat blamed herself. Unable not to look at the copy of the paper that, if Sergeant Drewd's hint was to be believed, contained an explanation of why Ephraim Brattle was now thought to be the most likely murderer of William Thackerton, she had not kept an eye on the boy's table manners quite as watchfully as usual. Luckily, his glass was all but empty. But there was mopping up to be done, a little scolding to be quietly done too, and a saucer to be inserted under the heavy white table cloth to lift the offending wet patch clear of the polished wood below.

So when a sudden 'Tcha' came from Mrs Arthur Miss Unwin thought it was an expression of irritation over the minor catastrophe directed chiefly against herself. But it was Mr Arthur, not at all concerned over Pelham's misfortune, who guessed the true reason for his wife's expression of annoyance.

'Something in your newspaper?' he asked. 'Not more scurrility about what they are pleased to call the Northumberland Gardens Tragedy, I hope?'

'And why should they not call it that?' Mrs Arthur replied, with unaccustomed sharpness. 'Surely it is a tragedy when your own father is foully murdered under his own roof?'

'My dear,' Mr Arthur answered along the length of the table, 'I wish you would not interrupt when there is an article in *The Times* here concerning events within this house. I think I ought to be allowed to try to master it without distraction.'

Mrs Arthur, behind silver coffee pot and silver tea pot, silver milk jugs and silver sugar basin, was clearly furious over this unjust accusation. But she elected, as she nearly always did, to suffer in silence.

'And not only events under this roof,' her husband went on, 'but events at the office as well. At my place of business.'

With that he plunged his head down into *The Times* again like a starved horse pushing its nose into a sagging bag of oats.

However, there was one person at the table blind to the performance he had put on for all their benefits. Little Pelham.

'Please, Papa,' he said. 'What means "event"? Why are we having events under the roof?'

'Hush, Pelham,' Miss Unwin said quickly. 'You must not talk to your papa while he is reading important things in the newspaper.'

'But they're things about us, Miss Unwin,' Pelham answered. 'Papa said so.'

'I dare say they are, Pelham. But little boys, you know, should be seen and not heard.'

'Yes, Miss Unwin.'

Slowly then Arthur Thackerton raised his eyes above the outstretched copy of *The Times*. He sighed.

'Apparently,' he said, addressing the air, 'the police have made inquiries at the office and they have found out that Brattle was not only Father's confidential clerk but that he is also, it appears, the grandson of a man by the name of Gunner, now dead, some sort of engineer, who is supposed, ridiculously I may say, to have been the inventor of our steam-moulding machine.'

Miss Unwin's thoughts raced. Thackerton's Patent Steam-moulded Hats, so much cheaper and so nearly as good as other hats, were, she knew, manufactured on the remarkable machines one of which, in miniature, crowned the tall silver Testimonial in the library. She had always understood, indeed it had been told her as gospel by more than one person in her first days in the house, that, although William Thackerton's father had not precisely invented the device he had been all but its sole originator. It was called, after all, the Thackerton Tube. Yet if it was true that the device had not been a Thackerton invention at all, that it should have been called – what was it? – the Gunner Tube, the invention of Ephraim Brattle's humble artisan maternal grandfather, then surely that grandson, the quiet, self-contained creature they were all used to seeing once a week in the house, had had a real and heavy grievance against the 'sole proprietor' of the Thackerton enterprise.

The possibility that he was William Thackerton's murderer had now become strong indeed.

But Arthur Thackerton had not finished imparting his information. He had paused to allow the full iniquity to become apparent of someone else claiming to have invented the device on which the family fortune rested. Now he added a summary of the final part of *The Times* article.

'It seems, I am glad to say, that the police are questioning Brattle at Great Scotland Yard. I suppose, indeed, that the arrest may have already been made, though apparently there is some doubt about the exact time the fatal blow was struck. I dare say Sergeant Drewd will be here again this morning to complete his inquiries.'

And, as if the mere mention of the Sergeant's name had brought him magically careering round the last corner of the course heading for the post, Mellings re-entered the room at that very moment to announce that he had arrived.

'See that nothing is placed in his way, my dear, about whatever questions he may want to put to the servants,' Mr Arthur instructed his wife. 'The sooner this business is finished and dealt with the better.'

So before beginning Pelham's lessons Miss Unwin had to have another brief interview with her tormentor of old. But it was only to tell him, once again, that she had heard quite unmistakably Ephraim Brattle's determined footsteps going up to the servants' attic on his way to bed at a time shortly before ten o'clock on the night of the murder. The Sergeant impassively recorded her testimony in a large notebook, not without licking a good many times the tip of his lead pencil. And that was that.

All through the morning, however, as she taught Pelham a poem from the *Juvenile Reciter* called 'The Bee' she was aware of an unusual hubbub in the house. No one was carrying out their daily tasks at quite the right time. There was the frequent sound of hurrying footsteps.

Once she caught, floating up the stairs, the sharp demanding tones of the Sergeant himself. She listened, unashamedly. Apparently Simmons, the papery-faced, was for some reason objecting to answering his questions. Then it became clear that she was insisting on staying with her mistress, to whom the doctor had earlier been called once again, on the grounds that she was too ill to be left alone. More hurrying steps. Then it seemed that Mrs

Thackerton must have told Simmons she could dispense with her services because after one final bark the Sergeant's voice was heard no more.

Miss Unwin went back to going over 'The Bee' line by line with Pelham and to wondering, as she could not prevent herself doing, whether what Mr Arthur had called 'this business' was really going to be finished and dealt with in only an hour or two more.

Would the Sergeant by all his close questioning be able to establish to the satisfaction of a future court that Ephraim Brattle had been truly the last person to have seen William Thackerton alive? That he had had the only real opportunity to have used that paper-knife dagger, as well as possessing that strong motive that had so unexpectedly come to light?

Only time would tell, she kept saying to herself. She must be patient. Perhaps even before the hour of Pelham's morning walk the burden she had stooped under ever since the moment Sergeant Drewd had seen that unfortunate blood on her sleeve would at last be lifted from her shoulders.

Chapter Thirteen

Sergeant Drewd, it appeared however, had not quite finished his interviews by the time for Pelham's walk. Miss Unwin was just setting off down the stairs with him when she realised that below in the hall the Sergeant was conducting what was presumably the last of the interviews, with the youngest and least in the household, John the page.

'One moment, Pelham dear,' she said. 'I think the police sergeant is in the hall. We won't disturb him. You can sit on the top step there for a little.'

Obediently Pelham sat himself down. Miss Unwin, as if she was not quite thinking what she was doing, descended a few steps more.

She very much wanted to hear what was being said in the hall. If this was the end of all the Sergeant's questioning she might very likely learn from anything she could glean whether he had finally come to the conclusion that he now had a cast-iron case against Ephraim Brattle. That would at last finally put her fears to rest.

There was another small consideration, too, that persuaded her into the unladylike action of eavesdropping. On that first fatal night when the Sergeant had conducted his questioning in the dining-room young John had been frightened almost out of his wits. He might well be as scared again now, and if he should be reduced to tears once more she could come quickly down the stairs and rescue him.

But it was not easy to make out exactly what was being said down below. The Sergeant and John were standing at the very back of the hall where the overhang of the staircase partially blocked them from view. However, idly descending a step or two more, Miss Unwin at last began catching enough of what was being said to come to some understanding of the situation.

'Yes, Sergeant, yes. True as I'm standing here.'

Well, at least John did not sound too distressed.

She failed to hear the next question the Sergeant asked or John's reply. But, again, his voice sounded quite confident.

Ought she to go back up to the top of the stairs where Pelham was sitting happily poking his fingers round the banisters in a game of peek-a-boo? If he realised she had deliberately gone down this far so as to overhear a private conversation it would be setting a dreadfully bad example.

John's voice floated up once more, sounding almost merry.

'No, I heard him, Sergeant. Honest I did. He had a funny way of coughing the Master, you couldn't mistake it.'

A quiver of alarm ran through her.

John had heard Mr Thackerton? Surely that must be after the time Ephraim Brattle had left the library. Otherwise the Sergeant would scarcely be interested.

So had Mr Thackerton been alive after that time some few minutes before ten o'clock when she herself had vouched for Ephraim Brattle going upstairs on his way to bed? That would mean unless the wronged confidential clerk had gone creeping back to the library again – and why would he ever risk doing that? – that he was not after all the murderer loose among them.

Recklessly now Miss Unwin moved down half a dozen steps more. She must hear every word she could.

'Now, lad, Sergeant Drewd ain't the man to tell a lie to. You learn that. Learn that now, and don't you try to forget it.'

'I ain't lying, Sergeant. Why should I lie?'

Why indeed, Miss Unwin, leaning over the banisters above, asked herself. Why indeed?

'So now then, me young shaver, if I was to tell you I had it on best information that Mr William Thackerton was dead mutton when Ephraim Brattle left that library, would you dare to tell me you heard Mr Thackerton a-coughing and a-spluttering after that time?'

Below, John was silent.

Above, Miss Unwin held her breath.

Then at last came the boy's voice from under the overhang of the stairs.

'I'd tell you it wasn't true, Sergeant. I'd have to tell you so, wouldn't I? 'Cos I did hear the Master coughing. Coughing the way he always did. Not spluttering. That'd be a lie all right. But coughing that little dry cough of his.'

Yes, Miss Unwin thought, hearing the confident, protesting tones floating clearly up. Yes, Mr Thackerton did have such a dry cough. He had it especially when he smoked a cigar, and in the evening in the library he had been smoking when she had seen him there.

So he had been alive then after Ephraim Brattle had left him. The Sergeant's newest case looked as if it had collapsed about him at the very last minute. He would scarcely like that.

His voice came to her ears again now, sharp and menacing.

'Now, you listen to me, lad. Listen to me, and I'll tell you a bit of a tale. There was once upon a time a criminal of my acquaintance. Let's call him, naming no names, let's call him Dirtyguts. Well, Dirtyguts had committed burglary. I knew it. He knew it. But devil a bit of proof had I got. He knew that. I knew that. So do you know what, young John?'

'No, Sergeant.'

There was a scared quaver in the boy's voice now.

'No, of course you don't, young John. But I'm a-going to tell you. So keep those big ears of yours well pinned back. In the pocket of Dirtyguts' coat when he was searched before witnesses what should I happen to find but a silver cruet from that very house he had burgled. Now what is the moral of that, my lad?'

'Don't know, Sergeant.'

'Then I'll tell you. The moral of that is that no one crosses Sergeant Drewd and goes away scot-free. No one. Never.'

There was a long, long silence in the hall.

Then John spoke again. Miss Unwin even thought she heard him swallow before he did so.

'Sergeant,' he said, 'I heard the Master cough. Honest and honest, I did.'

Well, it seemed she need not have feared John would succumb to bullying. He appeared to have acquired a lot more courage than he had had on the night of the murder.

But the case against Ephraim Brattle seemed now, beyond

doubt, in ruins. So the Sergeant's mind would be busy, surely, in mustering up again the case against Harriet Unwin. To be all the more strongly believed in for the upset his newest theory had received.

She bit her lip.

It would not be so easy now, not by a long chalk, to cajole the Sergeant into taking account of what she had found out about Mr Arthur. But if Ephraim Brattle could not possibly be the murderer of William Thackerton then it looked as if her own suspicions had been right all along. Mr Arthur had desperately needed money and his father's life stood between him and his acquiring it. Between him and the continued willingness, too, of the tiny womanly siren who had enslaved him.

She remembered abruptly the words Mrs Arthur had spoken at the breakfast table just a few hours ago. Those unusually sharp and bitter words. *Surely it is a tragedy when your own father is foully murdered under his own roof.* Yes, it had been a just rebuke. Mr Arthur had given little sign ever that he felt his father's death as a tragedy.

'Very well then, damn you, have your cough then. I'll look elsewhere. See if I don't.'

Sergeant Drewd's words, sharp as the crackle of musketry, interrupted her train of thought, and a moment later she saw from her high viewpoint his head with its heavily macassar-oiled hair crossing swiftly to the bell-pull to summon one of the footmen to let him out.

Barely had he rung when Joseph appeared, handed him that brown bowler hat from the hall-stand and unlocked the door for him.

He was gone 'to look elsewhere'. And where would that be? Down in the country where her own secret lay, easy for the finding? She very much feared that it would be.

But she did her best to shake the care off. There was nothing she could do to put matters right at the present moment. As soon as the Sergeant came back she would have to see him, if she possibly could, and begin to plant in his mind her own suspicions, her own certainties almost, about who had been responsible for the death of William Thackerton. But even if she had got hold of the Sergeant at this moment he would be in no mood to listen to anything she had to say. So back to her duties.

'Come, Pelham, or we shan't get as far as the Round Pond.'

'Oh, yes, Miss Unwin.'

Up Pelham jumped.

But in the hall, just as she was on the point of calling Joseph back to let them out, she checked herself. She had imagined that when Sergeant Drewd had delivered his *Damn you, have your cough then* to John the boy would have quickly retreated back to whatever work he was supposed to be doing. But he had not. Instead he was standing at the back of the hall, big hands stuck in his pockets, almost hidden beside the tall, ticking clock just where Hopkinson of the *Mercury* had tucked himself away before she had encountered him with such awkward results.

She turned and walked sharply back to where John was lounging, an expression on his face that looked like nothing so much as triumph, as if he had just emerged from a scuffle with a boy bigger than himself, a winner despite his inner doubts.

As she got close up to him – he had managed by the time she reached him to make his face blank, even a bit hangdog – she became conscious, too, of something else. Something so out of place that it took her two or three seconds to realise what it was, even to realise with which of her five senses she should recognise it.

The boy smelt of aniseed.

That was it. There was emanating from his mouth a strong odour of aniseed, so strong indeed that Sergeant Drewd too must have been very much aware of it. Then she saw what the source of the smell must be. John's left cheek was bulging. He had in his mouth, had had there during the whole course of his interview with the Sergeant, what had been known to her in her earliest days by the vulgar term of 'a gob-stopper', a large sugar ball, flavoured with aniseed, layered with different colours which while it was sucked revealed themselves one by one. During the whole of her desperate childhood she had experienced such a delight only on one solitary occasion when from a passing carriage a little rich boy had spat one out and she had swooped on it like a plunging carrion crow and tucked it straight into her own mouth.

Her first thought, when she realised what John had been doing during all the Sergeant's questioning, was to wonder again at the courage the boy had developed since his outburst of sobbing in the dining-room under the Sergeant's threats. But her second thought was quite different.

'John,' she said without any preliminary, 'where did you get that sweet you're sucking?'

With an audible click John pushed the aniseedy ball further back into his mouth.

'What sweet, miss?' he said.

'Now, John, it's no use pretending with me. You've got what's called a gob-stopper in your mouth, and I mean to know how you came to get it.'

For an instant plainly John contemplated not replying. His face flushed darkly and a mutinous look gathered in his eyes. But he was facing someone who had no doubts she would get her answer.

'Bought it, miss.'

'Oh, yes? And where did you get money enough to go buying yourself sweets?'

Again a moment of mutiny. Again only half carried out.

'I get me wages, don't I, miss?'

'Yes, you do, John. And I happen to know that your last month's wages very nearly all went on a new pair of white gloves which you had to buy in place of the ones you lost. Now, give me the truth. Someone put into your pocket the wherewithal to buy that sweet and a good many more, too, did they not?'

'No, miss. No.'

But the denials were hectic. Very different indeed, Miss Unwin thought, from the bravado with which he had told his lie to Sergeant Drewd. Because she had no doubt now that the boy had been lying through thick and thin in his interview with the Sergeant not many minutes earlier.

She turned to little Pelham waiting patiently by the front door to set off on his walk.

'Pelham,' she called, 'I think perhaps we can forget a little about being in mourning now. Would you like to take your hoop with you on our walk?'

'Oh yes, please, Miss Unwin.'

'Then go upstairs and fetch it from the toy cupboard like a good boy. I have got to go and see to something with John. I shan't be very long.'

She hardly waited to watch Pelham setting off for his hoop as fast as his chubby little legs would take him before she briskly ordered John to go ahead of her down the stairs to the kitchen area.

He made no attempt any longer to defy her. His face had lost much of its colour and his big lubberly hands hung despondently at his sides.

She ushered him smartly past the scullery where Nancy was busy at the sink peeling a large pile of carrots and went on to the nook between the servants' hall and the door to the area where there stood the truckle bed on which the boy spent his nights. Beside it was his box.

Miss Unwin did not stop to ask permission but knelt swiftly, grasped the box's lid and opened it wide. There on the top was the remains of a bag of gob-stoppers, some ten out of a dozen. She put them down on the floor beside her. Next came a few items of clothing, not very well folded. Miss Unwin plunged her hand straight beneath them and came up with a handkerchief tied at all four corners. It clinked a little as she lifted it.

She pulled apart the knot and poured the coins the handkerchief had held in a pile beside the bag of gob-stoppers. The sum amounted to twenty shillings and eight pence.

'So he gave you a guinea,' Miss Unwin said.

'No. Nobody ever –'

'Now, don't lie to me. I want to hear from your own lips who gave you so much money. Just that.'

A long, stuffy silence in the narrow nook of a sleeping place. John was staring at his ill-gotten wealth, spread in a shining pile of silver and copper on the bare grey-brown boards of the floor.

'It was Mr Brattle,' he whispered at last.

Miss Unwin had expected to hear nothing else. But her heart leapt up for an instant at the words.

'It was to get you to tell that story about hearing the Master cough and to stick to it through thick and thin, wasn't it?' she said.

Tears were rolling blotchily down the boy's face now. He sniffed hard.

'Yes,' he muttered. 'I – I –'

'Very well,' Miss Unwin said. 'You need not tell me any more now. But understand this, John, you will have to repeat it all to Sergeant Drewd at the very earliest opportunity.'

'Yes, miss. Yes. But will he – but what'll he do to me?'

'Well, you would deserve it if you were severely punished,' Miss Unwin answered. 'But I dare say the Sergeant will be so pleased to hear what you tell him that you'll escape lightly enough.'

With that she hurried up to the hall again. Pelham and his hoop awaited.

So, while Pelham bowled the hoop cheerfully along the wide pavements leading to Kensington Gardens, Miss Unwin gave herself over to thinking how she now stood. All seemed to be once again as fair as it had been when she had first heard that Ephraim Brattle might be the murderer in their midst. The position was, if anything, better, she reflected. The confidential clerk had now been exposed trying to provide himself with a false alibi for the time of the murder. Surely, only a murderer would need to do that.

For a moment she wished she had been able to deal with John while the Sergeant had still been in the house. He might already have left London to make inquiries about herself in the country, and to have her secret known, even when there was no question of her being seen any longer as a murderess, was something she would rather have avoided.

But in the meantime there was little Pelham. He was further away from her on the broad pavement than she could have wished, his hoop bouncing and singing in front of him. She picked up her skirt and ran.

Back from their walk Pelham's needs kept her steadily busy. His hands had to be washed after coming into contact with the hoop that had picked up the dust of the pavements. During luncheon he had to be watched with more than usual closeness. A second spilling accident was not to be thought of. After the meal he had to be settled down for his nap.

But as she attended to all these tasks Miss Unwin felt an inner sense of comfort. These were the things that ought to occupy her. No more cudgelling her brains over the mystery that had seemed to pervade the house like a miasma. No more journeying across London to confront ladies of doubtful virtue. No further need to enlist the aid of Vilkins in anything other than the everyday, ordinary tasks of filling Pelham's bath and bringing up her own simple supper each night.

So she was little prepared when, with Pelham happily asleep for his nap, she went to carry out her next duty, reading to Mrs Thackerton, to find that once again she was treading on the edge of a precipice.

Chapter Fourteen

Miss Unwin even felt a sense of deep pleasure in the fact that she was going to read to Mrs Thackerton once again. Of course her sitting-room would be unpleasantly stuffy, even though its hardly ever extinguished fire had been allowed to go out on this especially sultry day. Of course the ammonia odour of hartshorn would be hard to bear. Of course the dimness behind the half-drawn blinds would make it as difficult as ever to decipher the words on the pages of the book she would be given, and that book would be ploddingly dull, whichever it was. But reading to Mrs Thackerton was part of the everyday course of events in the house. It was part of the way things had gone from her very first days here. It had nothing whatsoever to do with murder, with sudden suspicions, with fluttering-winged striving to escape.

It was to be one of the days, she discovered as soon as she entered the room, when there was not to be conversation. After Mrs Thackerton's attack of the morning when the doctor had had to be fetched it was a wonder that she was not in her bed.

So, all there was was a thin hand extended in the direction of the book on the little side-table beside the brass-decorated coal scuttle. The volume proved to be a novel, *A Point of Honour* by Mrs Edwardes. It did not promise much.

But at least it is not *The Christian Year*, Miss Unwin thought. It was well enough to be pious but to read aloud for a whole hour those grey and plodding verses had been a strain on her patience. Yet had that volume been Mrs Thackerton's choice today she would not have grudged it. Its mild and unexceptionable sentiments would have been better far than extracts from whatever was now being said about the Northumberland Gardens Tragedy in *The Times* or the *Mercury*.

She embarked on her reading almost with eagerness. But hardly had she begun when Mrs Thackerton's weary hand was raised.

'Yes? Am I speaking too loudly? Does it pain you?'

'No, my dear, no,' came the invalid's feeble voice. 'I have got the headache it is true. But then I am seldom without that. No, I like to hear you read so. I like your vigour. Your youth.'

Silence fell then in the fuggy room. Miss Unwin wondered whether to ask again why her reading had been stopped. But eventually she got her explanation.

'It is my Godfrey's Cordial. I feel I should take a spoonful.'

'Yes, of course. Let me give it to you. Where is it?'

Miss Unwin peered round in the gloom.

'No, my dear. Beside my bed. Next door.'

'Ah, yes. Then I shan't be a moment.'

She got up from the low buttoned chair where she was accustomed to sit when she was reading and went to go to Mrs Thackerton's bedroom.

At least, she thought, the curtains will have been drawn back there and the blinds will be up now that the funeral is over so I shall be able to see.

She opened the bedroom door.

She was indeed able to see.

She was able to see in a single revealing instant the body of Simmons in her lavender stuff half-mourning dress, sprawled face downwards on the room's patterned green carpet.

For a long moment Miss Unwin stood in the doorway, transfixed. Almost she believed she was seeing a vision, that William Thackerton's terrible death must at last have suddenly unhinged her.

She shook her head angrily.

No, this was no vision. Simmons, quietly creeping, papery-faced Simmons, was lying there on the floor in front of her, dead.

That she was dead Miss Unwin did not doubt. But, again, she forced herself to be rational. How could she be truly certain that the still, sprawled figure was actually without life? Wasn't it possible that Simmons had simply fainted?

At once Miss Unwin went forward, dropped to her knees on the carpet beside the still figure, lifted one of the sprawled arms by the wrist and felt for a pulse.

Nothing. Nothing but a coldness, a less than body-heat.

Then, as she knelt there, Miss Unwin glimpsed the edge of a

stain that was soaking into the carpet beside Simmons's dry-skinned, scrawny neck. She lowered her own head almost to floor level and peered more closely. Protruding from underneath the body by the barest half-inch there was a small length of bright metal. She recognised it instantly. It was the top of the hilt of the second of the pair of Italian paper-knives from the library.

Miss Unwin wanted nothing more at the moment of realising this than to leap up, fling herself away from the dead body and scream and scream and scream. Instead, she closed her eyes for an instant, took one long, deep breath and then slowly got to her feet.

She went over to the bell-rope beside the bed and gave it a vigorous tug. Then she walked across to the door of the room which she had left open, closed it and stood waiting. She would have liked to have gone back to Mrs Thackerton, who would be vexed by the long delay in bringing her Godfrey's Cordial. But there could be no question of leaving Simmons's dead body to be discovered for a second time by one of the servants.

Yet when her ring at the bell was answered she almost wished she had after all gone to Mrs Thackerton. It was Joseph she found when she opened the door to the knock.

But, enemy or no enemy, there were things to be done. And without delay.

'Joseph,' she said, standing where she blocked his view into the room, 'another terrible event has occurred. I am sorry to say that – that your mistress's lady's-maid is dead. No, that she has been killed. She has been stabbed to death. Will you go at once to the police station and fetch an officer? If Sergeant Drewd is there, of course bring him. I will lock the door here now and go to Mrs Thackerton. Be as quick as you can.'

Much to her relief Joseph made no difficulties.

'Yes, miss,' he said. 'I'll fetch the Sergeant all right. Don't you worry about that.'

He set off down the servants' stairs at a run. Miss Unwin, feeling a little disturbed at something in the man's tone of voice, something she had no time to pin down now, went back into the bed-room, secured the Godfrey's Cordial, which she had already seen on the table beside the bed, and then returned to Mrs Thackerton.

She decided not to break the news to her. It would be a

124

tremendous shock. Simmons had been her maid for many years, and, although there had not appeared to have been the affection between them that there often was between a mistress and an old servant, learning of her brutal death could not but affect her. It might be best to suggest to Mrs Arthur that the news should be delayed even until the doctor had been fetched once more. Mrs Thackerton had looked as if Death was a near neighbour to her even before this calamity.

So, in the sitting-room she made some lame excuse for not having found the bottle of cordial more quickly, gave Mrs Thackerton the dose she wanted and then resumed reading Mrs Edwardes's insipid novel to her.

It was all she could do to concentrate on the words on the page in front of her and not betray in her voice the effect the appalling sight she had just seen had had on her. But she knew she must do nothing to rouse Mrs Thackerton's suspicions and she resolutely forced herself to make sense of the words she was reading, to speak them clearly and well.

But all the while she kept an ear open for sounds in the corridor outside, for the arrival once again in this house of death of the police.

In a little more than twenty minutes they came. There was the tramp of several pairs of feet, the sound of Joseph's voice raised in explanation and then a sharp tap at the door.

Miss Unwin laid down the book.

'I think that will be for me,' she said. 'A small matter requiring my attention. May I leave you?'

'Yes, yes. Go, my child. And thank you for your lively voice. I feel the better for it.'

Crossing to the door, Miss Unwin felt a sharp sense of dismay at the thought of what eventually must come to cause Mrs Thackerton to feel less well again.

But any such feelings were at once dispelled when she opened the door and slipped out. Sergeant Drewd was there.

He stood looking at her, his face as triumphantly grim as it had been when he had seen the bloodstain on her sleeve and had thought he had detected a murderess within an hour of his arrival at the house.

As he now must believe he had done after all, Miss Unwin thought. The idea of that had not come into her mind once up to this moment. She had found Simmons dead. She had been shocked, shocked to the point almost of letting out scream after scream. But she had known then that she must, if only to spare the invalid in the next room, control herself. And she had done so. She had suppressed all thoughts of the second murder other than the sheerly practical considerations, the need to keep the news from old Mrs Thackerton.

But now, at the sight of the Sergeant, cocky as a robin in his vivid brown suit, it came flooding back into her mind that a great part of his case against her for the murder of William Thackerton had rested on his belief – wrong though it was in fact – that she had been the first to discover his body. And now she had, in truth, been the first to discover this second corpse.

With a fierce effort of will she fought down the panic springing up within her. She had not killed Simmons any more than she had killed William Thackerton. She was innocent. Perfectly innocent. And she must behave in the manner of a wholly innocent person, let Sergeant Drewd look at her how he might.

'Ah, Sergeant,' she said, carefully closing Mrs Thackerton's door behind her. 'I am glad you proved to be near at hand. Has Joseph told you what has happened?'

'Joseph has communicated to me certain information,' the Sergeant replied. 'As a result of which I have returned to this house and now require you to surrender the key to Mrs William Thackerton's bedroom, which I understand you have in your possession.'

'Certainly, Sergeant,' Miss Unwin answered, still making herself remain cool in face of the uniformed constable and another man standing behind the Sergeant as well as of Joseph, lurking in the background, a barely suppressed smile on his bold-featured waxy face. 'You will understand that, having found Mrs Thackerton's maid dead in that room, I considered it my duty to prevent anyone entering unprepared.'

In reply the Sergeant simply held out his hand.

Miss Unwin took the key from the pocket of her dress and placed it in his upturned palm.

'Wilson,' the Sergeant said, turning to the constable, 'you will stay here with the def – with this lady while the police surgeon and myself make our examination.'

He marched off then along the corridor to Mrs Thackerton's bedroom and turned the key in its lock.

Miss Unwin waited where she was. She had bitten back the retort that she had no intention of running away. All she could do now was to stand there, straining to catch through the open door of the bedroom anything said there.

The words that she did eventually catch sent her yet deeper into cold anxiety. They were spoken by the police surgeon.

'No, Sergeant. Not very long. I would estimate well within an hour, certainly no longer. But it may have been very much less.'

She knew at once what murmured question of Sergeant Drewd's they had been the answer to. *How long has the corpus been dead?* And to the Sergeant's mind the answer he had been given could mean one thing only: that the person who had 'discovered' the body was in all likelihood the person who had plunged the second paper-knife into a second throat. Herself.

But could she prove to him that it was impossible for her to have done that? She put her mind to thinking.

But it did not take her long to come to the conclusion that no such proof was possible. Before coming down to read to Mrs Thackerton she had been with little Pelham making sure he had dropped off for his nap. He had, in fact, taken a little longer to do so than he often did after luncheon. But who was to know that? How could Pelham himself be relied on to say that she had stayed in his room? No, nothing proved that she had not run down the stairs to the library, seized the solitary remaining Italian-work knife, run up again to Mrs Thackerton's bedroom, where it was quite likely that Simmons would be busy tidying up or going through her mistress's clothes to see if her needle was needed anywhere, and had leapt upon her with murderous intent.

Always supposing there was any reason why she should want to kill Simmons. There was not, of course. How could there be?

But, even as she began to extract a tiny gleam of comfort from that thought, her reasoning faculty told her that the Sergeant would have in his mind already a perfectly good motive for her killing Simmons. It was definitely possible, he would say, that Simmons had seen her entering the library on the night Mr Thackerton died at an earlier time than she had claimed and that Simmons had decided to keep that secret with a view to blackmail.

What could she say in answer to that notion? There was nothing. She could only deny, as simply and directly as she could, that she had killed the poor creature whose body lay on the green Turkey carpet just inside that open door.

She braced herself to do this.

But she was not to be called on to do so as soon as she had expected. From Mrs Thackerton's sitting-room there came the sound of a handbell being desperately rung.

Without waiting to explain herself to Constable Wilson, Miss Unwin turned and hurried into the room. Was Mrs Thackerton undergoing another attack such as had necessitated calling the doctor earlier on? Was she even at this moment at death's door?

Her appearance might well have indicated that she was indeed suffering an attack. She was even paler than usual and her eyes were glitteringly bright.

'Mrs Thackerton, what is it? Are you ill?'

'No, no, my dear. Not ill. Not ill at all. But I am prey to anxiety. There has been such a disturbance outside. I have heard men's voices, strange men's voices. What is happening? Where is Simmons? She should have heard my bell. What is it, my dear? What is it? Has there been some new tragedy?'

Miss Unwin was silent, thinking hard. What should she say? Then she decided that, terrible though the truth was, it was all that would satisfy Mrs Thackerton now.

'Yes,' she said. 'I am afraid it is as you suppose. There has been another tragedy. I am sorry to have to tell you that your long-serving friend Simmons is –'

'No,' Mrs Thackerton almost screamed. 'No, no.'

'I am afraid that it is "yes",' Miss Unwin said hastily. 'Try to take it calmly. But poor Simmons is dead. She has been murdered too. In almost exactly the same manner.'

She watched Mrs Thackerton with double intentness. Would

that wan face convulse in the pain of a heart attack? Would those too bright eyes suddenly dim?

But neither event took place. Mrs Thackerton dropped her head back on to the silk cushions of her invalid's sofa and lay looking up towards the ceiling. There was a strangely calm expression on her face.

Miss Unwin, thanking Providence that she had been able to take the news so well, began thinking that as soon as possible she must get Mrs Arthur to keep watch in the sick room. She herself was likely to be called away at any instant. Called away permanently.

She was on the point of turning to ring the bell with the object of sending one of the servants for Mrs Arthur when a new outbreak of sound in the corridor brought Mrs Thackerton out of her strange spell of peacefulness.

'What – what is it? Miss Unwin, what is happening out there?'

But Miss Unwin had been able to make out through the thick door the actual words that had been said, even shouted, outside.

'Constable, didn't I give you an order? A strict order? What was that order, Constable?'

The constable's reply was muttered.

'Yes, Constable. To keep a strict watch on that woman. And what do I find? You have let her escape you. You have let a woman who has only just come from the scene of the crime, a woman with blood on her hands, escape.'

Miss Unwin strode across to the door and swept it wide.

'No, Sergeant,' she said. 'Let me tell you I scorn to escape from either the constable here or yourself. And let me tell you, too, that I am not a woman with blood on my hands.'

She stepped outside then and began closing the door behind her.

But not before a thin, demanding voice had called out.

'Miss Unwin. Sergeant. Please come here.'

Miss Unwin looked at the Sergeant. Should she do as Mrs Thackerton had requested? Or should she stay where she was, on the point surely of being arrested for a double murder?

However, it seemed that the Sergeant was fully conscious of what was owed to the lady of the house.

'Young woman,' he said to Miss Unwin, 'your employer is calling you. Go in. Go in.'

Miss Unwin turned and re-entered the darkened sitting-room. At her heels, dapper and quick, Sergeant Drewd entered in his turn.

'You called, madam?' he said to Mrs Thackerton. 'If it is in my power to be of any assistance, glad to oblige. Glad to oblige.'

'Yes, Sergeant, there is something you can do for me.'

'At your service, madam. What is it I can do for you?'

'You can listen to me, Sergeant.'

Plainly the Sergeant was surprised at the sharp tone in which the request had been made. For an instant his face went turkey-cock red. But he controlled himself.

'I shall greatly enjoy the privilege of listening to you, madam. To whatsoever you may have to say.'

'Well, I have this one thing to say only, and I trust you will hear it with attention.'

'Certainly, madam.'

'Then, Sergeant, do I understand you have implied that you believe the person who has killed poor Simmons committed the crime only just before it was discovered?'

'My investigations – well, in a manner of speaking, yes, madam.'

'In a manner of speaking only, Sergeant?'

'Well, yes. Er – that is to say, no, madam. I do believe it to be a fact, certainly, that the poor unfortunate woman was done to death only a very short time before the governess of this establishment purported to discover the corpus.'

'Indeed, Sergeant? Purported?'

'Yes, madam, I regret to have to inform you that such is the conclusion I have come to, taking into account a good deal of experience I have had in such matters.'

'I see.'

Mrs Thackerton fell silent. The ammonia smell of her hartshorn struck more strongly than ever on Miss Unwin's nostrils.

'Well then,' Mrs Thackerton said at last, 'I see that it is my duty to tell you, Sergeant, that Miss Unwin was here in this room with me for at the very least half an hour before I asked her to fetch some medicine for me from my bedroom. Does that alter your opinion of matters?'

Chapter Fifteen

Conflicting emotions swept through Miss Unwin's mind. First, sheer disbelief. It had seemed that nothing could prevent Sergeant Drewd acting on his fixed conviction of her guilt to the point of making an arrest. He had called her for everyone to hear 'a woman with blood on her hands'. Then, without the least hint of what was to come, relief had arrived.

Next, sweeping through as strongly as that feeling of bemused unbelief, came a huge wave of gratitude. Mrs Thackerton had, in a few simple words, made her safe. She had endorsed her innocence.

But then, in a new whirling gust, she asked herself confusedly why Mrs Thackerton had said what she had. It was not the truth. She had been in the sitting-room reading for barely five minutes. Yet Mrs Thackerton had stated calmly and clearly that she had been there for a full half hour, a length of time that put her clearly beyond the circle of people who could have plunged that Italian paper-knife into Simmons's throat.

'But – but, Mrs Thackerton,' she found herself saying. 'Why are you – I mean – I mean, are you certain that I was in this room reading for as long as that?'

'My dear, I have said what I have said. I am sure that the Sergeant has understood me. It was quite half an hour that you were here.'

'But –'

'No, my dear, let me be the judge of this. And now, Sergeant, I am not well, you know, and I must ask you to leave me to rest.'

'Of course, of course, madam. Sergeant Drewd is not one to give unnecessary trouble to a lady. I shall see to it that the utmost quiet is kept outside your room. I shall make it my business.'

He was as good as his word, though the orders he barked at Constable Wilson to secure the quiet he had promised were delivered almost as loudly as if the man had been on parade in front of him in a police station yard.

'Sergeant,' Miss Unwin said, when he had completed his arrangements, 'if you have no further need of me I should like to go and make sure Mrs Arthur Thackerton is aware of what has happened.'

The Sergeant looked at her. The twin points of his waxed moustache rose in unison as he gave her a ferocious glare.

'No, miss,' he said. 'I don't see as how I can put any particular questions to you at the present moment.'

'Then I will say good-day.'

'Yes, miss. Say good-day to Sergeant Drewd by all means. It is a good day for you. A lucky day, I would go so far as to opine. But, remember this, miss. Times change. Luck changes. A good day may turn into a bad day before all's done.'

'I do not forget such things, Sergeant, I assure you.'

Miss Unwin turned on her heel and marched off along the corridor, head high.

But as soon as she had turned the corner and set foot on the stairs to go down to Mrs Arthur very different feelings surged up in her.

She saw at once that she was by no means in safe harbour on any sensible reckoning. It was only Mrs Thackerton's extraordinary statement that stood between her and Sergeant Drewd's plain desire to have her in a cell. Statement? No, in the privacy of her own mind she could call those words by their true name. That extraordinary lie.

There could be no two ways about it. Mrs Thackerton had told the Sergeant a direct lie. In her frail state of health it might have been that she was a little confused about exactly how many minutes reading the first page or two of Mrs Edwardes's novel had taken. She could have believed, for instance, that it had taken ten minutes rather than five. But she could not possibly have believed that a whole half-hour and more had passed. No, she had lied to the Sergeant. It had been a deliberate attempt to put herself beyond the reach of the law. An act of extraordinary kindness, and one which she felt she had done nothing in particular to deserve.

Had she been weak to have allowed the lie to go unchallenged? Should she have chosen the truth at all costs and told the Sergeant roundly that she had been in Mrs Thackerton's sitting-room for only those five minutes?

Another uneasiness wriggled up in her mind. If the Sergeant somehow found out for certain the truth of the matter, would not her evasion just now count all the more against her? Might the Sergeant not hit on the notion that she had had some hold over Mrs Thackerton? That she had forced her to say what she had?

Well, it was too late now. What had been said had been said, and she had made no attempt to deny it.

So there was nothing for it but to trust to time to bring the real murderer to light when the lie that had helped her now could be forgotten.

Standing half-way down the first flight of the broad, carpet-covered staircase, with its brightly polished brass stair rods at every step, Miss Unwin asked herself once again who it could have been who had killed William Thackerton. There was no doubt, she thought, that whoever that had been had killed, too, poor Simmons. Simmons must have had some knowledge that was dangerous to that person, and she had paid dreadfully for her possession of it. She had paid in exactly the same manner as William Thackerton's death had been brought about.

So who was this person, the murderer? Was it, as she had believed until Sergeant Drewd had produced Ephraim Brattle as a suspect, Mr Arthur?

But, no, now it could not be. Mr Arthur was, surely at his office at this hour of the day. There would be plenty of people there who would have seen him, who could if necessary aver upon oath that he was there at the very moment of Simmons's death. Then was the murderer Ephraim Brattle? Ephraim Brattle who had bribed poor, greedy John into giving him an alibi for the time of Mr Thackerton's murder? But, no, again. Ephraim Brattle, too, would be at the office with dozens of people to witness it.

Then, as she slowly descended the stairs in deep consideration, there, walking across the hall below with his customary quiet, sober step, was none other than the person who had been in her mind.

'Mr Brattle,' she called out, before any more circumspect thoughts intervened. 'Mr Brattle.'

Ephraim Brattle, startled, looked all round him before he realised who it was who had called his name.

'Miss Unwin, isn't it?' he said at last when he had recognised her.

They were the first words he had ever spoken to her directly, though she had seen him on many occasions in the time she had been in the house as well as having heard all that the invaluable Vilkins knew about him.

'Mr Brattle, a word with you if you please.'

She had begun, and she could not now see how she could very well draw back. Nor, with some inner part of her, did she want to.

She descended the rest of the stairs while he waited for her at their feet, his round, solid, determined face showing only the very least signs of curiosity.

'Mr Brattle,' she said when she had come level with him, 'I have a somewhat curious question to ask you. Could we perhaps step into the dining-room there. I believe there will be no one in it at this hour.'

'As you wish.'

Ephraim Brattle doled out the words as if they were ha'pence, and money he could ill spare at that.

Miss Unwin preceded him into the dining-room, where the heavy green cloth had been put back on the long table after the luncheon dishes had been cleared. He carefully closed the door behind him and waited to hear what she had got to say, compact and settled.

For a moment her mind misgave her. Was she really going to accuse this quiet, self-confident person of committing murder? Was she actually going to tell him to his face that she alone knew that he had bribed John to provide him with an alibi for the exact time Mr Thackerton had been killed?

She might have been easier about doing so had she been sure that he had not been in the house at the time that Simmons had died. But had he been elsewhere? He was here now when, if he was anywhere, he ought to be at the firm's office and it was not so long since that paper-knife had been thrust brutally into Simmons's throat.

Miss Unwin felt sudden tears prick at her eyes, tears as much of fear for herself as of pity for Simmons. Resolutely she thrust back the thought of the moment of the poor woman's death.

'Have you been here in the house very long, Mr Brattle?' she asked without preliminary.

'An hour or so,' he replied, giving just the slightest indication of interest at the abrupt question.

One hour, she thought. Then he could indeed have been here when Simmons was killed. And he has admitted it. Well, Henry or Joseph would certainly know the hour at which he had been let in. He could really, guilty or innocent, do nothing else but agree to how long he had been here.

So, was she standing now facing a murderer? Was she standing within two feet of a murderer? One who had not hesitated, so it seemed, to kill a second time when he was in danger of discovery?

She glanced at the door which she had been foolish enough to let Ephraim Brattle shut. Its solidly thick wood would not be penetrated by any sound less loud than a full-throated scream. And she had, foolishly again, stepped quite far into the room before she had put her give-away question. Ephraim Brattle now stood between her and the only means of escape, a short, well-built figure, with square-toed boots planted firmly on the carpet beneath him.

But there was nothing else for it but to carry on where she had begun.

'I am surprised to find you here at all,' she said, not quite having resolution enough to ask at once why he had seen fit to give a whole golden guinea to young John. 'I should have thought that at this hour on any day but a Sunday you would be at Mr Thackerton's office.'

Best by far, she thought, not to mention that she knew he had spent some long time at Great Scotland Yard being questioned about Mr Thackerton's death.

'I should have been there,' Ephraim Brattle answered. 'I hope I may say that I have not been absent as much as half a day from my desk ever since I came to the house.'

'I am sure you have been most diligent. But you are here in this house now not that one.'

'That is because I was to meet Mr Arthur here.'

Miss Unwin could hardly believe what she had heard. Except that it had been said in such a short and straightforward way there could be no disbelieving.

'To meet Mr Arthur Thackerton? Here?'

'Those were my instructions. I dare say you know that I was taken last night to Great Scotland Yard under suspicion of having murdered Mr William Thackerton?'

'Yes. Yes, I had heard something to that effect.'

'Well, when I learnt that I was to be released this morning – there was no case against me, you know – I was told that Mr Arthur had urgent orders for Lancashire and would be at home here to give them to me.'

'And you have seen him here?'

Thoughts ran across Miss Unwin's mind like the flying shadows of clouds on a wild and windy day. Mr Arthur in the house here as well as Ephraim Brattle? Then he too must have been in a position to have killed Simmons. And, had he not to her certain knowledge had an excellent reason for having made away with his father? So, if Simmons had known by chance something which proved that, was it not likely at least that she might have thought the knowledge would keep her in high comfort into her old age if she held the threat of it over him? Certainly Simmons had always had the air of a person who hugged secrets to herself.

'No, I have not seen Mr Arthur yet. I understand he is in the library, while I had been put to wait in Mr Mellings's pantry. I had waited so long, indeed, that I was coming to see whether I had been forgotten when you called out to me just now.'

While Ephraim Brattle had been giving this reply – and it was the longest speech she had yet heard him make to anyone – Miss Unwin's thoughts had swung back to seeing him in the black light in which she had just envisaged Mr Arthur. There was the bribe to John. Surely there was no way of getting round that. Whatever reason this determined young man might have had for killing Mr Thackerton, and she was not sure that the reason Sergeant Drewd had seen him as having was altogether compelling, he had clearly shown by offering that bribe that he had something to hide.

'You are perhaps wondering,' she said, 'why I called to you, what it is I have to say to you.'

'Well, you have something to say, no doubt.'

And this is the moment, the inescapable moment, when I must say it, Miss Unwin thought.

'Yes, I have, Mr Brattle. I have to ask you this. Why did you give John that guinea?'

She braced herself for an attack.

But the round, determined face in front of her did not convulse in sudden murderous rage. Instead, it went a deep confused red.

'I – What guinea?'

'No, please, do not try to pretend with me, Mr Brattle. I will tell you exactly what I know. I was by chance within hearing when Sergeant Drewd was questioning John about your actions in the house on the night of the murder, and I heard John declare and swear that he had heard Mr Thackerton alive, and heard him coughing, after the time you had left the library. I saw the Sergeant depart then, evidently with his mind made up that he must release you at Great Scotland Yard. But there was something about young John ... Well, I will tell you just what it was. All the while the Sergeant was questioning him, I found, he had been sucking a sweet. Now I happened to know that he had recently mislaid his pair of white gloves and of course he had had to pay to replace them out of his wages. So Master John had no money for sweets. I questioned him then, and in no time he confessed to me who had given him a guinea. So now, Mr Brattle, I want to know why it was that you made him that gift.'

The dark flush had gradually left Ephraim Brattle's face while Miss Unwin had given him her long and circumstantial account. It had been replaced not with any murderous look – and that had much relieved her – but with an air of quiet steadfastness.

'You have told all this to the Sergeant now?' he asked.

'I have taken steps to see that he will be informed,' Miss Unwin lied boldly, once more measuring the distance between herself and the door. 'But, no, I have not yet had an opportunity of talking to him directly.'

'Then may I beg you not to do so?'

Ephraim Brattle looked at her hard and long.

She felt there was, curiously, nothing of a threat in the steady regard.

'If you will explain why,' she answered.

For the first time in all the weeks that she had known him Ephraim Brattle's face took on an expression that might have been a smile.

'It is because if you do the Sergeant will have every reason to believe again that I killed Mr Thackerton,' he said. 'And I did have good reason to, a better reason than he has ever suspected. Or, no, that isn't so. There's never a good reason to take a man's life, I believe. But you could say that I had had great provocation.'

'Provocation?'

'Yes, and I will tell you exactly what. Since you know that I was detained at Great Scotland Yard, I dare say you know too what reason I have to hate the Thackerton family. Mr Thackerton's father had cheated my grandfather, my mother's father, old Mr Gunner, out of all that he might have made from his invention, the Gunner Tube as I call it. It's the very key to the steam-moulding process for hat-making, you know.'

'Yes, I have seen the silver Testimonial to Mr Thackerton in the library.'

'A Testimonial to Mr Thackerton. That tribute should have been paid to my grandfather, only he was too simple a man to patent what he had invented with long trial and error over many years.'

'Yes, I see. And I suppose that does give you cause to hate and distrust the Thackerton family. But then why did you become Mr Thackerton's confidential clerk?'

'I will tell you why, and in all frankness. I took advantage of the fact that my name is Brattle and not Gunner to take a post in the firm, secretly as it were, with the sole intention of getting revenge for what had been done to my mother's father. I planned and plotted to work my way forward till I was in a position to do Mr Thackerton some real harm. In order to work my way up as I wished I had to make myself an excellent clerk, and that I did. I had to acquire an excellent knowledge of the workings of the firm. And that I did.'

Ephraim Brattle was looking at her now fixedly and steadily, as if by the very firmness with which he held her gaze he could drive the full import of his words into her mind.

'That was something that took me a good many years of patient endeavour to achieve,' he went on. 'And – will you believe me? – I found that during those years I had become a changed man. I do not know when or how it happened. But I knew in the end that I cared no longer for the revenge that I had worked so long and so hard to be able to take. I cared instead for the work I had learned to do. I know now, I can say it without boasting, as much as any man alive about the management of a hat manufactory, about the wholesaling of hats, about whom to employ and whom to get rid of. I know, I can safely say, a great deal more about it all than does Mr Arthur Thackerton, and more too than did Mr William Thackerton for all the years he had been "sole proprietor", for all the wealth he had made out of the business.'

'I am inclined to believe you, Mr Brattle.'

'So you should. It's the honest truth. Then, as I said, I found that I knew the work, and I wanted to do the work. So, when the time came, instead of taking what steps I could to ruin Mr Thackerton – and I could have done that in a year – I came to him, here in this house, and I asked him for a loan to start up in business for myself, in the straw hat line where we would not be rivals.'

'And Mr Thackerton refused you?'

Miss Unwin could see the scene for herself. William Thackerton had not been a man to dispense money that gave him no return in show. She saw the library as she had seen it on the night before the murder, the long table with its array of inkwells and penwipers, of stationery racks and blotters, with the glinting silver pyramid of the Testimonial at its middle, with its two Italian-work paper-knives. She could see Mr Thackerton, at ease in his chair, glowing cigar between his lips, as he had been when she had come to complain to him of Joseph's behaviour in the matter of sugar-mice. And she knew how brutally infuriating his attitude could be.

But she could not see, in her mind's eye, Ephraim Brattle, the Ephraim Brattle she had just come to know, being so infuriated that he had seized the nearer of those two paper-knives and plunged it recklessly into his employer's throat. She could not see it.

'Yes,' Ephraim Brattle said, his voice low, contained and unemphatic. 'Mr Thackerton refused me.'

'And when you had seen that his refusal would be adamant you left him,' Miss Unwin said. 'You left him and you made your way up to bed. I heard your tread passing the schoolroom door.'

'Was it the tread of a murderer? I ask you that.'

'No, Mr Brattle. It was not.'

Chapter Sixteen

Miss Unwin stood stock still after Ephraim Brattle had left her to go in search of information about whether Mr Arthur Thackerton still wished to see him. She asked herself how it had been that she had accepted so readily the young confidential clerk's explanation of why he had in panic given John that golden guinea bribe.

Nothing in strict reason, she told herself, made it now any less likely that Ephraim Brattle had killed William Thackerton and that later, to conceal evidence, he had murdered Simmons. Yet she had accepted his simple word, even though she had learnt that he had had even more provocation than she had hitherto believed. If Sergeant Drewd were to become aware both that he had bribed young John and that he had been refused a simple loan by the man he already had good reason to hate, then surely he would have him under arrest within minutes. But she, on the other hand, had been altogether convinced by that account of a rise in the Thackerton firm and of the effect it had had on that revengeful resolution.

Yet was it, nevertheless, her duty to inform the Sergeant of what she had learnt? Her duty as a citizen, and, more, in her own best interests? With Ephraim Brattle now no longer a suspect in the Sergeant's mind, she must herself be the person he was determined to see on trial for William Thackerton's murder.

An ugly thought came suddenly into her head. It brought such a cold sinking of fear that she had hastily to pull one of the tall dining-chairs away from the table and slide down on to it.

It was the abrupt recollection of the 'bit of a tale' the Sergeant had insisted on telling John when he had questioned him in the hall, his story of how he had deliberately put a silver cruet into the pocket of the burglar he had called Dirtyguts so as to obtain a conviction he could find no other evidence for. What if the Sergeant were to play such a trick on her now?

She could think of nothing unconcocted in the way of evidence that could possibly make anyone believe she had been in Mrs Thackerton's bedroom at about the time that Simmons had been killed. But she did not put it past the Sergeant to find or manufacture something to counter that untrue assertion of Mrs Thackerton's that she had been reading to her all that while. He might, for instance, she thought, bully one of the servants to say that she had been seen coming out of the library with her hand in the pocket of her dress perhaps holding the Italian paper-knife. Joseph would very likely agree to do that for him without any bullying. Unless his spite had at last worn itself out, he would need only the slightest hint of what was expected of him.

But, no. No, she must not allow herself to be frightened with false fire like this. She was a rational woman. She must think rationally. She must behave as if this were a rational world.

She forced herself to her feet. She did more. She made herself go upstairs and see whether Pelham had woken from his nap. They should begin his afternoon lesson soon. It was to go over the Sunday Collect for church next day, for him to understand it as best he might and to learn at least some of it by heart.

She had her duties. She would carry them out.

But her duties, earnestly as she buried herself in them, came eventually to an end. Little Pelham's head lay once more on his pillow, his long lashes rested on his soft cheeks, the nightlight on his mantelpiece burned with its tiny steady flame. Miss Unwin went back to sit in the schoolroom and wait for Vilkins to bring her up her supper.

Then there was nothing to prevent the grim thoughts from circling in her head.

For all that among them was that inspiring parallel of a story she had learnt that afternoon, Ephraim Brattle's determined rise through the ranks of the clerks in William Thackerton's firm, she could no longer see her own prospects in a rosy light. She had secured her governess post, something that once would have seemed far beyond her dreams, but only to find that her tenure in it was menaced from every side. Had it not been for that unexpected rescue by Mrs Thackerton it was very likely that she would not be sitting as she was at this moment looking out of the schoolroom window on to the quiet street, dusty in the exhausted heat of a long day, but instead she would be locked in a police cell under arrest on a charge of double murder. But, even if she had so far escaped that, Sergeant Drewd was almost openly vowed to getting past the obstacle that had been put in his way. To do that he might very well begin by investigating her past, if he had not begun to do so already, and when he found out about her lowest of the low origins he was more than likely to pass that information on to Mr Arthur. And Mr Arthur would then, almost for a certainty, rid himself of her services.

Arthur Thackerton, the man who in her eyes was in all probability the murderer who had struck twice under his own roof. Yet how could she move against him now?

A little while ago, when she had first discovered his secret, she might, given a good moment and using all her wiles, have planted in Sergeant Drewd's head the notion that Arthur Thackerton's nocturnal activities would bear investigation. She might have led the Sergeant on to go and see that spitfire seductress in Maida Vale and that would have given him the knowledge that William Thackerton's son had an excellent and pressing motive for his murder.

But now, when the Sergeant was doubly intent on proving that she herself had killed both William Thackerton and poor Simmons, now he was never going to listen to anything in the way of a suggestion or a hint that she might offer. So how was she to extricate herself from the dilemma? How was she?

A clatter at the door as Vilkins arrived with her supper broke the insistent circling of her thoughts.

As soon as Vilkins had come in she carefully butted the door closed again with a gawky hip.

'Lawks, Unwin,' she said, as she put down the tray which tonight held a piece of heated-up roasted hare instead of the usual chop, 'I been longing to talk all the livelong day.'

Miss Unwin looked at her, recalling in an instant the many childish secrets they had poured out to one another in the days long ago when they had been Vilkins and Unwin together and no more.

'Yes, I too have been wanting to talk,' she said. 'The times are as bad as any we've ever known, I think. There's no getting past that.'

'Simmons,' Vilkins said, putting a wealth of wonder into the name. 'Only think. I mean, keep herself to herself and never a word for the likes o' me, but all the same to go an' get herself murdered. In her bed.'

'Well, not in her bed, dear Vilkins. But in Mrs Thackerton's bedroom certainly.'

'An' you finding the body an' all. Was there blood all over everywhere then?'

'No. No, there wasn't all that much blood. A small stain on the carpet. That was all. Poor Simmons.'

'Well, don't give me no poor Simmons, all the same. Sly she was, an' sly she stays, dead an' all.'

Miss Unwin smiled a little.

'But we shouldn't speak ill of the dead, Vilkins.'

'I don't see the strength o' that, really I don't,' Vilkins answered. 'I mean, she ain't no different now she's dead, is she? Sly an' full of her secrets this morning, sly an' full of her secrets now. That's what I say.'

'And perhaps you're right. I seem to have got into ladylike ways, my dear, and sometimes they lead one astray.'

'I don't see you being led astray, Unwin. Not so very far leastways. Not for all the ladylike you get to be.'

'Well, I hope not. I hope not. Because I mustn't be led one inch astray over this business or I shall find myself in a police cell and up in front of a Judge at the Old Bailey.'

'That you won't, Unwin. That you won't, not if Vilkins can help it.'

'My dear, I'm afraid neither you nor anybody may be able to help it if Sergeant Drewd gets one solid piece of evidence that he thinks will undo me. He's waiting to leap on me, I know. Waiting like a garotter in hiding.'

'Well, but what evidence can he get? There ain't none, is there? You didn't never kill no one, Unwin, so he can't never put you in no police cell.'

'I wish I believed that as strongly as you. I wish I did indeed. But I suspect he means to dig out something, even if it's something he knows is false.'

'Yeh. I s'pose the likes o' him would. I never did trust no peeler.'

'And I had begun to trust them all,' Miss Unwin sighed. 'I had begun to, and how wrong I was. Let me tell you what I heard the Sergeant saying to John.'

'Not about old Dirtyguts?'

'Yes. How did you know about that? Did John tell you? I'm surprised if he did. I would have thought that young man would want to keep very quiet about his dealings with the Sergeant.'

'No, it weren't John. It were Joseph. Telling the tale, he was, an' laughing fit to bust.'

'Yes, I can see that that story would amuse Master Joseph. And he'll be all the more amused, I dare say, if the Sergeant tries such a trick on me.'

'On you, Unwin? But he couldn't. You're safe. There ain't no silver cruet he could slip into your pocket, nor nothing like it.'

'Well, I hope there isn't. I hope so indeed. Because if he were to do that, then there would be even less chance than there is now of me being able to put him on the road to Maida Vale that you went on, Vilkins dear.'

'Yeh. That's where he ought to be put, right enough. Up to see that lady there, an' learn all about 'ow much she owes an' who's got to pay the bills.'

'How I wish he could be persuaded to do that. How I wish he could be persuaded that he had thought of going there in the first place, because unless he feels that it's his idea he'll never consent to make any such move, I'm sure of that. But with the feelings he has about me now I don't see how it's ever to be done.'

'I could do it,' Vilkins said. 'I could go up an' tell him straight. You keep your 'ands off of girls what's too good for you, I'd say, an' go up along to Maida Vale, to an address what I could give you, an' ask there what Mr High-and-Mighty Arthur Thackerton does of a night an' 'ow much he 'as to pay to be able to go on doing it.'

Miss Unwin tried as much as she could to keep a smile off her face as Vilkins concluded her tirade. But her friend of old knew her too well.

'No, you're right, Unwin,' she said. 'A chap like that Sergeant wouldn't never take no heed o' me, not however long I went on at him.'

'I'm afraid that's so, Vilkins dear. He won't listen, however hard either of us tries to make him.'

'So what we do then? What we do?'

'Hope,' said Miss Unwin, though she felt furious with herself to be reduced to as feeble a course forward as merely hoping.

Vilkins seemed as little impressed.

'I don't see as 'ow 'ope'll do you much good,' she said.

'Well, neither do I. But it seems that all that I can do is to hope. To hope that some turn of events will make it clear to the Sergeant that he is looking in the wrong direction. But I shan't rely on hope for ever, my dear. Tomorrow is Sunday, and I suppose nothing will happen then. But if by the end of Monday there's been no change, then I shall do my best to tackle Sergeant Drewd, come what may.'

'You'll tell 'im what I'd like to tell 'im?'

'Something of the sort, Vilkins dear. Something of the sort. And if he doesn't believe me, or if I can persuade him first that he has thought of it all for himself, well, I can't be much worse off than I am at this minute, can I?'

'No, Unwin,' said Vilkins sturdily. 'That you can't.'

But Miss Unwin could be. And she was.

It was almost at the start of that Sunday which she had confidently spoken of to Vilkins as being a day when 'nothing will happen'.

They were going to church, Mrs Arthur, herself and Pelham, the servants having been despatched to early service. Mr Arthur had never been a churchgoer when he was simply Mr Arthur and he evidently saw no need to change his ways now that he was properly Mr Thackerton, for all that his father had appeared regularly at St Stephen's for Matins and had taken good care to put more in the collection than any other parishioner and to make sure that the sidesman knew of it. When he had been alive the carriage was always used for the outing, rain or fine, although the church was barely five minutes' walk from the house. But now that he was no longer there the coachman had let it be understood that it would not be convenient to get the horses round from the stables on a Sunday morning, and Mrs Arthur had not had the strength of mind to order otherwise.

They were going to be in good time for the service despite having to go on foot, however, and as they neared the church Miss Unwin noticed that there was quite a crowd gathered on the pavement outside. She put this down at first to the fine weather. It was in fact so hot that they had been constrained to cross the road earlier to keep in the shade.

Now, opposite the elaborate ironwork gates of the narrow churchyard, they began to cross back again. But, before they had reached the far pavement with Mrs Arthur walking a little ahead and for once holding Pelham's hand, a sudden loud voice bawled out from the knots of idlers on either side of the gateway.

'That's the one. That's the governess.'

Although she had clearly made out the words, Miss Unwin could not believe that she had heard what she had. *That's the governess*. The shout could only refer to herself. And now that she looked at the crowd more sharply she saw that they were hardly the regular churchgoers at respectable St Stephen's, not even the servants from other houses in the district who usually occupied its back pews. They were nothing less than a collection of roughs. But why should one of them have called out that she was there, that the governess had come?

She learnt why at once.

'Murderess!' shouted another voice, loudly and terribly clearly.

Miss Unwin saw Pelham dart a look back towards her, a look that showed more of fright than understanding. Nor did it seem that his mother had gathered what was happening any more than he had. She was walking sedately forward towards the far pavement and the church gates, head tilted high, seemingly oblivious of the vulgar mob.

Miss Unwin wondered for a moment whether she should hurry forward and take Pelham's other hand to reassure him. But at once she knew she must do nothing to associate him with herself, especially as in the wake of that first 'Murderess!' almost everyone in the two knots of people on either side of the gateway was now shouting.

Luckily the very volume of the noise was obscuring what was being yelled for the most part. Once or twice, as she walked slowly forward some two yards behind Mrs Arthur, she caught some particularly clear shout.

'Let 'im seduce yer, did yer? Dirty cow.'

'Not fit ter look arter anyone, never mind a child.'

For an instant she longed to clutch her skirts and dash full pelt up the path and into the sanctuary of the cool interior of the church. But at once she despised herself for the thought.

No, she was innocent. If the ignorant shouted and catcalled, let them. Only the truth could hurt.

By the time they had gone through the gateway the noise had penetrated even the ladylike aura which Mrs Arthur surrounded herself with. Miss Unwin saw her suddenly look back at the jeerers on the pavement and it was evident that now at last she had understood what they were calling out.

'Come, Pelham, come.'

Her voice was high-pitched and not far from sudden hysteria.

At something like a run she hurried into the church. Her disappearance brought a renewed burst of noise from the crowd, a sort of ironical cheer. A voice called 'You should have sacked the filthy creature long ago.'

Miss Unwin, her face set, walked the last few yards up to the church porch at the same pace that she had walked the rest of the way. But she more than half-expected to feel a stone come flying through the air and strike her on the back.

Inside the church she made no attempt to go up the aisle to the Thackerton pew near the front, but sank on to her knees on a hassock in the first vacant place she saw.

But even then she was aware that at once the person sitting on the bench next to her had moved sharply away.

Chapter Seventeen

Miss Unwin paid little heed to the service that Sunday morning. The thought of the shouts and jeers of the crowd outside made her shudder each time they entered her mind. There must be gossip all round the district, for miles around, to attract such roughs to the church just to see herself. In the public houses where the men servants of the area went to drink her name must have been bandied about. The vilest things must have been said about her. The scandal hinted at by Hopkinson of the *Mercury*, on the basis of that quarter-minute and by Mr Commonsense of *The Times*, read by dozens of butlers as they ironed its inky sheets, must have been discussed, embroidered on, laughed over in the coarsest way.

And tomorrow, when there were newspapers published again, Horatio Hopkinson would tell the world at length about the murder of poor Simmons, would speculate afresh over its implications. Then things would go from bad to worse.

Once she could have borne it all, however filthy the rumours. Long ago such tittle-tattling, however much neighbourhood tongues wagged, would not have touched her. In those days she had been low and there was nothing that could have sunk her lower. But now, now she had climbed up to the slippery perch she rested on, each word she imagined being said of her was like a slap in the face.

At last the congregation embarked on the final hymn. With a twist of irony that she was able to recognise through all her misery, it proved to be that favourite of the children's hymnodist, Mrs Alexander, 'All Things Bright and Beautiful' with its unbending description of the social order, 'The rich man in his castle, the poor man at his gate, God made them, high or lowly, and ordered their estate.'

In her distress Miss Unwin found it hard to say to herself, as in better times she had, that this was only the opinion of one woman versifier. Instead she found herself questioning whether by moving from the low estate into which she had been born she had indeed sinned against an immutable law. Were those jeers and catcalls her punishment? Was there to be yet worse to come?

Angrily she shook off the thought. No, she had risen in the world by her own good efforts, aided by kindness that she had had no right to expect. But those efforts had been hard indeed to make. She had toiled, she knew, far more than she would ever have had to have done had she been content to remain the maid-servant she had become, like Vilkins, when they had both left the parish workhouse together. She deserved to be at the height, such as it was, that she had risen to. She did deserve it, and if she was to be cast down from it now it would be an injustice that cried out for remedy.

But would Mrs Arthur Thackerton see any injustice there? It was scarcely likely.

She could imagine that as soon as they had returned from church Mrs Arthur would tell her husband about 'the disgraceful scene' outside the gates, even if it was not repeated when, in a few minutes' time, they had to leave. Then there would come the unyielding words of dismissal, and this time no threat of taking legal action would save her. Mr Arthur would know very well that such expense was beyond her purse. He would act ruthlessly and he would act quickly.

She might well sleep in a different bed this very night. At the Governess's Benevolent Institution, if she was lucky. At somewhere yet more bleak if they denied her the right there to call herself a governess any longer.

> 'All things bright and beautiful
> All creatures great and small
> All things wise and wonderful,
> The Lord God made them all.'

The final repeated chorus of the hymn came to its triumphant conclusion. A few last organ notes reverberated in the high roof of the church. The Rector and the choir filed out. In the nave the worshippers in the back pews waited respectfully for those in the front ones to leave.

Miss Unwin saw Mrs Arthur coming towards her down the aisle with Pelham's small hand clutched in hers so tightly that the tips of his fingers were a pulsating red.

She stepped out from her place to join them.

'Stay where you are,' Mrs Arthur hissed like a snake about to strike. 'Stay where you are, and do not try to come to the house till I have taken Pelham back.'

Miss Unwin flinched and moved into her pew again. The words were no more than she had expected. But they had hurt.

She wondered with an inner sinking whether the crowd that had assembled for the pleasure of abusing her had dispersed.

The last reverberations of the organ had died away. She listened intently. A few of the congregation as they neared the doors had begun speaking to each other in voices discreetly low. But it was not difficult to hear sounds from outside.

There seemed to be no shouting. Only there came to Miss Unwin's ears the raised voices of neighbours greeting each other.

She stepped aside to allow the other people in her pew to leave. The women among them, without exception, clutched their skirts tightly around themselves so that there was no possibility of them even touching her. But this no longer upset her. She had been scorned enough already.

Besides, when she got to No 3 Northumberland Gardens, she knew for certain now something worse than scorn awaited her.

At last she thought that Mrs Arthur and Pelham would have got sufficiently far ahead for her to be able to venture out without causing Mrs Arthur the terrible shame of being seen with her. She hurried past the few remaining members of the congregation who were standing talking in the sunshine – were they discussing the dreadful Thackerton governess? What if they were? – and made her way back towards Northumberland Gardens, deliberately choosing to walk in the full glare of the sun by way of accepting some punishment somehow to mitigate the wrath that awaited her when the door of No 3 opened to her ring on the bell.

Should she even ring at the servants' bell as a sign of humility? No. No. No. She would not. She had earned the right to use the visitors' bell and she would exercise it.

The door opened almost as soon as her gloved finger had touched the bell-push.

Henry was there in the full glory of his livery, wig on head powdered to a fine whiteness, green plush braided coat well-fitting across wide shoulders, white breeches snowy as his wig, stockings taut across the well-shaped thighs that had as much as anything secured him his post. Then, peering further into the hall, which was deep in shadow after the glare of the sun outside, Miss Unwin saw, drawn up for the sole purpose of confronting her, a grim party of three.

In the middle stood Mr Arthur, tall, flushed of face between his well-brushed Piccadilly Weeper whiskers, mouth set in a fierce line under his moustache. To his left stood Mrs Arthur, in her go-to-church finery, and still with the furious expression that had been on her face when she had hissed her warning to follow only at a great distance. And, unexpected but no surprise, on Mr Arthur's right there was Sergeant Drewd.

As she took a pace into the hall past the impassive Henry, the Sergeant stepped forward in his turn.

'Miss Harriet Unwin,' he said, rolling the syllables on his tongue.

Miss Unwin drew back her shoulders and advanced to meet whatever fate awaited her.

'Yes, Sergeant. You were waiting to see me?'

'Waiting, yes. To see you, yes. To have a word with you, yes indeed.'

'Then perhaps we should step into the dining-room,' Miss Unwin said. 'I do not think the servants will have begun to lay the table for luncheon yet.'

'Ah, no, miss,' Sergeant Drewd retorted. 'I don't see this as what you might call a dining-room matter. What I have to say can be said where we are. Just exactly where we are.'

He gave a glance to each side and shot another in the direction of Henry standing, tall and impassive in his green livery, beside the door he had just closed.

Yes, thought Miss Unwin, you want your audience.

She felt a sudden inner sinking. Was what the Sergeant wanted an audience for to be the arrest in the case of the murder of

William Thackerton and the subsequent murder of Simmons? It looked very much as if it was.

Had he then contrived now to find something he saw as being good evidence against her? But what was there to find? Had he, perhaps, though, while she and Mrs Arthur had been out at church, succeeded in making his way to Mrs Thackerton in her bedroom and there persuading her into retracting the claim that had seemed to prove her own innocence of the murder of Simmons?

Or, worse, had he now manufactured some 'Dirtyguts' trick or other, and was he about to spring that trap?

'I have just one question to ask you, miss,' the Sergeant went on, secure of his spectators. 'Just one question and that is all.'

'Very well, Sergeant. I shall do my best to answer.'

But what question would it be? Would she have a good answer to it? Almost certainly not, if the Sergeant was so sure of himself in putting it to her. But, even if she did, would that of itself be enough to lift suspicion from her shoulders once again?

Sergeant Drewd came stepping forward towards her, and, as he reached her, whipped round his right hand, which he had been holding stiffly behind his back, and thrust it almost into her face.

She looked down. He seemed to be holding, bunched in his fist, a small piece of white cloth, a corner of it drooping down in front.

'Now, miss. What I have to ask is this, this and this only. Do you recognise the handkerchief I am holding in front of you?'

Still somewhat dazzled from the effect of the strong sunlight outside, Miss Unwin had not realised that what the Sergeant had been holding out to her was a handkerchief. She blinked now and peered at it more closely.

She saw on the corner that hung down from the Sergeant's fist two initials worked delicately into the fine fabric. The letters H and U. Her own initials.

'Yes,' she said, puzzlement seeping into her brain like an on-coming mist. 'Yes, I do recognise it. It is one of my own handker-chiefs, a very precious one I was given by –'

She hesitated for a moment.

'A precious handkerchief I was given by a former pupil.'

It had been the gift, in fact, of the young lady whose leaving home to be married had been the cause of her own elevation in the world from lady's-maid into lady. The embroidery had been done, in greatest secrecy, by her young mistress on a particularly fine piece of cambric.

The only handkerchief of such material that she possessed, she never used it but kept it carefully in the top drawer of the chest in her bedroom. What was it doing here now, in the Sergeant's hand?

'So,' the Sergeant said, dipping a look quickly back over his shoulder to make sure his every word was being closely followed. 'So, miss, you don't attempt to deny that this particular handkerchief is your particular property?'

'I do not, Sergeant. Why should –'

'Then, miss, do you deny what this handkerchief is stained with?'

With a flick of the wrist that would have done credit to a professional conjuror Sergeant Drewd turned the fragment of cambric so that the larger part of it, until now hidden inside his fist, was visible.

On it Miss Unwin saw a dark brownish stain which she knew at once was blood.

There appeared, too, to be some little glinting specks of black adhering to the brown-red stain, but she took no immediate notice of them. Blood on my handkerchief, she thought instead. Blood on a handkerchief that I have been made to admit is mine. Whose blood can it possibly be? Surely not Simmons's? Yet for the Sergeant to be flourishing it in the way he is can mean only that, yes, he is claiming that it is Simmons's blood.

Did I have it with me when I found her body, she asked herself then distractedly? At once she knew that she had not. The cambric gift was not something to be tucked into her sleeve on any day of the week. Indeed, there had never been a single occasion while she had been at Northumberland Gardens that she had chosen to wear it.

No, beyond doubt it ought to be in the top drawer of her chest in her bedroom. Yet here it was in Sergeant Drewd's hand.

He was playing the Dirtyguts trick on her. He must be.

'Sergeant Drewd,' she said, making her voice as coldly cutting as she could manage, 'from where was it that you took that handkerchief, which I acknowledge to be mine?'

'I take it?' the Sergeant answered, with a look of slyly concealed triumph on his face. 'I assure you, miss, I did not take this handkerchief, which you have admitted before witnesses to be yours, from anywhere at all. It was brought to me, this object was. Brought to me by a reliable and public-spirited person, who will if necessary aver to the fact in court.'

Miss Unwin felt yet more confused.

'What do you mean by "brought to you"?' she said.

It was all she could rise to in answer.

'Sergeant Drewd is a man who's apt to mean what he says, miss. As perhaps you'll come to know.'

'I dare say, Sergeant. But I ask you once again. Where did you get this handkerchief which ought to be in a drawer in my room? Who was this person who brought it to you? And – and what is that stain on it?'

'Well, now, miss, what would you say the stain is? Allow me to show it to you more clearly. Allow me.'

And the Sergeant thrust the little piece of cambric as close to Miss Unwin's face as he could without actually touching it.

'Take it away,' she burst out in fury. 'Take it away.'

At once she regretted her anger, because the Sergeant had immediately turned round to Mr and Mrs Arthur with a look on his face as much as to say *See the guilty thing start back from the evidence of her crime.*

'Well, miss, what do you now say that this handkerchief is stained with?'

'I would say,' Miss Unwin answered, remotely as she could, 'that it seems to be stained with blood, though whose blood that might be I cannot say. Did one of the servants cut herself? Did she snatch up the handkerchief when she happened to be in my room for some reason? Is that it?'

'Won't do, miss, won't do at all,' the Sergeant said. 'Supposing I was to tell you where this handkerchief was found. Do you think you might sing to a different tune then?'

'I have no idea where the handkerchief could have been found.

As I told you, it ought to have been found, if it was found at all, in a drawer in the chest in my bedroom.'

'Well, it was not, miss. I can assure you of that. It was found, I'm very much inclined to believe, exactly where it was hidden.'

'Hidden? Hidden by whom, Sergeant?' Miss Unwin countered.

The Sergeant lifted the waxed ends of his moustaches with a sharp smirk.

'By whom, miss? By whom? That's as may appear in due course. That's as it may appear to a Judge and jury in due course.'

'What do you mean by that, Sergeant?'

Miss Unwin felt herself uttering the challenge as if she was watching herself from a far height, a figure dressed in her grey stuff half-mourning frock and quiet grey mantle, still clutching her prayer-book in her gloved hand. A figure striving to contest every point being made against her. Because she knew very well what the Sergeant had meant. He meant that he now felt he had enough evidence to arrest her on a charge of murdering Simmons and very probably on one of murdering Mr Thackerton too.

No sooner had she admitted this fully to herself than the Sergeant spoke the words.

'Harriet Unwin, I arrest you on a charge of murdering one Martha Simmons on or about the fourth of the present month, and I caution you that whatever you say will be taken down and may be used against you.'

From the pocket of his violently checked brown suit he produced his fat notebook.

Miss Unwin said nothing.

Chapter Eighteen

Despite her dismal predicament, Miss Unwin found in herself a sharp quirk of amusement at the way, no sooner had the words *I arrest you* been spoken, than Mr and Mrs Arthur, as one, turned on their heels and presented their backs to her. It was as if, she thought with a lively bitterness she had hardly known she possessed, they were a long-matched, loving couple sharing at once their every idea.

For a moment she contemplated calling out to their swiftly retreating figures *Miss Rhoda Bond of Maida Vale*.

But this was no time for petty revenges. Her own troubles had crowded in fast upon her.

Henry, by the front door, was almost as quick as his Master and Mistress to act on Sergeant Drewd's words.

'Will you be wanting a cab then, Sergeant?' he asked.

'Yes. Cab to the door, quick as you like,' the Sergeant answered.

There followed some long silent minutes while Miss Unwin and Sergeant Drewd waited together in the empty, marble-floored hall with only the echoing tock-tock-tock of its tall clock to be heard.

Miss Unwin once or twice was on the point of speaking. She wanted chiefly to ask who the 'reliable and public-spirited' person had been who, the Sergeant had said, had brought him her precious cambric handkerchief stained with blood. She wanted, too, to know where it had been found. The Sergeant had said to her – she heard again the very tone of his brisk words – that she would sing to a different tune when she learnt where that was. But he had not told her. Evidently he had felt he had learnt enough now to make his arrest without noting her demeanour when he produced that revelation.

But each time she brought herself to the pitch of demanding answers to the questions a wave of discouragement washed over her. She had been arrested. The words that she had striven so hard to avoid having said to her had been spoken. It was done. Nothing that she could say now could make them be withdrawn. Whatever she told the Sergeant now he was not going to answer with a merry laugh and say it had all been the merest mistake.

She was altogether in doubt, too, about what would happen to her next. She was going to be taken away. But would she be hurried off to Great Scotland Yard or to the nearby police station? And when she got to whichever of the two it was to be, what would happen then? Presumably she would be questioned. But would this be by Sergeant Drewd once more, or would some superior officer now take a hand?

Whichever it is, she reflected amid the blank confusion this unknown future presented to her, the time to put up her defence would be at that interrogation. If she could find a defence to put up. But it would be then that she must convince the authorities that she was the victim of a terrible error.

If that was possible. If the magistrates' court first and the Judge and jury at the Old Bailey afterwards did not inexorably await her.

At last Henry arrived with the cab, a four-wheeler, and Sergeant Drewd led her out to it. She cast one glance backwards as she was hustled along the path to the gate.

How much she was leaving behind in this house she had lived in for not much more than three short months. Little Pelham first of all. They had got on well together. She had pledged herself to his future, and he had gobbled up everything she had given him to learn as if they had been so many creams and custards. Then there was Vilkins. Vilkins, who, when she had first encountered her here, she had for a moment wanted to disown as part of a past to be blotted out for ever, but who from the start of the ridiculous business of the missing sugar-mice had been a staunch and welcome ally in an unfriendly world. There was her work, too. In teaching Pelham she had been acquiring knowledge fast herself, learning how to teach, how to encourage, how at times to reprimand. Besides that, there had been what she had taught herself in the quiet evenings in the schoolroom, her steadily advancing grasp of French grammar and vocabulary, the volumes of history she had devoured, and Lyell's *Geology* and those two books of Mr Darwin's.

She had even developed some affection for the house itself, new and ostentatious though it was. But its broad stucco front with its tall windows glinting and gleaming from their regular cleaning, the solid front door with the daily whitened front steps leading up to it and the two well-polished brass bells beside it, all these had come to mean something to her. They had given her a sense of solidity, a feeling of security. Even the two clusters of spotted-leaved laurels on either side of the path leading to the steps, dust-covered in summer through they were, grime-smeared after winter, had contributed their share to that feeling by their very sombreness, by their stubbornly continuing existence in soot-permeated London.

Would she ever see the house again? It was horribly unlikely. Even if, when she was questioned, she managed to find such convincing answers to everything that she was allowed in the end to emerge a free woman, it was extremely doubtful that Mr Arthur would consent to have her on the premises again. The best she might hope for was that he would agree to provide her with a letter she could show to any future employer.

Sergeant Drewd reached past her and opened the cab door.

'Get in, miss,' he said.

Miss Unwin dipped her head and climbed into the interior of the vehicle. It smelt of straw that had been wetted a hundred times and now had dried to powderiness. The Sergeant climbed in behind her after giving the driver a muttered instruction she had been unable to hear. With a groan the cab jerked into motion.

It was the local police station that proved to be their destination. Sergeant Drewd hurried her in and past a long counter presided over by a uniformed sergeant and heavy with great black-bound registers of various sorts. Behind this there was a broad corridor down which the Sergeant led her, his boots clunking loudly on its bare greyish floorboards.

At the far end they came to a small lobby with two ranks of barred cells leading off it. The sight of the bars, thick and close-set, sent an actual shudder of suddenly realised loss of hope through Miss Unwin's frame.

To be put behind bars: it had been the threat that had hung obscurely over all her childhood. Obscure but real. How many of the children she and Vilkins had grown up with had ended behind bars, she asked herself? She could not know, but felt safe in guessing that it might be as many as half of their playmates – in what little play they had had.

A constable was sitting at a bare wooden table in the middle of the lobby with yet another black-bound register open in front of him. He was scratching laboriously with a squeaky quill as he made a new entry.

'Brought you a female on a charge of murder,' Sergeant Drewd said to him.

He looked up. A drop of thick black ink fell from the end of his pen and made a large blot on the open page below.

'I don't see how I can 'commodate her,' he said. 'I don't see it at all.'

'Then you'll have to stir yourself and make shift,' the Sergeant answered. 'She's to be kept here till Mr Superintendent Heavitree comes over from Great Scotland Yard. Them's orders.'

'But I'm full right up,' said the constable. 'You know how they come pouring in on a Saturday night, Sergeant. Drunk and disorderlies by the dozen. No, by the score. I'm full right up, I tell you.'

'But not so full as you can't take one female, up on a charge of murder,' Sergeant Drewd stated.

The constable, who had begun trying to scoop up the blot on his register with the ball of a fat finger, gave a huge, puffy sigh.

'I'll have to put her in the solitary with Old Fits then, that's all,' he said.

'You do that then, Constable. You do whatever you have to, but just have her ready and waiting for Mr Heavitree.'

The constable got ponderously to his feet and led the way all along one of the ranks of cells to the far end. There was a pervasive odour of carbolic overlaid in whiffs with the sharp tang of vomit. Miss Unwin tried not to look through the bars of the cells against which her skirt was brushing. But she could not altogether avoid getting an occasional glimpse of the cells' occupants, and what she saw did nothing to raise her spirits. There were women lying on the floors, apparently still dead drunk after the excesses of the

160

night before. There were others, standing close to the bars, whose profession was startlingly clear from bright broken feathers adorning battered hats or from brass-heeled shoes boldly flaunted, let alone the occasional shouted coarse endearments with which they greeted the constable.

At the end of the row a small cell faced up the rank. The constable took a heavy key from the bunch at his belt and unlocked its door. Only when Miss Unwin was urged inside did she get a good sight in the gloom of the single person occupying the confined space, so far back was she sitting and so black were her clothes.

She was a woman of perhaps sixty with a long, pale face, wearing a black bombazine dress from which odd pieces of material sharply jutted. Her black straw bonnet, too, had more of its straws projecting, it seemed, than lying in place. Across her bony shoulders was a black feather boa, or at least the remains of one, with scanty feathers spiking out at all angles. Altogether she looked like nothing so much, Miss Unwin thought, as a bedraggled, wind-blown rook.

Her eyes had been fast closed when the cell door was opened and she made no move when, with a booming clang, it was shut and locked.

'Old Fits,' the constable announced from the far side of the bars. 'I dare say she won't do you any harm, now she's had her sleep.'

Miss Unwin stood looking down at her companion, so ominously introduced. There was just room on the bench and after a little she cautiously went over and slid down on to it.

She had meant to go over in her mind all the facts of her situation with the intention of having her arguments ready for Mr Superintendent Heavitree when he came from Great Scotland Yard. But hardly had she recalled once again the moment when Joseph had come out of the library and had said to her that Mr Thackerton had been stabbed – and he had truly done that, she told herself, and all his assertions to the contrary were no more than spite – when from beside her there came a croaking voice.

'Mrs Fitzmaurice,' it said. 'Mrs Honoria Fitzmaurice.'

'I beg your pardon?' she answered, hardly believing what she had heard.

'It is customary, I believe,' her bedraggled companion on the narrow bench replied, 'for one lady to give her name to another when that lady first announces hers.'

And the voice was, Miss Unwin noted, beyond gainsaying ladylike.

She took a cautious look sideways. But it only confirmed her first opinion: here was a drunken, out-at-elbows creature sleeping off the excesses of a Saturday night rampage. But she supposed that she had better answer in the vein in which she had been spoken to.

'I beg your pardon, ma'am,' she said. 'You surprised me in a moment of reverie. Allow me to introduce myself. Miss Harriet Unwin.'

'Ah, Miss Unwin. A good enough sort of person, I suppose, though by your dress I should say you are some sort of governess in half-mourning. Yes, a governess.'

Despite the faint note of contempt, Miss Unwin answered civilly as she could.

'You are perspicacious, ma'am. I am, or perhaps I should say I was, a governess.'

'And what are you now, if you are a governess no longer?'

Miss Unwin found the question a little difficult to answer.

'I suppose I am a lady in a prison cell, charged – charged with murder,' she said, in a voice scarcely above a whisper in the end.

Mrs Fitzmaurice, Old Fits, gave a sharp little laugh.

'And I am a lady in a prison cell charged only with drunkenness and being disorderly,' she said.

'But I feel obliged to tell you,' Miss Unwin added, 'that the charge against me is wholly unjust.'

Again Mrs Fitzmaurice gave her spiky little laugh.

'Shall I tell you that the charge against me is unjust?' she said. 'No, I scorn to do so. I was drunk last night. Whether I was disorderly or not, I cannot say, though I think it likely. And I tell you this: I hope I shall be as drunk or drunker again tomorrow. Otherwise life would be unbearable.'

Miss Unwin hardly knew what to reply. She thought about the black, spiky figure beside her. There could be no doubt from her voice and manner that her claim to be a lady was true. But how far down she had sunk. Because from the great whiffs of stale gin she received each time Mrs Fitzmaurice had turned towards her it was clear that her confession to being so drunk the night before that she had not known what she was doing was sadly true.

The need to find a reply was spared her, however. Mrs Fitzmaurice, after a barely suppressed groan and once more closing her eyes, opened them again and went on.

'Yes, unbearable. That is what life is for me, now and always. Unless one way or another I can get enough drink to blot out everything that I see or hear around me.'

Once more she let out her pointed little laugh.

'A governess,' she said. 'Let me tell you that I had governesses through my hands as if they were housemaids once. Yes, governesses for my children one after the other. And where are they now? They have forgotten me, forgotten me entirely for all the consideration that I used to show them. If they passed me in the street, they would turn away in disgust. And so would my children. Yes, my very children would disown me. Disown me, and go crawling to their beast of a father.'

Suddenly a hand, plainly engrained with dirt on top of its dead pallor, shot out and grasped Miss Unwin by the forearm.

'Yes, my children would have nothing but pretty words for the father who walked out on them and on me. Yes, walked out on me, and left me to manage how I would. Can you wonder that I began to take a little more wine than I should have done? Do you despise me for that? Do you? Do you?'

'I hope I do not,' Miss Unwin said.

'Oh, yes, Miss Mealy-mouth, the governess. You hope you do not. But you do. You think you would never do such a thing yourself. Don't you? Don't you?'

Miss Unwin sighed.

'To be truthful, ma'am,' she replied, 'in my present circumstances I cannot answer for what I might do.'

Mrs Fitzmaurice raised herself a little on the bench, giving another deep groan as she did so, and peered down into Miss Unwin's face, breathing on to her yet another sickly whiff of stale gin.

'Hm,' she said. 'But I doubt if you would do anything very

terrible. I see some spirit in you. And you needn't bother to try and contradict me. I see more spirit in you than ever I had. If I'd had spirit, my girl, I wouldn't have taken to the bottle. I wouldn't have drunk all the wine that wretch left in the house. I wouldn't have run up bills at the wine merchants until they took me to court. I wouldn't have sunk down to where I am, to where I'd give the devil my soul for just one nip of gin.'

'But I'm sure –'

'No. I don't thank you for your being sure. I don't indeed. Look at this. Look.'

From where it rested on the floor at her side Mrs Fitzmaurice picked up a black straw reticule. She flourished it directly in Miss Unwin's face.

'Yes. Yes, I see it. Your reticule.'

The old woman laughed then. Not the sharp little spiky laugh of earlier on, but a long, high-pitched giggle that ended in her choking.

'But you don't know the trick of it,' she gasped at last. 'You don't know the trick of it. You don't know what will happen when my good and dear friend Mrs Childerwick comes to see how I am after my night of drunkenness. My dear friend Mrs Childerwick, the laying-out woman, with the smell of the corpses on her hands. The lowest of the low, my fit companion.'

'I am afraid I do not understand.'

'And so you shouldn't. So you shouldn't. Because he doesn't understand either. That pig-headed constable who always starts me off in this cell because he thinks while I'm drunk enough I'd tear out the eyes of those trollops in there, as no doubt I would. As I most certainly would.'

Miss Unwin began to edge away along the bench. Then she stopped herself. If this was a lady she was seated next to, in whatever extraordinary circumstances, she owed to her ladylike assistance and comfort.

'I'm sure that you are painting a worse picture of yourself than you need,' she said.

Mrs Fitzmaurice produced her short, jabbing laugh again at that.

'I am sure that I do not,' she answered. 'But I have yet to tell

164

you about Mrs Childerwick, my friend, and I suppose that you are trying to turn the conversation, thinking it is something you had rather not hear. But hear it you shall, my girl. Hear it you shall, because perhaps one day you'll come to it, too, despite the spirit I see in your looks.'

'I am quite willing to hear whatever you have to tell me.'

'Quite willing, quite willing.'

Mrs Fitzmaurice laughed again, with spite. But a moment later she turned, bathed Miss Unwin anew in a waft of old gin fumes, seized her arm and began again.

'No, let me tell you. Let me tell you all about my little device. About what I have sunk to. When Mrs Childerwick appears, and I hope to God she doesn't delay much longer, she too will be carrying a cheap black straw reticule, the very image of mine. And she will put it down just at the foot of the bars. Then, as we talk a little, I will put my reticule down on this side of the bars exactly beside hers. And then – and then –'

She gave another eldritch cackle, so unlike her usual sharp laugh.

'And then when she goes she will take my reticule and I will take up hers. And in it I'll find – I'll find – Ah, God, I had better find, a quartern of gin.'

Mrs Fitzmaurice launched herself upright at the thought of the succour that was on its way and went over to stand and peer through the barred front of the cell, looking more than ever like a wind-blown rook, all spiky, jutting-out feathers, as she waited for the laying-out woman.

But evidently there was no sign of her, because in a minute or two she turned, came back to the bench, sat herself wearily down, uttered a long groan and closed her eyes.

Miss Unwin sat beside her, hearing the occasional shouts and curses coming from the other cells and trying not to let them recall to her, as they all too vividly did, the wild disorderliness of her earliest days. Instead, she attempted to concentrate on the course of her troubles up to the moment when Sergeant Drewd had arrested her. But the spectacle of Mrs Fitzmaurice, the thought of her descent to where she was really even lower than she herself had been when she had begun life, so invaded her head with drab thoughts that she could not give her own situation any logical consideration.

She must, she supposed, have been sitting in a stupor of unthinking misery for the best part of an hour when she was roused by the sound of brisk steps approaching the lobby at the other end of the row of cells. At the noise Mrs Fitzmaurice had woken too. She looked up with an air of elated expectancy, but almost at once lapsed into slumped silence muttering 'Not Mrs Childerwick, not the Childerwick style at all.'

From the lobby came the sound of voices, of brisk orders being given. Then the constable came in sight, tramping down towards the cell jingling his heavy bunch of keys.

'She ain't gone for you then?' he observed, seeing Old Fits with her eyes firmly shut. 'Ain't had a go at you? Well, that's something, I suppose. And now you're wanted. Mr Superintendent Heavitree wants to see you.'

He unlocked the door, motioned Miss Unwin out, re-locked the door and then led her, swinging his keys as if he were a monk of old swinging an incense-swirling censer, through his lobby and back along the bare-boarded corridor she had come down before. Near its end there was a door to the left. The constable opened it and ushered her into a small room with lime-washed walls and a single high, barred window.

In its centre was a table with a bentwood chair in front of it and on the other side a similar chair with wooden arms occupied by the man she guessed must be Superintendent Heavitree.

Her spirits rose at the sight of him. He had none of the sharp knowingness of Sergeant Drewd. Indeed, his appearance was very much the opposite, a large, comfortable-looking figure wearing a suit of quiet grey tweed with a thick watch-chain running across the waistcoat. The eyes beneath the grey jutting eyebrows appeared to be regarding her with a look that might well be kindly and his face, lined and wrinkled with experience, was framed in a pair of stout mutton-chop whiskers.

He rose to his feet as she entered.

'Ah,' he said, 'Miss Harriet Unwin. Well now, let's see what we can do about you.'

Miss Unwin went forward and sat in the chair he indicated.

A small glow of hope sprang to life within her. Superintendent Heavitree might be a detective officer, but he looked, surely, as if he was a man who would listen. And all she needed, she told herself, was someone who would listen to what she had to say and draw the conclusions warranted by the facts she had at her disposal.

'I am at your service, sir,' she said.

'I'm glad to hear it. Very glad.'

Mr Heavitree put his hand on to the button of a domed brass bell that was the only object on the table between them.

'Now,' he said, 'let me just ring for a shorthand-writer, and then we'll get your confession down on paper all in the proper way.'

Chapter Nineteen

Miss Unwin felt as if she had heard not a mere suggestion that a shorthand-writer should now record her confession, but a Judge himself pronouncing sentence on her at the Old Bailey ... *that you be taken from hence to a lawful prison and from thence to a place of execution, and that you be there hanged by the neck till you are dead ... And may the Lord have mercy on your soul.*

That someone she had seen as both kindly and intelligent should without so much as hearing a word she had to say assume that she was a double murderess and wished to confess: it was the worst shock that had yet come to her. It was worse, far, than hearing Sergeant Drewd bouncily say the words that had put her under arrest. It was worse even than that first moment when the Sergeant had seized on the splash of blood on her sleeve on the night Mr Thackerton had died.

She very nearly allowed Superintendent Heavitree to tap his outstretched fingers down on to the knob of the domed brass bell and summon his shorthand-writer. But she had some spirit left.

'No, sir. There is no question of my confessing to anything. I should like you to understand: my arrest was a grave mistake on the part of Sergeant Drewd.'

Superintendent Heavitree shook his head from side to side.

'Perhaps you feel bound to say that, my dear,' he answered. 'But let me sincerely advise you: it will do you no good. No good at all.'

'On the contrary, since I am guiltless, saying so as clearly as I can should do me nothing but good.'

'Ah, but, my dear young lady, you are not guiltless, you know. I wish you were. I wish you were. Do you think I like having to come here and talk to a young creature like yourself, well knowing that not once but twice she has taken away a person's life? But, no, my dear, you must make up your mind to it. Confess everything to the very last word, it's the only way. Then, when you've done that, we'll set about seeing if we can't make out some sort of defence for you, find some exonerating circumstance.'

'But there is none, Mr Superintendent. There cannot –'

'Now, I'm sorry to hear you say that, my dear. And I'm not sure that I even believe it's true. You tell it all to me just as it happened, and I'll see if I can't show you that perhaps you didn't act in quite such a bad light after all.'

'Superintendent –'

'Now, my dear girl. No anger, I beg of you. No shouting. That sort of thing doesn't become a young lady. Not at all. Now –'

But now it was Miss Unwin's turn to interrupt.

'Young lady?' she said. 'You call me a young lady. Do you know, Mr Superintendent, just how much of a young lady I am, or just how little of one? Hasn't your precious Sergeant Drewd found that out yet?'

The kindly glow in Superintendent Heavitree's eyes was replaced at once by a long look of cool shrewdness.

'So that's the way of things, is it?' he said.

He shook his head.

'You know,' he went on, 'it's astonishing how often something of that sort turns up in a murder case. You wouldn't think the bounds of society are broken as often as they are. You'd think, if you hadn't had my sad experience, that people stayed in the station in life in which it had pleased the Almighty to place them. But, no. Time and again I've come across something like this. I must see that Drewd acquires the full particulars. They'll be needed at the trial.'

'But, Mr Superintendent,' Miss Unwin said, her blood up. 'Whatever my origins, I did not murder Mr William Thackerton. Nor did I murder Mrs Thackerton's maid, Simmons. What proof that I did has Sergeant Drewd obtained?'

'I am sorry to find you taking that tone, my girl,' the Superintendent answered. 'I am sorry indeed. But, since you ask, I'll tell you. The Sergeant, who is as keen an investigator as any in the Detective Department, has obtained, firstly, a cambric handkerchief with your initials embroidered on it stained with blood.'

'And where did he obtain that handkerchief?' Miss Unwin

demanded. 'A handkerchief which I have already agreed belongs to myself. Where did he get it?'

'He got it, young woman, from where it might have been expected to be. From where you had hidden it. In the coal-scuttle in the room next to where you killed that poor soul Simmons. In among the sea-coals which you might well have believed would have been tipped on to the fire in that invalid chamber and burnt, except that with the particularly hot weather of the past few days for once the invalid did not require a fire.'

In Mrs Thackerton's coal-scuttle, Miss Unwin thought. So that was what those little glinting black specks she had noticed had been. Coal dust. So her handkerchief, stained with blood – But with whose blood? Could it have been with Simmons's own? – had been placed in that coal-scuttle. And found there by whom? Not by Sergeant Drewd himself. He had told her that 'a reliable and public-spirited person' had brought the handkerchief to him.

'Well, if my handkerchief was found where you say, Mr Superintendent, then I tell you that it was put there by someone who wished to implicate me in the crime, or who wished to injure me. Who was it who brought the handkerchief to Sergeant Drewd?'

Miss Unwin already had her suspicions, suspicions of the person who had already shown his wish to injure her. She waited with impatience while the Superintendent consulted some sheets of close-written paper he had pulled from an inner pocket of his comfortable grey tweed suit. He turned over two or three of them. Then he looked up.

'That handkerchief was brought to Sergeant Drewd by one Mary Wilkins or Vilkins, second housemaid at No 3 Northumberland Gardens,' he said.

For a moment Miss Unwin felt as if the grey scrubbed boards beneath her chair had split apart and sent her tumbling to the nether regions.

Vilkins. Vilkins betray her. Vilkins play the Dirtyguts trick on her at the instigation of Sergeant Drewd. Her childhood companion, her friend when friendship was the only thing either of them had had in the whole world. It was unbelievable. It was impossible.

Then, yes, she thought, it is impossible. Quite impossible.

'Superintendent,' she said, 'I am afraid I do not believe you.'

Superintendent Heavitree shrugged his massive shoulders.

'It's written here, plain as plain in Drewd's report,' he said.

He put his finger on the sheet in front of him and traced out the words.

'At or about ten-thirty a.m. the second housemaid, one Mary Wilkins or Vilkins, came to me carrying a coal-scuttle which I had previously observed in the sitting-room appertaining to Mrs Thackerton, widow of the deceased. In that scuttle, closely attached to a large piece of sea-coal at the bottom, I observed a cambric handkerchief with a reddish or brownish stain upon it, which I later ascertained to be blood. I asked the said Wilkins or Vilkins under what circumstances she had made her discovery. She answered that while she was cleaning the aforesaid room she had occasion to notice that the coal-scuttle was not full. Wishing to remedy this, she requested Joseph Green, second footman, who was present –'

'Stop,' said Miss Unwin.

The Superintendent looked up.

'You asked me to give you the full particulars, my girl,' he said.

'Yes, and I understand now how that handkerchief got into the scuttle. Joseph Green put it there.'

Superintendent Heavitree shook his head.

'Come, miss,' he said. 'That's nonsense. How could Joseph Green have got hold of your handkerchief, the handkerchief you have more than once admitted to be yours, and got blood on to it? Come now, that was the blood of the murdered woman, and you must know it to be so.'

'No,' said Miss Unwin.

The answer had come to her in a blessed moment of illumination. She had suddenly seen herself in the basement of No 3, had seen herself there on one of the days long ago they seemed, when in her first weeks in the house she had ventured into the kitchen quarters and had noticed, hung to acquire a proper gamey flavour, Mr William Thackerton's favourite dish, a brace of hares. The blood that dripped from them had been collected in little bowls hung from their necks, and even after Mr Thackerton's death hare had still been served regularly. She had been given a left-over leg of hare for her supper on the very night that Simmons had been murdered. Yes, Joseph would have had access to a convenient supply of fresh blood.

'No, Mr Superintendent, the blood on my handkerchief is by no means necessarily that of poor Simmons. It could well be from any meat that came into the kitchen. From the blood caught from a hung hare for instance, and hare is a dish served regularly in the house, I can assure you of that.'

She saw from the look on the Superintendent's face that this was a possibility that had occurred neither to him nor to Sergeant Drewd. But, as plainly, she saw a moment later that he was not going to let such a consideration alter his fixed belief in her guilt.

'Blood from a hare,' he said, with clear scorn. 'You're telling me, are you, that Joseph Green deliberately splashed a handkerchief of yours with hare's blood and put it in that coal-scuttle? Now, don't go making things worse for yourself by wild accusations of that sort. Why should Joseph Green wish to do a thing like that?'

'Because – Because of the stolen sugar-mice,' Miss Unwin replied.

But even as she spoke the words she saw how ridiculous the whole story of the sugar-mice and of how she had set the elaborate trap that had caught Joseph would look to the Superintendent's eyes. It must look absurd, set against the grim reality of murder.

Yet there was nothing else for it but to tell the story, now that she had uttered that give-away phrase. So tell it she did. Even in her own ears it sounded doubly ridiculous now.

'I see,' the Superintendent said when she came to a lame end with it. 'I see. And that is all you have to tell me? All this balderdash, all this nonsense about sugar-mice is supposed to account for Joseph Green stealing one of your handkerchiefs, dipping it in the blood from a hanging hare and then placing it in a coal-scuttle and directing the attention of the young woman Vilkins to it? Is that what you are saying?'

'Yes, it is,' Miss Unwin replied.

But she could not bring much conviction to the words.

'I see. And you go on to claim that you did not murder the maid Simmons?'

'Yes, I do.'

'And that you did not murder Mr William Thackerton?'

'I did not.'

'Well then, young woman, suppose you tell me who did commit those two murders. Suppose you tell me that.'

Miss Unwin, presented at long last with the opportunity of putting to a police officer who might listen the facts she had discovered to Mr Arthur Thackerton's detriment, felt the irony of her situation at its keenest. Superintendent Heavitree might, she felt, have heard what she had to say with sympathy, despite his original conviction of her guilt, had she not just the moment before produced her long, involved and, on the face of it, ridiculously unlikely tale about Joseph, the blood-soaked handkerchief and the stolen sugar-mice.

But after hearing that, after saying in round terms that it was sheer balderdash, what credence would the Superintendent give to her account of Arthur Thackerton's love-nest in Maida Vale? He would ask her how she had come by the information, and she would have to tell him that she had sent Vilkins as a sort of inquiry agent over to Maida Vale, and go on to retail to him her public-house conversations and her visit with the cats-meat man to the mews to see a gig with leopard-skin seats and milk-white harness.

He was not going to accept very much of that. Yet tell him she must. It was after all, surely, the truth of the matter. It was not herself who had murdered Mr Thackerton and Simmons but someone else under the roof of No 3 Northumberland Gardens. And who could that have been? Just possibly Ephraim Brattle. But that dourly ambitious young man's account of what had happened the night Mr Thackerton had died she had absolutely believed from the very weight of the adverse circumstances he had freely told her of. Or it could be Mr Arthur, against whom she had certainly collected a great deal of circumstantial evidence. Yes, it must be Mr Arthur, unless there was some altogether unlikely other person whom she had never suspected at all or had hardly suspected, someone apparently out of any consideration but who yet by virtue of some logically unconnected circumstance might, despite all appearances, have turned murderer, Or murderess. But, no, such a supposition was too far-fetched to be worth a moment's thought. No, Mr Arthur was the sole person possible.

'Very well, Mr Superintendent,' she began, making her voice as steady as she could, 'you ask me who did commit the two murders, and I will tell you whom I earnestly and sincerely believe it to be. It was –'

She came to a full stop.

Something had been niggling at her mind during the last stages of this fraught interrogation. Something she had said, or the Superintendent had said, had fired a tiny powder-train inside her head. It had burned steadily on, acknowledged by her only as an irritating distraction, as she had tried first to produce an account of the sugar-mice business that would seem moderately sensible and then to marshal her thoughts to present a case against Mr Arthur persuasive enough to overthrow the Superintendent's fixed conviction of her own guilt.

That irritating something had burned and fizzled its way along the thin line of powder that had lain ready prepared in her head, little though she was aware of it. And now, suddenly, it had exploded within her.

She knew now, knew past uncertainty, just who, extraordinarily, unexpectedly, had killed William Thackerton and had then gone on for a yet more urgent reason to kill Simmons. She knew just why, in every logical step.

All she lacked, curiously, was a final willingness to name the name.

'No, Mr Superintendent,' she said, 'I am unable, after all, to tell you who the guilty person at No 3 Northumberland Gardens is.'

'Well, yes, my dear young woman, of course you are. Don't think now that I hold it against you that you contemplated such a thing. It was very natural, very natural.'

The Superintendent looked at her almost as if she was a dog and he was about to pat her on the head because at the last moment she had not taken the joint of beef off the butcher's stall.

'So now,' he went on, his hand reaching out once more towards the bell on the table in front of him, 'shall we call in that shorthand-writer and get this business over once and for all?'

'No, sir,' said Miss Unwin. 'I have nothing more to say.'

'Really? I cannot persuade you? It is for your own good, you know. A full confession is much the best way.'

'I have nothing to confess.'

Superintendent Heavitree pushed himself lugubriously to his feet.

'Very well then. We shall bring you up before the magistrates tomorrow morning. They won't have any doubts about committing you for trial, you know. And then it'll be the Old Bailey.'

He shook his mutton-chop-whiskered head at her.

'The Old Bailey,' he repeated. 'You won't like that, you know. Never mind what comes after. You won't like the Old Bailey at all.'

'I dare say I shan't, sir. But it seems I have no alternative.'

'So hard,' Superintendent Heavitree murmured. 'So hard. So convinced in evil, and so young.'

At the door he turned to her once more.

'Is there nothing I can do for you?'

'Why, yes, sir,' Miss Unwin answered. 'If I am to remain here till the magistrates sit tomorrow morning I would much welcome a change of apparel. Would you be so good as to have a message sent to No 3 Northumberland Gardens. Perhaps the second house-maid, Mary, could come round with what is necessary.'

'Yes, yes, my girl. I'll see to that. I'll see to that. It's the least I can do. And, remember, if you should change your mind . . .'

'I do not think I will do that, Mr Heavitree. But thank you for your consideration.'

When Miss Unwin was taken back to the small cell at the far end of the row of women's accommodation she found that Mrs Fitzmaurice was no longer there. She wondered whether Old Fits's friend, the laying-out woman, had come in time to smuggle her that quartern of gin before she had been put into one of the communal cells alongside the other drunks and the trollops she was now sober enough not to attack. She hoped she had. She hoped the old bedraggled lady had had something with which to raise her spirits before she had been plunged into such brutally uncongenial surroundings.

Then she sat, all alone, on the narrow bench and thought over the astonishing sequence of events that had flashed into her head at the very moment she had been about to try to make the case against Arthur Thackerton to Superintendent Heavitree.

It had been a phrase of the Superintendent's that had set spark to the powder-train that had eventually exploded in illumination in her head. *Why should Joseph Green wish to do a thing like that?* Those had been the words that had set alight the thin trail of gunpowder that had lain, unbeknown to her, all the while in her mind.

The Superintendent had asked the question when she had accused Joseph of staining her handkerchief with hare's blood and putting it in the coal-scuttle in Mrs Thackerton's sitting-room. She had known it must be Joseph, determined she thought once again to spite her, who had for the third or fourth time played a malicious trick on her. It could have been no one else, since apparently Sergeant Drewd had had no direct hand in the business, and Joseph, so Vilkins had told her, had overheard the Sergeant's story about Dirtyguts the burglar.

Then, as she had readied herself to answer the Superintendent, her outer mind had seen the cause of Joseph's malice as the stolen sugar-mice. But her inner mind must have rejected that explanation even as she was about to put it to Superintendent Heavitree. And rightly so, she saw now. Because Joseph's action in putting the handkerchief in Sergeant Drewd's way was of much too serious a nature to be actuated by the petty malice she had supposed had inspired it.

No, Joseph had stained her handkerchief with blood for the sole purpose of making it appear that she had been Simmons's killer, thus deflecting any possible suspicion from her real murderer. Himself.

Chapter Twenty

It had all run on in Miss Unwin's mind quickly as if a live spark had been travelling, hissing and fizzing, along a real line of gunpowder. Joseph had murdered Mr Thackerton. Sergeant Drewd had been right at least about one thing: the person who had discovered Mr Thackerton's body had been his murderer. She must have seen Joseph, she thought, coming out of the library within minutes of the instant he had seized that Italian-work paper-knife, so ready to hand, and had thrust it in a blaze of fury into Mr Thackerton's throat. He had been white as a sheet then. She had remarked on it.

Had thrust the knife into Mr Thackerton's throat. No. Into his father's throat. Into the throat of his natural father.

She had seen that, too, in her explosion of light. It was the reason that lay behind the murder, Sergeant Drewd's missing motive. What had shown her the truth of the matter was simple: nothing more than the sudden recollection of Joseph standing in the hall on the day after she had failed to persuade Mrs Arthur to take any action against him for his repeated thefts of the sugar-mice. It had been as the family had been going into breakfast after Morning Prayers, and Joseph had triumphantly confronted her, sticking the thumbs of each hand into the pockets of his white uniform waistcoat. She had taken the gesture at the time as being a mere parody of his Master's most typical attitude. It had not been so. It had been a natural gesture passed down from father to son.

The cut of Joseph's face should have confirmed the relationship for her. He looked very like Mr Thackerton. He had the same over-large features. It was only that she had always thought of him as a servant and of Mr Thackerton always as a gentleman, her employer, that had prevented her noting the plain likeness.

It had, too, been only that she had thought of Simmons as being a servant as well, a lady's-maid of long standing, that had prevented her seeing her as, in the distant past, Mr Thackerton's mistress by whom he had had his natural son. No wonder when she had told Mrs Thackerton that her 'long-serving friend Simmons' was dead she had almost screamed a 'No'. She had not been rejecting the fact of the death: she had been denying the friendship.

Why, she herself had even been forced to think about such relationships crossing the bar of society by that dreadful letter signed Commonsense in *The Times*. That self-satisfied correspondent had declared that when men had invalid wives they were known to go 'seeking solace' elsewhere. He had implied that Mr Thackerton had recently sought solace with herself and that in a lovers' quarrel of some sort she had stabbed him. But the truth of it was, the truth of it must have been, that long ago Mr Thackerton had sought his solace with a maid who had once been a seductive, china-delicate person: for all that in her last days she had become a dried-up, papery-faced figure hard to imagine as ever having been pretty.

Because Simmons, too, had resembled her natural son. Both she and Joseph had had those remarkably long incurving teeth in those long faces.

Joseph, it was absurdly clear to Miss Unwin now, was in his looks an exact mixture of the most notable features of his father and his mother, of Mr William Thackerton, gentleman, and of Martha Simmons, lady's-maid.

No wonder Mr Thackerton had hesitated in such an odd manner when she had told him which one of his servants it was who had been stealing his goods. He had held back the thunderbolt of instant dismissal because it was the man whom he had eventually been persuaded by Simmons to employ. No wonder that Joseph had been able to say that he had had no more than 'a wigging' from the Master. Mr Thackerton would not have dared to award any punishment more severe than a mere rebuke.

Then, on the last night of his life when Joseph had taken him his whisky and seltzer and had had the opportunity of another private conference, it was plain to her now what must have passed between them. Joseph, emboldened by his success in brazening out a crime as serious in Mr Thackerton's eyes as theft of his goods, must have demanded that he himself should step into old Mellings's shoes as butler. He had spoken before of doing just that one day, and it had seemed ridiculous in someone who was only a second footman in the house and a notoriously lazy and careless servant too.

But Joseph had had his ambitions to rise in the world, though plainly he had always intended to do so without the labour of earning that rise. Then, when his father had refused his request, as doubtless astonished at such effrontery he would unhesitatingly have done, Joseph had seized that paper-knife and lashed out.

Then ... then – Miss Unwin's fast-working mind saw it all – Joseph had stripped from his hand the white glove that had become soaked in the jetting blood from Mr Thackerton's neck, had crossed to one of the conveniently open windows of the library and had thrown it together with its fellow down into the enshrouding laurels beneath. From these when he had, providentially for him, been sent to Great Scotland Yard to summon police assistance it would have been altogether easy to collect the damning evidence and somewhere on the way to Westminster get rid of it for ever. And that very night, no doubt, amid all the confusion in the house he had had no trouble in abstracting lubberly John's gloves and making them his own, leaving poor John to have to buy a new pair out of his scanty wages and so be susceptible to Ephraim Brattle's unnecessary bribe.

Everything fell into place in the light of this account of what had happened at No 3 Northumberland Gardens the night William Thackerton had died. Even such a minor domestic detail as John losing his gloves. Why, she had noticed just before that terrible confrontation with William Thackerton's blood-splashed body the way Joseph's sweaty fingers had left marks on the silver salver with the seltzer and the whisky decanter on it which he had kept holding out stiffly in front of himself. She had seen that, and it had meant nothing to her. Then.

Even Simmons's air of always being in possession of some secret or other, which Vilkins, poor simple Vilkins, had noted, was accounted for. And, of course, this accounted too for Mrs Thackerton's strange falsehood about how long she herself had spent reading to her at the time of Simmons's death. If Mrs Thackerton was a rejected wife, then it was natural enough for her to feel a sort of awed admiration for somebody ready to beard her overbearing husband as well as performing the simple task of keeping little Pelham in order. It must have been only out of this feeling of admiration – Mrs Thackerton had openly expressed it more than once – that she had lied to save her.

Yes, everything fell into place. But not a shred of it was capable of proof.

How could she have explained to Superintendent Heavitree that Joseph Green and Simmons both had noticeably long teeth? How could she ask to see him now and tell him that? How would she be able, in giving evidence in her own defence at the Old Bailey trial, to point out that Joseph Green had placed his thumbs in his waistcoat pockets in exactly the same manner that murdered William Thackerton was wont to do?

No, she knew who had killed both Mr Thackerton and his mistress of long ago, Simmons, but it was she herself who would be tried for those murders and who could produce in answer to the charge scarcely more than the assertion of her innocence.

She sat on in her small cell, time and again butting up against this dilemma and each time backing off from it with not the least dent made in its iron surround. She was not guilty of the murders for which she was behind bars here now. She knew who was guilty. She could prove nothing.

At last, early in the evening, there was the sound of voices in the lobby at the far end of the row of cells. Miss Unwin thought she recognised a familiar one and her heart leapt up at the prospect of seeing a friendly face at last.

It was Vilkins, indeed, who came towards her along the row of the communal cells. Vilkins, her round red face under her garishly decorated wide straw bonnet looking like a disconsolate moon. Vilkins, carrying on her arm a large basket containing no doubt the change of under-garments Superintendent Heavitree had agreed to ask to have brought in.

The constable escorting Vilkins took the ponderous key from the ring at his belt, let her into the cell, locked the door behind her and said gloomily that she could tap on the bars when she was ready to be let out again.

'Lawks, Unwin, you're in trouble all right now,' Vilkins said as soon as the constable had regained his distant lobby.

Miss Unwin managed a pallid smile.

'Yes. Yes, I'm in worse trouble than I ever thought I would be during the worst of our childhood days together,' she answered.

'What they going to do with you?' Vilkins asked. 'They ain't a-going to hang you right off, are they?'

'No. No, my dear, they won't quite do that. They're going to take me before the magistrates tomorrow. The magistrates will find that there is a case to answer, and I will be remanded in custody for trial at the Old Bailey.'

'The Bailey, but – But, Unwin, that ain't very good.'

'No. No, it isn't good at all, my dear. I am innocent of all they allege against me, but I cannot see how I can prove it to them. Vilkins dear, I know who did commit those two murders, but there's nothing that I can see that I can do to prove what I know.'

'You know? Who was it then? Was it that Joseph?'

'Why, yes. Yes, Vilkins, it was. But – but how did you know too?'

'Nasty piece o' work,' Vilkins answered. 'Always was. I always knew it. Only I didn't like to say so to you, Unwin, 'cos you'd of asked me for proof an' all, an' I don't understand nothing o' that. But I knew it were Joseph all along all right.'

'Well, I wish I had been ready to listen to you while I was still out in the world and could perhaps have done something about finding that proof. Though what that could have been I don't know.'

'No, well, if you don't, you don't. But it's a poor look-out now, Unwin, I'll say that much.'

Vilkins shook her head beneath her over-large bonnet.

'Yeh,' she added. 'That Joseph. I knew all along. An' then this afternoon, too. This very afternoon.'

'What this afternoon?' Miss Unwin asked idly.

Too late, too late, she kept thinking to herself. All too late. Why did I not come to the same conclusion as Vilkins, if on better grounds, while I was still free and in a position somehow to do something about it?

She listened idly to Vilkins's reply to her idle question, asked only so as to keep saying something to her old friend in this doleful predicament.

'What this arternoon? Why, only him a-trying to break into old Simmons's room, that's all. Dare say he thought there'd be some pickings there for him. Dare say he thought that.'

Miss Unwin sat up straighter on her narrow bench.

'Trying to break into Simmons's room?' she asked. 'Tell me about that. Did he succeed? How did he come to be doing it? How did you manage to see him?'

'Oh well, that's easy. I 'ad to go up to me own room 'cos I tore me apron somehow an' Mrs Breakspear told me to put on another. Though I didn't see why I should. 'Tweren't a very bad tear.'

'No, I'm sure it wasn't. But what was Joseph doing trying to break into his moth – into Simmons's room? And did he succeed?'

''Course he didn't. Not with me coming along an' disturbing him. 'Ow could he of? Pretended to be doing something else, didn't he? Made a joke of it. But I know he'll be back, trying again. He wasn't making no joke about trying to get in there in the first place. I dare say he'll be at it this very moment, if he knows I'm out o' the way.'

'Vilkins,' Miss Unwin said with urgency. 'There must be something in Simmons's room that Joseph thinks would prove him guilty. He must be trying to get hold of it. And he must be stopped. Sergeant Drewd has got to be told, quickly.'

'No need to tell 'im,' Vilkins answered. 'He was the one what looked through all old Simmons's things an' then had the room locked up. He won't be interested in Joseph trying to get in there.'

'No. No, I suppose he won't be. But what about Superintendent Heavitree? No. He'll have gone back to Great Scotland Yard, if he hasn't gone home long ago. Oh, what can I do? What can I do?'

'Yeh,' said Vilkins with lumbering sympathy. 'You're in a right pickle, Unwin, so you are. An' you a lady, too. That's what makes it worse, you know. That's what makes it all the worse.'

Miss Unwin, whose head had sunk to her breast in despair, looked suddenly up.

It was simply what Vilkins had said about her being a lady. It had put her in mind, by an unaccountable leap of thought, of her cell companion of the morning, Mrs Honoria Fitzmaurice, Old

Fits, lady at the bottom of the long slope up which she herself had climbed a little way and had been hurled back down. It had put her in mind of Mrs Fitzmaurice and the trick she had boasted of playing with the aid of her lowest-of-the-low friend, Mrs Childerwick, the laying-out woman.

'Vilkins,' she said. 'Vilkins, you and I are of the same height and the same figure, are we not?'

'Always was,' Vilkins answered sturdily. 'Could always put on one another's pinafores, such as they was, turn and turn about, couldn't we?'

'Yes, yes. We could. And you are wearing that wonderfully big bonnet of yours.'

'Yeh. I like 'em big. The others laugh at me about it. But I like it the way it is.'

'Listen, Vilkins. I want to change clothes with you. I want to change clothes, then call the constable to let you out but go out myself instead. They won't come to look at you in here till nine o'clock. They told me that. It's when they give the prisoners bread and cocoa. I want that time – I suppose it's not much more than an hour and a half – to go back to No 3 and there, if I can, get into Simmons's room before Joseph does.'

'But you won't be able to break in there, Unwin,' Vilkins said, apparently quite undismayed by the extraordinariness of the plan that had been put to her. 'You won't because Joseph couldn't, an' he tried hard enough, believe you me.'

'But I will get in, Vilkins, I will. You see, I have an advantage over Joseph. I have a good memory for what has been said to me.'

'Well, memory won't get you past that door. It's a good 'un. A real good 'un.'

'No. But my memory has told me already that Mrs Thackerton said to me once that she has kept a set of keys to the house even although Mrs Arthur has taken over conduct of the household. I can get the key to Simmons's room from her set, Vilkins, and then I can get in there and find what Joseph is so sure is to be found and what Sergeant Drewd evidently missed.'

'Then go on, Unwin. Go on.'

And Vilkins instantly began pulling off her lavender stuff half-mourning dress.

Chapter Twenty-One

It did not take long for Miss Unwin and Vilkins to exchange dresses and pass over servant's shawl for governess's grey mantle. Once the change was completed Miss Unwin hid her head inside Vilkins's large straw bonnet, took Vilkins's purse, which she had accepted the loan of after some demur, and with its metal clasp set the bars of the cell ringing.

In the lobby at the far end she was able to see the constable's shadow move as he heaved himself out of his chair. Then she turned away and pretended to be looking down at the cell's occupant seated in the gloom on the narrow bench.

Clump, thump, clump. She heard the constable's steps approach and forced herself not to look round.

'You've been long enough,' came a grumbling voice at last, accompanied by the heavy jingling of keys.

'Yes, sir, I'm sorry,' Miss Unwin said, answering quickly for fear that Vilkins might speak by mistake and keeping her voice to a murmur.

Still with her head turned towards Vilkins, she heard the key squeal once in the lock of the cell door. Only then did she turn, muttering a quick 'Goodbye then, miss' for Vilkins's benefit, and scurry, head still lowered, out into the corridor.

Behind her the cell door swung closed with the same booming clang it had made when she had first been put into the dark confined space alongside Mrs Honoria Fitzmaurice.

'You're in a great rush all on a sudden,' the constable complained. 'Wait, can't you?'

Without turning, Miss Unwin flung out an answer, picking up again in her fear the coarse mode of speech of her earliest days, something she thought she had for ever banished.

'I'm wanted back at me place. They'll create something terrible if I'm any later.'

'You're all the same, you girls,' the constable replied, immensely to her relief. 'Well, you can find your own way out. I'm not going chasing after the likes of you.'

Miss Unwin hurried away, face well concealed inside her large bonnet, slipping like a wraith back along the way she remembered from having been marched in by Sergeant Drewd. In little more than half a minute she found herself standing outside the police station on the wide pavement. A free woman.

Then, to her delight, she saw a hansom come slowly trotting along the street with no passenger inside.

At once she hailed it, thanking Vilkins once again in her mind for providing her purse. Every moment might count if she was to get back to Northumberland Gardens before Joseph attempted to break into his mother's room once again.

But the trip in the hansom, that wonderfully light vehicle specially designed for rapid movement through city streets, was in the event too quick for her. She had hardly sat in its gently swinging seat for three minutes before the cabbie was drawing up outside No 3 Northumberland Gardens. She had had no time at all to think how she was going to get into the ever-locked house in order to obtain the key to the room in the attics that might mean everything to her future.

Here she was, dressed in Vilkins's lavender maid's dress. So how could she ring at the visitor's bell to have Henry, or worse Joseph, open the door to her? On the other hand, were she to ring at the servants' bell, she would be let in at the door down in the area by most probably Mrs Breakspear, and the cook would hardly admit Miss Unwin, the governess, by this unaccustomed way without a host of questions.

But time pressed. She passed up to the driver, high-perched behind her, the sixpence of his fare through the little trap in the hansom's roof, set foot on its iron step and descended to the pavement. And still no answer to her dilemma had come to her.

For a moment she stood looking up at the house, the house that only that morning she had been convinced she would never see again. Tears pricked at her eyes at the thought of how near she was to the secret that lay in Simmons's room and how far away.

But her dilemma remained.

She went up to the gate, opened it and set off with leaden steps along the path towards the white-scrubbed steps leading up to the imposing front door and its two either-or bells.

Then, floating up from the area beneath, she smelt a richly mixed aroma. It was the Thackertons' dinner. The mingling smells of what might be rich turtle soup, well-cooked plaice sweet and fresh, roast mutton too, it seemed, and most probably a fowl and the spiciness of a substantial pudding.

The Thackertons' dinner. It was being served at that moment. What a mercy, she thought, that Mr Thackerton had always insisted on dinner on Sundays being eaten at the same time as on weekdays and not, as in other households more considerate of servants, in the middle of the day. And serving at the table, however few diners were seated at it, there would be Mellings himself and both Henry and Joseph. So if the visitors' bell rang at this unusual hour one of the maids would answer, and whichever of them it was would be a much easier figure to confront than the footmen. A sharp word from Miss Unwin and, with a little luck, even Hannah for all her customary unwillingness to take orders from the governess, would retreat and allow her to set foot indoors.

Miss Unwin put a finger on the visitors' bell and let it peal loud and long.

Then she waited, counting the seconds.

She had reached only 'twenty-three' when she heard footsteps on the far side of the door. Would they be Henry's or Joseph's after all? No, surely, they sounded too light and too rapid.

Then the door swung open, a little hesitantly. It was Hannah standing holding it.

'Ah, Hannah. I am happy to tell you that the misunderstanding has been satisfactorily cleared up at the police station. I will go up to my room now, and when Mr Arthur has dined I shall come down and tell him.'

Already she had gained entrance.

'Oh, yes, miss, yes,' Hannah said, blinking in surprise. 'Only the Master ain't dining at home tonight. But Mrs Arth – but the Mistress is here, of course.'

'Yes. Good. Then I shall see her.'

Miss Unwin longed to race up the broad stairs in front of her before Hannah took in the clothes she was wearing. But there was one thing more that she had to find out.

'And Mrs Thackerton?' she asked. 'Is she dining downstairs this evening?'

'Oh, no, miss. Mrs Thackerton ain't at all well still. She's in bed. Fast asleep in her bed, I dare say.'

'Yes. Of course. Poor Mrs Thackerton.'

Then at last she could make for the stairs, and go up them, if not at a telltale run, at least with reasonable haste.

Once out of Hannah's sight, in fact, Miss Unwin did take to her heels. She had a tremendous amount to accomplish, and very little time to do it in.

First, without any hesitation, she made her way to Mrs Thackerton's sitting-room. Outside its door she listened hard for a few seconds. She had to be sure that there was no one there, not Mrs Thackerton up unexpectedly from her bed, not say Nancy, promoted from the scullery to duties upstairs.

All seemed silent. Slowly Miss Unwin opened the door. The room beyond was almost in darkness. The blinds were half-lowered as they almost always were, and the fire had still not been lit. And there was no one there.

Miss Unwin closed the door swiftly behind her and looked all round. Mrs Thackerton, though she had said that she still held the keys of the house, had said nothing about where it was that she kept them. But they were at least much more likely to be somewhere in here than in the bedroom next door.

The invalid sofa. The little piecrust table next to it, with a medicine glass still on it. The mantelpiece, but nothing on its green cloth with the green-and-gold fringe except the clock ticking quietly away under its glass dome and the photographs in their silver frames – Mr Arthur as a boy in frocks, Mr Arthur at Eton, Mr and Mrs Arthur on their wedding day, little Pelham in his mother's arms, little Pelham naked on a bearskin rug, little Pelham in his first sailor suit.

Then there was the bookcase. But there was nothing behind its glass front besides Mrs Thackerton's books, the works of piety and the dull, dull novels. In the far corner, a hanging shelf with half a dozen pieces of Meissen ware on it. Just as it had always been.

But next to the fireplace there was the side-table, and it had two narrow drawers under it. Miss Unwin, while she had been reading to Mrs Thackerton or having the undemanding conversations which occasionally had taken the place of reading, had never seen either of these drawers open.

She crossed over to the table and did a most unladylike thing. One after the other she jerked the two private drawers wide.

It was in the second that, together with a pile of lavender-coloured writing paper and a few dried-up pens, she found them. A large assorted clutter of keys on two linked rings.

She picked them up, thrust them into the pocket of Vilkins's shapeless dress and hurried out. As quickly she mounted the stairs to the schoolroom landing.

There she had intended to go through the baize door leading to the last part of the servants' stairs, those going up to the attic bedrooms. But on the landing she hesitated. Pelham. How was he? Who had seen him to bed in her absence? Was he happily asleep as he ought to be? Or was he perhaps lying awake still, lonely and worried by the startling change that had occurred in the even tenor of his life?

She crept to his door and eased it open.

In the dim light of the still bright evening outside coming through a gap in the curtains she saw that he was, in fact, asleep. But, stepping nearer, she realised that his face was flushed with heat and, yes, there were surely the smudges on his cheeks of tears that had not long dried. And no one had lit the nightlight. If he were to wake when it had got thoroughly dark he would be yet more distraught.

She turned and went across to the schoolroom where, safely out of reach on the top of the tall toy cupboard, she kept a box of lucifers.

Hardly pausing to discard encumbering bonnet and shawl, she hurried back with the matches into Pelham's room. There, turning from the bed so as to shield the sudden burst of light and the harsh scrape of the lucifer on its box, she struck the first match that she had been able to take hold of with fumbling fingers. Mercifully it lit at one stroke. She carried the little flame carefully to the mantelpiece and applied it to the wick of the nightlight. It caught and began to burn steadily.

Thrusting the lucifers into Vilkins's pocket alongside the two rings of keys, she closed the door carefully and softly behind her and then went to the servants' staircase and rapidly mounted upwards.

But, up at last where she wanted to be, she realised that, ridiculously, she did not know which room off the narrow corridor there had belonged to Simmons. All she did know of this part of the house, the women servants' domain, was that one of the rooms was shared by Vilkins and Nancy. Supposing she tried one of the doors and it was that one and Nancy was there. That alone might put an end to her quietly getting into Simmons's room and giving it the thorough search that was likely to be needed.

Yet there was no time to be wasted. Downstairs dinner might have nearly come to its end and Joseph, free of his duties in the dining-room, might come creeping up here to make a new assault on the locked door.

The locked door. Yes, weren't there bound to be signs on it of Joseph's first attempt?

There was little light up under the roof, only what came in through one small window at the end of the narrow corridor. But Miss Unwin went rapidly from door to door, stooping and peering, and hoping. And at the fourth one she looked at she saw, quite clearly, a whole line of scratches along its edge near the lock.

Hastily she pulled out Mrs Thackerton's two linked key rings. Which key was the one she wanted?

Rejecting the larger ones as obviously having more important uses than to give a servant some privacy, and discarding too some of the smaller ones as belonging almost certainly only to cupboards, she saw with dismay that there were still plenty of possibilities left. Nothing for it but to try them systematically one by one, shifting each rejected key to the far side of her gripping fingers as it failed to do the trick for her.

The business took her more than ten minutes. Three times she thought she had at last found the right key, only to feel it stick when it had turned half-way in the lock. One of them jammed, and she felt a hot flush of frustration run all the way down her back at the thought that she would not be able to free it. She imagined the door in front of her remaining obstinately unopenable till it was too late and Vilkins had been discovered in her place at the police station and a hue-and-cry had located her here.

But at last after patient wriggling with fingers wiped clean of sweat the key turned back and she was able to slip it out. The very next one she tried opened the door as sweetly and easily as if it had been used on it every day.

She almost stumbled into the room and only after standing there breathing deeply and trembling for long moment after long moment did she remember to take the hanging bunches of keys out of the lock and shut the door behind her. Then at last she brought her mind to considering where in the room what she sought might be hidden.

It was a chamber only a little smaller than her own, the privileged room of a privileged servant. The bed, like hers, had tall brass rails at head and foot. Its mattress, too, looked lumpy as her own, she reflected, as she dropped the heavy keys on to it, carefully examined the bedclothes neatly folded on top and passed her hand underneath it from end to end.

The only other pieces of furniture were a chair, clearly relegated from the dining-room when newer furniture had been bought, and a chest of drawers on which there stood a wash-basin with a ewer in it and, behind, a notably large looking-glass with a fine pair of hairbrushes on its shelf.

Yes, she thought, I was right. Once long ago Simmons was a woman who paid more than a little attention to her appearance, enough to have caught the eye of the younger Master of the house.

She began pulling out the drawers from the chest. If Sergeant Drewd had searched the room, as Vilkins had told her he had, he would have been hardly likely to have missed anything in them. But he would not have known that there was something well worth the finding hidden somewhere under the room's low ceiling, something that Joseph certainly believed to be here. And if that something was a document of some sort, perhaps Joseph's secret certificate of birth, then it might well have been hidden behind the drawers.

But her supposition proved incorrect. Nothing was fastened to the back or bottom of any of the drawers nor to the inside of the chest.

So where else?

She stood thinking furiously.

Unlike her own room on the floor below there was here no fireplace. So nothing could have been thrust up the chimney.

Where, if she had wanted to hide something herself, would she have put it? Of course, under a loose board in the floor.

She dropped to her hands and knees and began feeling carefully all over the worn drugget that covered the entire floor. Under it everything seemed firm. Would she have to prise up a board that Simmons had nailed down? It seemed unlikely. Nowhere had she seen any tool that Simmons could have used for that purpose, and somehow she could not see that sneaking, papery-faced figure gliding up here with a claw-hammer purloined from wherever tools were kept in the basement.

Then, on the far side of the room, within a foot of the wall, a plank under her pressing outstretched fingers rocked. She pulled back the drugget with tearing hands. And, yes, in a short length of board there where there ought to have been nail heads there were instead empty black holes.

With scrabbling fingernails she pried at the board's edge. It came up.

Before she had got it quite clear she was able to see that underneath, lying among the brownish rubble between the joists, there was a small packet wrapped in oilskin.

She had been right. Joseph's attempted break-in had indicated that there was something to be found in the room. And that something could only be something to Joseph's disadvantage, something that would show clearly that he had had a strong motive for murdering his natural father, and perhaps his mother too. Something that would prove to Superintendent Heavitree and to Sergeant Drewd that she was not a murderess.

'And what are you doing here, Mary, my girl?'

She had recognised the voice before two syllables of the sentence had been uttered.

Joseph's.

Chapter Twenty-Two

Miss Unwin scrabbled round on the floor at the sound of Joseph's threatening question and lunged to her feet. But she was trapped, she realised, in the furthest corner of the room with the chest of drawers to one side of her and the wall to the other. She was as far from the door as it was possible to be, but at least she was standing upright and facing her enemy.

Because she had no doubt that, the moment Joseph realised that the figure in the lavender dress was not Vilkins but herself, the enmity between them would blaze out. Joseph's words as she straightened up and faced him confirmed this to be the utmost.

'The blasted governess, by God. How did you get out of a cell, my fine miss?'

'Never mind how I got out of the cell you did your best to put me in,' Miss Unwin replied, feeling stir in her veins a readiness for battle learnt in a hundred hard-fought childhood scuffles and, she believed, altogether forgotten. 'Never mind how I got out, it's time now you were put in, Joseph Simmons.'

It might have been wiser of her not to have said so plainly that she knew Joseph was the murderer in the house and what lay at the back of his crime. But she hardly believed any fair or flattering words were going to get her out of her present predicament. The glowering look on that long, waxen face, which she saw with renewed force now as a plain cross between father's and mother's, told her she was not going to quit the room alive unless she could fight her way out.

For some moments each of them now stood looking at the other, neither dropping their glance by as much as a quarter-inch.

'Yes,' said Joseph eventually, 'you've stood in my way too long, curse you. I don't quite see how I'm to get out of this new scrape you've got me into, but I dare say I'll think of a way. I've done it each time before, ain't I? And no thanks to you neither.'

'It wasn't me who got you into your scrapes,' Miss Unwin answered. 'It was your own greed and your own pride and nothing more.'

'Was it, my girl? Was it then? Well, I'll tell you what's going to get me out of it now. Now and for ever. This.'

And from the tail pocket of his green plush livery coat he whipped a long and ugly kitchen knife.

'Brought it up to force the door,' he said. 'But it'll stand me in better stead now.'

Miss Unwin looked at him across the width of the room, conscious suddenly of how small it was. One good lunge forward and Joseph would be well within striking distance, penned as she was in the corner. And she had nothing with which to parry any blow from that dark iron blade.

Was she going to have escaped the hangman's rope only to end her life at a murderer's hands? Was all that she had done with her days on earth, her slow, hard rise, to come just to this? A squalid death in a little room?

A shiver of fear went uncontrollably through her.

She saw in Joseph's eyes as he stood menacingly in the doorway that he had observed it. And that he delighted in it.

Her hand dived into the wide pocket of Vilkins's dress, grasped the square box of lucifers she had dropped into it, pulled it out and all in one movement sent it shooting across the room right at Joseph's face.

It would have done him little harm had it caught him fairly between the eyes. But he had had no time to see just what it was she had flung at him and he side-stepped from it and ducked down his head. The box struck the door-post behind him and clattered to the floor.

But, while his eyes had been momentarily off her, Miss Unwin had acted. She jumped out of her cramped corner beside the chest of drawers and, free to move, she reached across and seized from the far side of the chest the heavy earthenware ewer from where it stood in the basin there. To her relief, the moment she began to lift it she knew it had been left full of water. She had something heavy in her hands. A weapon. A weapon that could inflict real damage.

She raised it high in the air and stood with legs frankly apart, in an altogether unladylike stance, ready to throw or to swing.

Joseph at the door smirked.

'Going to make a fight of it, eh?' he said. 'That's more than the other two did.'

'Yes, the other two,' Miss Unwin answered, grasping at a sudden hope that she could after all make this man quail from a sense of shame. 'Your own mother and your father. Both dead at your hands.'

But Joseph was not to be weakened so easily.

'In my way, both of 'em,' he said. 'In my way. He owed me, owed me. And he thought he'd never have to pay. And she, she'd have betrayed me sooner or later. I saw she was ready to do it.'

Miss Unwin moved a little to one side.

Could she, if Joseph came forward at all, yet make a dash for the doorway, get through, slam the door in Joseph's face, escape?

Or would she have to bring her heavy jug hard down on his head? So hard that it might kill him?

Could she do that? Could she kill?

She was not sure. She knew how to fight, to fight to win. That she had learnt bitterly in her earliest rough-and-tumble days. But to fight to kill? That was a different matter. Could she do that?

Joseph had not moved from the door as she had shifted her position. But now he began to advance, taking short quarter-steps, careful to keep his balance, not for one moment taking his eyes off her. And with the dark kitchen knife held ready.

Ready to strike.

There could be no doubting that. Joseph had killed. He had struck and killed twice already. He was not going to hesitate at a third time.

Six inches nearer. And another six. Already he was within furthest striking range. He might want to get a little closer before he struck out with that black-splodged knife. But not much. Two more small careful steps only.

Miss Unwin saw that if she was to take the initiative she must do so at once. And she knew that, slim though her chances were against that long, dark knife, if she was to stand a chance at all she it must be who moved first.

And, yes, she would do it. She could do it. She could strike with force enough to kill. Strike for the temples.

She launched herself. Heavy ewer, outstretched arms, taut body, springing legs. All one. All intent to the last on striking home.

She was aware that Joseph was stooping to get under her rush with that black knife. She brought her arms hard down to counter the move and felt a jarring stop go all through her body.

As if it was a series of different pictures, she saw the ewer in front of her break. She saw pieces flying off. She saw the water it had contained spin out in a single sheet. She saw Joseph's arm at its fullest reach, with the knife extended from it.

She felt a rip at the sleeve of her dress, knew the blow had cut through to the flesh beneath, knew she was falling forward unable to prevent herself.

Then for an instant she knew no more.

But still she was able through the blackness to direct it to depart. To force herself back to full alertness. To know that, sprawled on the floor half in and half out of the doorway, she would be at the mercy of the killer she had hurled herself on if her one desperate blow had not gone home.

She shook her head, and the blackness went. She put out her hands flat on the drugget in front of her and pushed upwards with all her might. She felt her knees press into something yielding and for an instant feared she would slide and fall.

But somehow, lunging and struggling, she got clear, scrabbled at the doorpost and got to her feet. She whirled round to face –

To find that it had been Joseph, lying inert on the floor, that she had been kneeling on, to see a thick coil of blood creeping out from beneath his head.

Then, though she had begun to tremble till her legs felt like water, she went back into the room, fell to her knees beside the turned-back corner of drugget, and plunged her hand deep into the hole that the floorboard she had removed had revealed. She grasped the oilskin packet lying there and, still on her knees and shaking now as if she was racked with the ague, she tugged the oilskin clear of the single thick folded sheet of paper it protected. Then she opened the sheet and saw in an instant what it was.

The birth certificate of Joseph, not Green, but Simmons, born of Martha Simmons and – it was there clear to see – William Thackerton.

She had proof at last, better proof by far than any assertion of similarity of looks or gesture, that the man who lay insensible in the doorway there, the man who had tried to take her life, had good reason to have committed the murders that had taken place under this roof.

She was freed of the burden. Freed. Freed.

Sergeant Drewd handed Miss Unwin into the four-wheeler he had waiting outside the house with punctilious politeness.

'Well now, miss,' he said, all bouncing cheerfulness, as he settled down beside her, 'we'll soon have that – hum – fellow-conspirator of yours out of durance vile. What a fine ending to the case, eh? What a triumph it is.'

He rubbed his hands briskly together.

'I'll tell you something,' he said, as the cab swung and jerked into motion, 'This is the first time Sergeant Drewd has made use of a lady collaborator. The very first time.'

Miss Unwin checked unspoken a sharp query about just what had been the extent of that collaboration. She hardly had the spirit to put it in any case. The events of the hour or more since she had knocked Joseph unconscious had been so crowded that they had drained her of what little energy she had left.

Between recurring bouts of faintness she remembered herself calling out for help after she had read the wonderful document that cleared her of all suspicion. She had called and called again, she seemed to remember, and it had been little Pelham, of all people, who had eventually heard her.

He had come exploring up the stairs to the servants' attics and had found her – how she had got there she never knew – kneeling beside the newel-post at the top of the stairs, clutching it for support.

'Oh, Miss Unwin,' he had said, 'you're back. 'You're back. Hip, hip, hoo – Oh, Miss Unwin, are you ill? You're all blood on your arm.'

'Yes, Pelham, I'm not very well. Can you go down and fetch Mellings and perhaps Mrs Breakspear. They'll look after me.'

Then she had become yet more confused, seeing only a succession of faces all asking questions which she doubted whether she had properly answered at all. Till at last Sergeant Drewd's violently checked brown suit had swum into her vision and she had made a huge effort to be coherent enough to explain matters fully to him.

'Joseph Green, Joseph Green,' he had said. 'I've had my eye on that fellow ever since we took that cab ride together from Great Scotland Yard the night Mr Thackerton was killed. There was something about the way he said you had been the first to discover the body that never rang true to me. You can't put much past me in that line, you know. Not very much at all.'

'No, Sergeant. I am sure no one could.'

Then she had had to explain about Vilkins, since the Sergeant had not up till that moment thought to inquire how it was that someone he had left in a police station cell was back in the house where the murders had taken place.

By that time Mrs Breakspear had bathed her cut arm and had bound it up with clean rags, and soon afterwards she was let go back to her own room where she had contrived to take off Vilkins's torn and bloody lavender dress and put on her own best grey merino with the tiny trim of lace at its neck.

'Whoa, whoa,' she heard the cabby call from his seat in front of them. The swaying growler came to a halt. The Sergeant opened its door, jumped smartly out and then turned and offered her his arm to make her own descent. She took it. She would have liked to have demonstrated her independence by refusing. But she knew that if she did her weakness might very well cause her to stumble and fall.

So, on the Sergeant's arm, she entered once again the police station, passed through the battered counter in the front office with its jumble of black-bound registers and waited while the uniformed sergeant on duty there was given Sergeant Drewd's account of the successful conclusion of his inquiry.

Then they went, as before, along the broad, bare-boarded corridor to the lobby guarding the station's cells. The same constable was sitting at the table there, still painfully inscribing names in his big book, though doing so now by the light of a single stub of candle in a lantern.

For a moment Miss Unwin believed she had somehow slipped backwards in time and was about to go through all her experiences of the day once again, to hear Mrs Fitzmaurice wake from sleep and introduce herself with such imperious formality, to learn about the laying-out woman, Mrs Childerwick, and the concealed quartern of gin, to be questioned by Superintendent Heavitree and asked once more to make a full confession, to conceive her plan with Vilkins and to go back, head concealed under her big straw bonnet, along the same corridor that lay in front of her, calling out in her voice of old 'I'm wanted back at me place, they'll create something terrible ...'

Then she pulled herself together. No, these thoughts had entered her dazed head for no better reason than that the poor constable labouring away at his writing had to stay on duty for long, long hours.

She hardly listened to Sergeant Drewd telling the fellow that he wanted to see 'as a matter of urgency' the prisoner in the end cell.

Then the constable was lumbering ahead of them, lantern held high, and by its dull orangey light she was able to make out, at last, stretched full length on the bench at the back of the little end cell, dressed in her own clothes so that it might have been herself lying there, her friend of old, Vilkins, comfortably snoring.

And, as the constable set down his lantern to unlock the door, she saw the mug of cocoa and slice of bread that ought to have been her own frugal supper still standing untouched just inside the bars. Vilkins must not have dared to take them for fear their deception would be given away.

'Vilkins, Vilkins,' she called as the cell door swung open.

She rushed in and flung herself down beside her friend.

'Vilkins, it's me, Unwin,' she said, careless altogether now whether the Sergeant knew of her lowly origins or not. 'Vilkins, I've come back to take you out of here. It's all right, Vilkins dear. Everything's all right now. Joseph caught me in Simmons's room and he tried to kill me too, and they know now he murdered Mr

Thackerton and Simmons as well. They've already brought him here to a cell. It's all as right again as right can be.'

Vilkins sat up, shaking her head to clear it. She scratched at her big red dab of a nose.

'Well,' she said, 'that ain't so bad then, is it?'

SHADOW
OF A DOUBT
June Thomson

At Hawton Hall, an expensive and successful private
clinic, Claire Jordan disappears: she is the timid,
grey-haired wife of handsome and confident Dr.
Jordan. Can she possibly have walked out on him?
The admiring women who surround Dr. Jordan –
assistant, secretary, housekeeper – know he had very
little attention to spare for his nervous wife. And they
share his passionate concern that no breath of
scandal should mar the clinic's reputation . . .

*'There is a fine deep understanding of what people
are like, how they think, what makes them do as they
do.'* H R F Keating, The Times
'The writing is unusually perceptive and graceful.'
Daily Telegraph

CRIME   0 7221 84360   £1.95

'This book really puts Mrs Thomson among the elite...'
Birmingham Post

Bedridden, impoverished and almost forgotten, Max Gifford is at the end of his career as a painter. In artistic terms, his achievement has been considerable, yet recognition and reputation elude him still. Only the loving care of his wife – a woman young enough to be his daughter – prevents him sinking into cynical despair.

But then the owner of a smart London gallery proposes a major exhibition of his work, a suggestion to which Max and his wife readily agree. Here at last is their passport to fame and fortune – until a brutal murder puts an end to their dreams.

For as Detective Chief Inspector Finch will discover, buried deep in the artist's Bohemian past, amid the lingering bitterness of old, unhappy, far-off relationships, is the reason that has driven a person or persons unknown

TO MAKE A KILLING

June Thomson

'Imaginative and convincing... as always, the author depicts characters and their relationships with skill and art'
Times Literary Supplement

CRIME   0 7221 8438 7   £2.25

Also by June Thomson in Sphere Books:
SOUND EVIDENCE

A Mind To Murder

PDJames

'THE NEW QUEEN OF CRIME'
NEWSWEEK

One Friday evening the peace of the exclusive Steen psychiatric clinic was shattered by a woman's scream. Death had come to the Steen, and in the basement sprawled the body of the Administrative Officer, with a chisel in her heart. Summoned from the party he was attending, Superintendent Adam Dalgliesh arrived to investigate a killing, which from the first, he sensed would provide one of the most complicated cases of his career . . .

'A classic twist . . . somewhat of a triumph.' *Books And Bookmen*.

'Writing and characterisation of neurotic intelligentsia, well above average . . . readable all the way.' *Observer*.

'. . . with suspects ranging from the hall porter and the anaesthetist up to the trick cyclists themselves . . . altogether an excellent book.' *Sunday Times*.

CRIME   0 7221 5189 6   £1.95

And don't miss P. D. James' other novels in Sphere paperback:

INNOCENT BLOOD
COVER HER FACE
UNNATURAL CAUSES
SHROUD FOR A NIGHTINGALE
AN UNSUITABLE JOB FOR A WOMAN
DEATH OF AN EXPERT WITNESS
THE BLACK TOWER
THE SKULL BENEATH THE SKIN

The body of a young man lay slumped on the
floor of an abandoned house, his face brutally
smashed in. It looked like a clear case of murder
for Detective Inspector Finch.

But like the sign post at a country crossroads, the
evidence that could lead him to the killer seemed to
point in several directions at once. On the one hand,
there were the victim's underworld associates; on the
other, there was the man's lover, a senior Foreign Office
official and a perfect blackmail target.

And there were other possibilities as well, but Finch
didn't realise it at the time – at least, not until he'd
thought again about that vital piece of

SOUND
EVIDENCE
June Thomson

'A fine, deep understanding of what people are like,
how they think, what makes them do as they do.'
H. R. F. Keating, *The Times*.

'Few can match this author's careful characterisation
and precise settings.'
Christopher Wordsworth, *Observer*.

'Rivalled only perhaps by P. D. James, June Thomson is
a long way ahead of most detective story writers.'
London Mystery Selection.

CRIME   0 7221 8437 9   £1.95

A selection of bestsellers from SPHERE

FICTION

HOOLIGANS	William Diehl	£2.75 □
UNTO THIS HOUR	Tom Wicker	£2.95 □
ORIENTAL HOTEL	Janet Tanner	£2.50 □
CATACLYSM	William Clark	£2.50 □
THE GOLDEN EXPRESS	Derek Lambert	£2.25 □

FILM AND TV TIE-INS

SANTA CLAUS THE NOVEL		£1.75 □
SANTA CLAUS STORYBOOK		£2.50 □
SANTA CLAUS JUMBO COLOURING BOOK		£1.25 □
SANTA CLAUS: THE BOY WHO DIDN'T BELIEVE IN CHRISTMAS		£1.50 □
SANTA CLAUS: SIMPLE PICTURES TO COLOUR		95p □

NON-FICTION

HORROCKS	Philip Warner	£2.95 □
1939 THE WORLD WE LEFT BEHIND	Robert Kee	£4.95 □
BUMF	Alan Coren	£1.75 □
I HATE SEX		£0.99 □
BYE BYE CRUEL WORLD	Tony Husband	£1.25 □

All Sphere books are available at your local bookshop or newsagent, or can be ordered direct from the publisher. Just tick the titles you want and fill in the form below.

Name _____

Address _____

_____

Write to Sphere Books, Cash Sales Department, P.O. Box 11, Falmouth, Cornwall TR10 9EN

Please enclose a cheque or postal order to the value of the cover price plus:

UK: 45p for the first book, 20p for the second book and 14p for each additional book ordered to a maximum charge of £1.63.

OVERSEAS: 75p for the first book plus 21p per copy for each additional book.

BFPO & EIRE: 45p for the first book, 20p for the second book plus 14p per copy for the next 7 books, thereafter 8p per book.

Sphere Books reserve the right to show new retail prices on covers which may differ from those previously advertised in the text or elsewhere, and to increase postal rates in accordance with the PO.